I0689561

HEXADECAGON
A CITY ON ITS KNEES

FROM THE MINDS OF

SEAN J. TOWSEN & CRAIG S. PALMER

Towsen & Palmer Authors
towsenandpalmerauthors.com
info@towsenandpalmerauthors.com

Table Of Contents

Prologue

As Detective Coffey raised the yellow tape that cordoned off the area—a familiar motion that he had performed countless times before—he noticed that something was different. This time, the tape felt unusually taut in his hands, almost as if it had been wrapped with a silent disdain.

The afternoon cool air seemed to vanish from his lungs, leaving him breathless, and with it, a piece of his own spirit seemed to fade away, as though each breath carried the weight of everything he had experienced. For a moment, he paused and allowed himself to be truly present in the here and now—something he had not done in a long time.

The familiar, suffocating heaviness of anger, frustration and the relentless burden of his work washed over him. It was as though he could feel the same emotions burning through the young rookie's eyes as they observed him entering the scene, each of them hardened by the horrors they had witnessed. Their souls seemed worn down, already scarred by the darkness they had been forced to navigate, yet it was clear the worst had not yet passed. A fleeting thought crossed his mind, almost like a whisper:

Was it wrong to feel so alive?

He wondered to himself, *Why now? What have I done to deserve this? If this is the penance I must pay, then surely, I'm already in Hell.*

With deliberate caution—as if performing a sacred and somber ritual—Detective Coffey carefully pulled back the shroud that concealed the grim truth beneath it. Each movement was measured—a quiet reverence in his actions—though there was no escape from the inevitable. He approached with caution, aware of the horrors he was about to uncover, yet accepting that it was something he could not avoid.

The woman's form seemed delicate, almost fragile, her age unmistakably etched into the lines of her face. Time—it seemed had not been kind to her—her features, once vibrant, now appeared worn and weathered. But there, despite the ravages of age, was a smile, frozen on her lips as if caught in some long-forgotten moment of peace.

However, her body told a far darker story. Beneath the smile, it bore the grotesque marks of violence—mutilation and suffering that could not be hidden by the passing of time. It was difficult to reconcile the image of this frail, elderly woman with the capacity to inflict pain on another. Yet, as Coffey's eyes lingered on the scene before him, he knew the answer to that question all too well. He had seen enough to understand the darkness that had taken root, a truth that hung heavily in the air, unspoken but deeply understood. Michael knew what she was capable of.

Sean J. Towsen & Craig S. Palmer

This book is dedicated to the unwavering hearts who stood by us - our Wives, our Family and our Friends, whose faith in us never faltered, whose love never dimmed.

And to our Dads, now echoes in the wind, stars in the night sky - gone,

yet forever etched in our souls.

Chapter 1

An Artist's Ambition

In the early years of the Twentieth Century, the Lower East Side of Manhattan had become home to millions of newly arrived immigrant families. This influx of people created a tight-knit community, where Katz's Delicatessen quickly emerged as a central gathering spot. Every Friday, the neighborhood would gather to indulge in franks and beans—a beloved Katz tradition—as well as their world-famous pastrami on rye. It is here, just outside this historic establishment, that our story begins—on a rainy June morning in 1987.

Young Detective Charles William Coffey sat patiently in his Plymouth Gran Fury, waiting for his partner, Peter "Mac" Mackenzie. At that very moment, Mac was inside the deli, carefully selecting just the right amount of deli meats to be piled high on his rye bread—a sandwich that was nearly too overstuffed to manage.

"What the hell is taking him so long?" Charles muttered to himself, his frustration growing as he absentmindedly examined the length of his fingernails, ensuring each one was perfectly even. His fingers, a small obsession of his, were aligned just right, each nail precisely the same length as the others. While his attention was absorbed in this odd ritual, he took the time to glance at his surroundings.

Charles let his eyes wander across the street to the apartment buildings that lined the block. Just next to them stood a very old synagogue, its architecture standing proudly as the jewel of the neighborhood.

"Why would anyone want to defile such a holy place?" Charles thought, a sense of disbelief washing over him as he noticed the ugly graffiti plastered across the synagogue's sidewall and even on the front door. "Seems the neighborhood is not what it once was," he said out loud, shaking his head in disappointment. As he turned to his left, he saw a towering new apartment building under construction—a stark, modern structure that felt like a stain on this once-historic stretch of land. At least Katz's Delicatessen had managed to endure through the years, still standing proud amidst the changes.

The dashboard clock flickered, reading 7:17 a.m., and Charles noticed the first signs of traffic building up on this unusually rainy New York City morning. His gaze shifted, and he caught a glimpse of Mac emerging from Katz's, shuffling toward the sidewalk with a purposeful but distracted gait. He barely glanced left or right as he made his way back to the patrol car. His breakfast—now wrapped in a napkin and cradled carefully in his arms—looked almost like a newborn, as if he feared it might be

harmed in the chaos of the busy street. As Mac made his way across, he narrowly avoided two or three cars that hardly slowed down, honking impatiently as they zipped by. Charles couldn't help but think that perhaps the drivers were just as irritated by Mac's presence as he was. The man always seemed to be in everyone's way—moving at his own pace and oblivious to the world around him.

Mac slowed his pace as he walked around the back of the patrol car and made his way toward the passenger side. With a lazy but determined motion, he managed to open the door using just two fingers, and then he practically collapsed into the seat beside Charles, soaked to the bone.

"Took you long enough, Mac. Can we go now?" Charles snapped. His voice was sharp and showed no sympathy for his partner's likely discomfort. Mac didn't say a word in response, but instead gave Charles a childlike grin. Without uttering a single word, he raised his right arm, holding his sandwich carefully in hand, and gestured forward, signaling for Charles to leave their parking spot.

Before Charles could drive off, Mac excitedly unwrapped his sandwich with exaggerated movements, then took a huge bite of the deli delight. "Charlie boy, you gotta try this," he called out, trying once again to tempt his partner into joining him for a bite of his on-the-go breakfast. Charles glanced at him briefly, his eyes briefly narrowing, then he turned his attention to the rain outside, momentarily shutting Mac out, preparing himself for the irritation of the next few minutes. Just as he was about to take a second bite, Charles caught sight of an unappetizing mix of mustard, tomato, and thick butter oozing from the sandwich and spilling onto Mac's scruffy beard. Mac, appearing surprised by the mishap, just laughed it off, which only irritated Charles further.

The truth was, Charles was disgusted by Mac. It wasn't subtle; Mac knew it, and Charles knew that Mac knew it. Every action, every moment, every behavior that Mac exhibited only served to remind Charles of how little he could stand him.

Although Mac was fifteen years older than Charles, their dynamic often gave the impression that Charles had assumed the role of the lead detective between them. Mac had long since faded from his prime, a "has been" in every sense of the word, while Charles was a mediocre "never will be," slightly better but still stuck in a rut. He was the kind of guy who'd be the poster child for the "BUY 2 GET 1 FREE" frozen dinners—eating alone in his apartment while watching the 6 p.m. news from his sofa, far from the grand success he'd once envisioned.

What was about to unfold as Charles and Mac left the deli that day would alter the course of Charles' life in ways he could never have imagined. Every facet of his being—the way he saw the world, the way he viewed himself— would undergo a profound transformation, evolving into something entirely unfamiliar. In that moment, he would begin a journey of change so deep and far-reaching that not even Charles himself could have predicted the person he was about to become; and it all stemmed from the person he never became.

Suddenly, the old dispatch radio crackled to life, its sound somewhat muffled and distant, as a voice came through:

"Unit No. 34, come in, over. "Unit 34, do you copy? "Dispatch, this is Unit 34, over," Mac responded.

"Unit 34, is Detective Coffey with you, over? "Dispatch, yes, Coffey here." "Detective, we have a possible 10-57, a victim located at the corner of John and William Street in the Financial District. Officers are already on scene, and your presence is requested, over. "Dispatch, that's miles away! It's all the way across town. At this hour, the area's bound to be backed up. Is there another unit closer? "Detective, your presence has been specifically requested at the scene. Do you copy, over? "Charles, growing increasingly frustrated with the dispatch officer on the other end, muttered a curse under his breath.

"Why the hell would I need to be called to a scene that's not even in our district, Mac?" "I'm not sure, Charlie boy, but it sounds serious. At least it gives me time to finish this delicious sandwich," Mac replied, trying to lighten the mood with a bit of humor, though deep down, he sensed that this was no ordinary call. "Dispatch, it'll take us at least half an hour to get there, but we're on our way. Over and out.

"As Charles and Mac made their way downtown, the city streets felt more chaotic than usual. They passed through Chinatown, driving beneath the Manhattan Bridge, a spot Charles suspected would be jammed with traffic. They then passed under the Brooklyn Bridge and navigated through several inner-city parks, including Thomas Paine Park. As they drove by, Charles caught sight of a small group of children playing hopscotch on the sidewalk. His eyes lingered on one boy whose foot brushed the line of the squares. Charles felt a fleeting sense of justice, a memory of simpler days. He thought about his own childhood, growing up in wide-open spaces, where the trees and woods now stood in stark contrast to the cold, concrete jungle around him. He wondered how a child could feel at home in this environment, surrounded by so much steel and stone.

They finally reached the traffic lights at the intersection of Vesey Street, and soon entered John Street, maneuvering through the bustling Financial District. The area was alive with ambition, as people rushed past one another, all driven by the relentless pursuit of wealth. But something had shifted in the air. It was as though a heavy, oppressive cloud had descended over the scene when Charles and Mac arrived. "We're two blocks away, Mac, and I can't even get this damn car through. Move!" Charles yelled out of the window, his voice almost drowned out by the blaring siren. To make matters worse, construction workers had blocked the sidewalk with their scaffolding, adding to the chaos.

"Too much construction these days... can't these buildings get any taller?" Mac grumbled, his voice tinged with nostalgia for the old days when neighborhoods had a sense of community, before the city turned into a rat race where everyone was trying to outdo everyone else. "It's like a whole new world now, eh, Charlie boy?" Mac said with a melancholic tone, the sadness evident in his voice as he glanced around the ever-changing cityscape.

As Charles and Mac approached the scene, they both simultaneously noticed something peculiar about the middle of the intersection—it was eerily devoid of cars or people. Yet, just off-center, on the ground, something caught their attention. At first glance, it appeared to be a body, lying motionless as if it had been struck by a vehicle. Perhaps dispatch had been right after all. A handful of NYPD officers were already on the scene, but they were vastly outnumbered by the growing crowd—roughly twenty to one, when compared to the general public. Crime scene tape had already been strung up across William Street, from one street corner to the next, blocking off access to the intersection. The tape stretched between the poles that held the road signs above, forming a barrier between the streets. In addition, there was more tape blocking off traffic on John Street, running from one side of the street to the other, effectively halting all traffic in both directions. The scene was bizarre, and the level of protocol for what appeared to be a hit-and-run was unusual.

Charles and Mac both stepped out of their car at the same time, and Coffey glanced at the dashboard clock: 8:08 a.m.

Meanwhile, less than half a mile away, in the direction from which Charles and Mac had just driven, a distinguished, well-built man with striking blue and green eyes was taking in the beauty of a sculpture nestled among the trees in Zuccotti Park. He sipped on a freshly purchased café latte, his thoughts distant as he wound down from a productive night. The project he had worked on was very dear to him, and now, with the sun rising, he could finally relax. He had been awake all night, and while he had heard the distant sound of a police siren moments before, it hadn't disturbed his peace. On the contrary, the sight of the patrol cars rushing past, their sirens blaring, brought him an odd sense of warmth and satisfaction—like the feeling an artist experiences after a successful gallery exhibition. The sound of the siren felt like a subtle acknowledgement from the universe, a recognition that his hard work was about to pay off, and his efforts were finally coming to fruition. He couldn't help but feel excited by the thought.

Back at the scene, Charles lifted the crime scene tape over his head and approached the awning that had been set up to protect the evidence from the rain. Peering beneath it, he saw a body unmistakably lying in the middle of the street. The victim lay there, seemingly at peace, an eerie calmness surrounding them, as though they were merely asleep. But the sight of the prosthetic hand, its unnatural appearance, alluded to something far darker. Charles slowly crouched beside the lifeless body, his eyes scanning the scene with growing unease.

"Look at this," he muttered, his voice thick with disbelief, as he carefully examined the wrist where the hand should have been. His gaze shifted up to meet Mac's, his face reflecting the same confusion. Neither of them spoke a word in response, the silence only deepening the uncertainty.

Charles stood up, surveying the scene before turning to a group of officers huddled nearby under umbrellas.

"Who was first on the scene?" he asked, his voice sharp, as he scanned the group.

An officer ran up to him and Mac. "Sir, that would be Officer O'Connor, Sir. He was the first on the scene."

"And where is he?" Charles inquired.

The officer pointed to a man sitting about twenty feet away on the sidewalk, a cigarette dangling from the corner of his mouth and a cup of coffee in his hand.

"Officer O'Connor!" Charles called out, his voice cutting through the air. The man looked up, then slowly stood up and made his way toward the detectives.

"What do you want?" Officer O'Connor asked, his tone dripping with arrogance. O'Connor was one of the so-called "golden boys"—his family had a long history of serving in the force. His father had worked alongside Mac before retiring. "That's what do you want, Sir, to you" Mac muttered under his breath, stepping in to defend his partner's integrity.

O'Connor shot back with a sarcastic apology. "I'm sorry, I thought we didn't have time for formalities."

"Watch your mouth!" Charles snapped, his face turning red with irritation.

"Whoa, whoa—okay, I'm sorry already, Sir," O'Connor said, raising his gloved hands in mock surrender.

"You were first on the scene, right?" Charles asked, trying to keep his temper in check.

"Yes, Sir," O'Connor replied. "We got a call from dispatch about a possible 10-57. My partner and I were nearby, so we responded. When we arrived, a crowd had already started to form, so we pushed them back. I checked the body for signs of life, and that's when I noticed the fake hand. It was clear this wasn't an accident, but we were all in shock, so we called it in as a hit-and-run."

"But why call me?" Charles asked, clearly puzzled. "What's my involvement here?"

In response, Officer O'Connor simply reached into his jacket pocket and pulled out a white envelope. He handed it to Detective Coffey, who took it with a raised brow. The front of the envelope read:

To Charles William Coffey
"This was found on the body, Sir," the officer said, his voice tense. Charles' eyes widened with disbelief. "You mean you found this on the body!?"

He stared at the envelope in his hand, stunned and in shock.

With careful precision, Charles opened the envelope, aware that every move could disturb vital evidence. His gloved fingers trembled slightly as he peeled back the paper, determined not to damage it. As he began to draw out the contents, a flash of vibrant color caught his eye—bright red and green, an unmistakable combination of balloons. Slowly, he pulled the object free, and it became clear: it was a birthday card. The image on the front was playful and innocent—children were seen laughing, swinging on a playground, and others were blowing up balloons in the corner. In the center of the card, a birthday cake was surrounded by smiling family and friends. Beneath the joyful scene, in bold, cheerful letters, it read:

Hip Hip Hooray
You Are 1 Today

Charles carefully unfolded the card, his fingers gently lifting the top edge, almost as if he were handling something fragile. As he opened it fully, he found the inside empty, save for a single, striking detail. Across the smooth, unmarked surface, in flawless calligraphy, the words were written with precision and elegance. The delicate strokes of the pen were impeccably formed, each letter flowing into the next with a graceful rhythm. The message read:

Pleased if some Souls (for such there needs must be)
Who have felt the weight of too much liberty
Should find brief solace there, as I have found
I am Reason, I am Liberty

Charles stood frozen in disbelief, completely overwhelmed by the unexpected turn of events. His mind raced, perplexed by what he had just read.

He couldn't form coherent thoughts, nor could he decipher his emotions— he was lost in a haze of shock. All he could force himself to say, his voice sharp and demanding, was, "Give me an evidence bag, Mac, quick!" His instincts kicked in, and he clung to protocol, despite nothing of what he had just experienced as being logical.

"Where's the Doc?" he asked, his eyes scanning the scene in search of the county coroner.

"Here he comes, Sir," Officer Smith replied, his gaze focused on the approaching figure.

Dr. Stanley Bullard, the county coroner, came into view, walking briskly toward the scene. He appeared slightly out of breath as he reached them, offering an apologetic smile. "Gentlemen, I'm terribly sorry I'm late. My tires were slashed this morning. I walked out of the house and found them flat, lifeless, so to speak—had to take the missus' car to get here."

Charles didn't have the patience to acknowledge the Doctor's late arrival. "Never mind that, Doc," he said quickly, trying to keep things focused. "We haven't examined the body yet."

Dr. Bullard nodded, immediately switching to his professional demeanor as he knelt by the victim. "Gentlemen, it appears we have a Caucasian male, around 35 years of age. No clear cause of death at the moment, though... his right hand is missing. It seems the wound has been cauterized, and the replacement hand has been sewn on with remarkable precision." He paused, studying the replacement carefully. "The prosthetic hand appears to be made of a latex or silicone of some kind from what I can tell."

"Anything else?" Charles asked, as he absorbed the details.

"Yes," Dr. Bullard continued. "There's no identification on the victim—no wallet, no social security number, nothing. His left hand's fingerprints have been entirely burned off and all his teeth have been removed. It looks like the perpetrator went to great lengths to conceal the victim's identity."

"Can you get DNA, Doc?" Charles asked, his voice tight with urgency.

Dr. Bullard sighed, shaking his head slightly. "It might be possible, Detective, but it's unlikely. DNA analysis is still in its early stages. If the victim had been to a clinic in the past year, we might have a chance at a trace."

Charles nodded, pressing on with another question. "Time of death, Doc?" Dr. Bullard hesitated, assessing the scene with his practiced eye before answering. "It's difficult to say, Detective. Considering the rain, I'd estimate the time of death to be somewhere between 24 and 72 hours ago."

Dr. Bullard continued his meticulous examination of the body, carefully inspecting every detail as his hands moved with practiced precision. Meanwhile, Mac glanced over at Charles, his expression filled with concern and confusion. He subtly motioned his head, a silent signal to move to the side for a private conversation.

"Charles, what does this mean?" Mac whispered urgently. "Are you involved in this? Do you know the victim?" His voice carried a note of confusion and suspicion.

Charles shook his head quickly, frustration bubbling beneath the surface. "No, Mac! I don't know what's going on here!" He took a deep breath, trying to maintain his composure despite the swirling chaos around him. "I don't know the victim, okay?"

Mac's gaze softened slightly, but the unease didn't fade. "Well, Charles, whether you like it or not, you're involved now."

Charles clenched his jaw, fighting to remain calm as the situation slipped further out of his control. "Mac, for the last time, I don't know what's going on! I don't know why I was called here, and I definitely don't know who that guy is!" His voice trembled.

Mac held up his hands in a gesture of surrender, his tone calming but firm. "Alright, Charlie boy, calm down. We'll get to the bottom of this. I promise."

Before Charles could respond, Dr. Bullard intervened, his voice professional but final. "I wish I could give you more, Detectives, but I need to get the body on the slab. I'll be in touch once I've completed my examination. I cannot rule out foul play at this point in time but in all honesty, I don't think this is a hit and run.". His words clipped as he moved toward the gurney, signaling that his work at the scene was done.

As the doctor walked away, Charles knelt down once more beside the victim, his mind racing as he took in every detail before the body was removed. He studied the man closely, making a mental inventory of what little he could gather.

The victim wore a jacket that looked worn and frayed, one that could easily have been picked up from a thrift store. Could he have been homeless? Charles thought briefly before dismissing the idea—he was clean-shaven, a detail that made the assumption far less likely.

The jacket itself caught his attention—a deep yellow stripe ran down the sleeves, and a red line down the middle, with some kind of logo on the chest. Charles squinted, trying to make out the faint design. He thought he saw a "C" and a "B," but it was too unclear to be sure.

His mind wandered to unanswered questions, a flood of them crashing through his thoughts. *Who are you?* He asked silently. *Where did you come from?* The mystery deepened. *How did you end up like this?* The mystery of the scene was unsettling. *What drove someone to do this to you?* And finally, the question that gnawed at him the most: *What do you have to do with me?*

After navigating through the crowd of onlookers and fighting the heavy weight of their own turbulent thoughts, Mac and Charles finally made their way to the car, their minds clouded with confusion and unease. They drove through some of the city's most prestigious buildings, heading toward the police headquarters, where both men were part of the Major Crimes Unit. The drive was quiet, filled only with the sound of the engine and the occasional hum of the streetlights, yet Charles couldn't shake the storm of questions swirling in his mind.

As Mac maneuvered the car into the undercover parking area, the engine's rumble coming to a soft stop, Charles leaned back in his seat, his gaze still fixed ahead, lost in his thoughts. He turned to Mac, his voice laced with frustration and uncertainty. "Mac, I don't know what the hell is going on. I've been holding this card in my hands the whole way here, trying to make sense of it, but I'm just... lost. I don't know what to think of this."

Mac glanced at him briefly, his expression serious but trying to offer some reassurance. "Well, Charlie boy, I can tell you one thing for sure: the Cap's gonna assume the worst, you know how he gets."

With that, they both exited the car and made their way toward their office. As they approached, a deep, booming voice echoed down the hall, a familiar sound that made both men pause. It was Captain Stevens—his voice unmistakable and filled with authority, though they couldn't quite make out the words from that distance. Whatever was coming, they both knew the storm was far from over.

"Coffey... Mac... get in here... now!" The voice of Captain John Stevens thundered through the hallway, sharp and commanding. Charles and Mac exchanged a brief but knowing glance. Neither of them needed to say a word—the weight of the situation was clear. Both men knew that the conversation ahead would be tough, and deep down, they understood that what they were about to face was only the beginning of something much larger.

"You wanted to see us, Cap?" Mac asked, his voice calm but resigned, as he stepped into the Captain's office. The question was rhetorical—Mac knew the Captain's anger wasn't open to debate.

"Sit down, both of you," Captain Stevens barked, his tone clipped. There was a slight tremor in his voice that suggested just how upset he was. The heavy silence of the room seemed to press down on them as they took their seats.

The Captain didn't waste any time. "Can either of you tell me what the hell is going on here?" He stood up from behind his desk, walking across the room with a sense of barely contained frustration. "You show up at a scene across town—miles from where you were stationed—all because some jackass left a damn letter for you, Charles? What do we know about the victim, any clues yet, Detectives?" His voice rose with each word, the disbelief and anger apparent in his sharp tone.

Mac, cleared his throat and spoke up. "No, Sir, we've gathered everything we could from the scene. But there's nothing usable right now—no fingerprints, no blood, nothing we can work with."

His words were measured, trying to keep the situation under control despite the tension mounting in the room.

The Captain turned his focus to Charles, his gaze intense. "And Charles, what about this letter? What does it say?" His question was direct, his impatience growing by the second.

Charles hesitated, taking a deep breath before answering. "It's not a letter, Cap. It's a birthday card."

The Captain's eyes widened in confusion. "What!?" he exclaimed, his voice filled with confusion. "A birthday card? Are you serious?"

"Yes, Sir," Charles replied calmly. "It says 'Happy 1st Birthday.'"

The Captain's frustration reached a boiling point as he paced back and forth, muttering to himself. "Now what the hell can that possibly mean?" His words grew more agitated, and he stopped by the window, staring out into the distance as if hoping the answer would come to him from the city streets below. He ranted for a moment, his anger bubbling over as he shook his head. "What kind of message is this supposed to be?"

Charles barely registered the Captain's outburst. His mind was elsewhere—lost in the web of confusion that had been gnawing at him since they'd first encountered the victim. He couldn't stop turning over the details in his head, trying to make sense of it all. He even thought back to his early days on the beat, wondering if there was anyone from his past who might be capable of this kind of act, but nothing came to mind.

Before he could dive any deeper into his thoughts, the Captain's voice boomed from across the room, dragging him back into the present. "What do you have to say for yourself, Detective!?" The words rang out with a force that left no room for argument.

Charles snapped back into focus, his voice firm but laced with sincerity. "Captain, I know it sounds insane, but I swear to you, I don't know anything about this victim. I've never seen him before in my life."

The Captain's gaze hardened as he stepped closer, his voice dropping to a low, commanding tone. "Well, Charles, you better get to the bottom of this. Something tells me we haven't seen the last of this son of a bitch. Get on it."

As Mac and Charles left the Captain's office, their footsteps echoing in the hallway, Charles couldn't shake the feeling that there was something more to this case. A thought lingered at the edge of his mind—someone from his past, a name he couldn't quite place, but one that seemed to pull at him with increasing urgency. Could that person be connected to all of this?

"Hey Mac, do you remember that perp they caught a while ago? His name was Jimmy... something... I can't quite recall. It was Bradshaw's case, wasn't it?" Charles asked, trying to piece together the details.

Mac responded almost immediately, his voice sharp with clarity. "Jimmy 'Two Tone' Taylor."

"Yeah, that's the one! The guy who skinned his victims alive," Charles said with a shudder. "What happened to him? Is he out now?"

Mac's expression hardened as he answered, "That bastard died in prison about two years ago. Didn't make it long."

Charles was momentarily taken aback. "But what's with the name 'Two Tone'?" he asked, still trying to grasp the full horror of it.

Mac let out a grim sigh, his eyes narrowing as he explained. "Well, they found out he made a coat out of the skin of his victims. He called it his 'coat of many colors.' That's why they started calling him 'Two Tone.'"

Charles recoiled, visibly disturbed. "That's seriously messed up, Mac. Like, really sick."

The two detectives arrived at their desks, the familiar weight of their job settling in. They began sorting through the items collected from the crime scene, carefully placing them on the murder board. Charles pinned the photograph of the victim to the board, labeling it with "John Doe" in stark, simple letters. Nearby, he attached photos of the street where the body had been found, marking them with "Cnr John and William Street, Manhattan." The final piece of the strange puzzle was the birthday card they had discovered at the scene. Charles pinned it to the board with an unsettling calm, as though it were a cheerful holiday greeting—yet the atmosphere in the room was far from festive.

As the harsh light of the office illuminated the photos and evidence, Charles stared at the board, frustration building. "Mac, we don't know anything about this victim. Where he came from, who his family is, not a damn thing."

Mac leaned back in his chair, sighing deeply. "This is a first for me too, Charlie boy. Normally, cases like this would go to Bradshaw and his team, but the Captain's making it clear we're the ones handling it. He insists, especially since that birthday card has your name on it."

Charles looked even more confused. "Yeah, I don't get it! "

Mac gestured towards it. "I mean, it's a birthday card. What the hell could it mean? It's nowhere near your birthday, so that's not it. And it's a card for a one-year-old, but neither of us have a one-year-old at home."

In that moment, Mac seemed to lose focus as his mind drifted back to a distant, foggy memory. "I was just thinking about Judy's first birthday," he said quietly, a lump forming in his throat. "I don't really remember much, except that Darla spent the whole day baking the cake while I..."

Charles, sensing his partner's pain, tried to offer some comfort. "It's okay, Mac. That was a long time ago," he said softly.

Mac nodded, a distant look in his eyes. "Yeah, you're right, Charlie boy. What do you say we call it a night?"

The two detectives left the station. The air felt thick, oppressive, as if the weight of their work had followed them out into the night. The ride home seemed longer than usual.

Mac glanced at Charles before pulling away from the curb. "I'll see you tomorrow, Charlie boy. I'll pick you up around seven."

Charles gave a small, concerned smile. "Thanks, Mac. Just... don't go throwing your money away under the witch's dress tonight, okay?" His voice was full of genuine worry for his partner's drinking habits, especially after the exhausting day they'd had.

"Yeah, yeah, I hear ya," Mac muttered, a faint, knowing smile on his face. He slammed his foot on the gas, tires screeching as he sped off into the night.

Charles resided in a modest apartment on the Upper East Side of Manhattan, tucked within a small, aging building. It wasn't much, but it was his sanctuary—his home. He approached the building's front entrance with the usual tiredness from the day's grind. With a quick glance around, he fumbled in his trench coat pocket, pulling out his set of keys. He carefully selected the fourth one on the keyring, the one clearly labeled "Front Door-Building," and slid it into the lock. The door had always been a bit finicky, and Charles had learned over time that a small tug combined with a slight upward lift was required to turn the key and gain entry.

He stepped inside and started his usual ascent up the staircase, the creaky old steps familiar underfoot. But as he climbed, an unsettling feeling crawled up his spine. It was as if someone was watching him, though the sensation was elusive, hard to place.

The stairwell had a small, grimy window at the top of the landing, and Charles paused, feeling the weight of the gaze he couldn't shake. His eyes darted toward it, and through the murky glass, he could make out the silhouette of a man standing next to the phone booth, just beyond the reach of the streetlight. The man's eyes seemed to be fixed on him, but the darkness made it impossible to see his features clearly.

Then, the man did something odd. He raised his hand, slowly turning his fingers forming the shape of a gun, aimed directly at Charles. The hair on the back of his neck stood up and without thinking, Charles turned and bolted back down the stairs, fumbling for his keys as he reached the bottom. He hastily unlocked the door and stepped out onto the sidewalk. His heart pounded as he saw the same man slip into a waiting cab. The car revved and sped off into the night, leaving Charles standing in confusion.

Who was that man? Was he simply waiting for a cab?

Charles couldn't shake the unsettling image of the man with his hand shaped like a gun. His mind raced as he climbed back up the stairs, this time with his keys already clutched tightly in his hand. He reached his apartment door and began to insert the first key labeled "Front Door - Apartment." That's when he noticed something strange. There, next to his welcome mat, was a small mound of freshly turned soil—perfectly shaped. Charles paused for a moment, perplexed. His plants were all on the back balcony, and his neighbors had no plants that would spill over near his front door. The sight struck him as out of place.

With a sense of urgency, he threw open his front door and rushed inside. He grabbed his broom and dustpan, not allowing a single trace of the soil to remain. He swept it all up quickly. His nerves already frayed after the day that he had been through.

At first glance, Charles Coffey appeared to be an ordinary man, nothing more than a typical city dweller in a small, nondescript building. But a closer look would reveal that beneath the surface, there was more to him that meets the eye.

The sudden click of the remote echoed through the quiet apartment as he turned on the TV, his attention shifting away from the unsettling events of the evening. The screen flickered to life, displaying the familiar, glossy news anchor for the 6 p.m. broadcast. The news was his usual escape, a brief distraction, but even as the images of the city flashed across the screen, Charles couldn't shake the feeling that he was being drawn into something much bigger than himself.

Breaking News: *A body was discovered earlier today in the Financial District. Authorities are tight-lipped about the victim's identity, with no further details released at this time. However, the Chief of Police has stated that the investigation is being treated as a "high priority." We will continue to follow this developing story and bring you updates as they become available. In other news, the New York City Zoo this morning welcomed...*

Charles sat motionless, his gaze fixed on the television screen. His eyes moved over the images, yet his mind wandered far away, detached from what he was seeing. The sounds of the program washed over him, but they failed to register in his consciousness. Suddenly, the microwave beeped, a sharp "ping" cutting through the silence. With a mechanical routine, Charles rose from his chair and retrieved his frozen lasagna dinner. Tonight, it was lasagna. Tomorrow, it will be chicken tikka. The same meal choices, day after day, week after week.

Once he had finished, he carefully washed his knife and fork—the same utensils he used every night. He washed them three times, as was his custom, before drying them meticulously. They were then placed with precision into the top right-hand drawer of his kitchen, marked clearly with the label "Utensils." Alongside them, he had prepared the exact amount of salt and pepper for the week, a task he completed every Sunday without fail. His obsessive-compulsive tendencies were as much a part of him as breathing, a constant and often overwhelming presence in his life.

Charles often found himself lost in thought, reflecting on the source of his "problem," as he called it. He traced it back to his childhood, to the rituals his mother had practiced. The compulsive cleaning, meticulous organization and hygiene routines. These habits had been ingrained in him at such a young age that they had become second nature and almost uncontrollable.

That night, after Charles switched off the mind-numbing television program, his mind refused to quieten. The thoughts of the day spun in a chaotic whirl, each one pulling him deeper into a web of questions that refused to untangle. He stood up, his body moving toward the bed mechanically, but sleep felt like an impossible destination, just out of reach. His mind was too cluttered, too overwhelmed by the weight of unanswered questions and mounting worries.

What the hell is going on!? he thought, frustration bubbling up within him. *Why me? What have I ever done to make someone single me out like this?*

The inscription inside that birthday card haunted him. *Why does that style of writing feel so familiar?* A wave of recognition crashed over him, but he couldn't quite place it. *I know that inscription from somewhere...*

Charles tossed and turned, his mind racing faster than he could keep up. *Who is the victim? Do I know him?* The face in his mind seemed so familiar, but where had he seen it before?

Could it be that guy from the corner store down the street? He thought of the man who worked there, someone he'd seen countless times. Do they look alike? The resemblance was striking, yet there was a disconnect in his gut. It didn't make sense. *No, it can't be him. I saw him just two nights ago as we drove by on the way home.*

The unease lingered, gnawing at the edges of his thoughts. *Is the perpetrator someone I know?* The question felt like a tightening vice around his chest. *But how? He must know me, right?*

The more he turned it over in his mind, the more he realized there was not a single clue, no trail to follow. *Where did this person come from? How could they know me without me knowing them?*

It was maddening, and as the minutes ticked by, the mystery only seemed to deepen, leaving Charles trapped in a spiral of unanswered questions and mounting anxiety. Charles lay tossing and turning in his bed, his body drenched in sweat, the sheets tangled around him as he fought to escape the nightmare that gripped him.

Meanwhile, on the far side of the Narrows Bridge, a series of events were unfolding in the shadows—an unspeakable act was taking place. Little did Charles know that what was happening miles away would soon haunt him in ways he could never have anticipated, leaving him shaken, horrified, and utterly sickened to his core.

"Are you comfortable?" came a distorted, unnerving voice through a speaker mounted high on the left hand corner of the ceiling in the dimly lit room.

"Who are you?!" Vincent shouted, panic rising in his chest as he strained against the blindfold that covered his eyes. He was seated on a hard, cold chair, alone in the middle of a room that felt foreign, unfamiliar.

"The question, Vincent," the voice replied, now with an eerie calmness, "is not who am I, but rather, who are you?"

Fear gripped Vincent's heart as his mind raced, his body trembling uncontrollably. He felt a growing, mortifying sensation—an undeniable pressure—and in that moment, he realized with horror that he was completely naked. A wave of humiliation washed over him as he felt the warmth of urine running down his left leg, soaking into his skin. The floor beneath him felt strange, too—a soft, uneven texture, almost like grass. It made no sense. His confusion deepened as he noticed the coldness of the room, mingled with the faint scent of dampness or fresh rain, adding to the unsettling atmosphere.

His mind, already on the edge, struggled to piece things together. He had no recollection of how he ended up here, in this room, in this situation.

"Please, Sir, please, let me go... please!" Vincent begged, his voice trembling with terror, his throat raw from his desperation.

"Vincent..." The voice spoke again, this time lowering in tone, growing more menacing. "I'm not here to hurt you. I'm here to help you. To help you understand yourself. To help you see who you really are, deep inside. And most importantly, Vincent, to understand why you are here."

A scream tore from Vincent's throat, his terror overpowering his ability to think clearly. "Someone, help me! Please!"

"Don't worry, Vincent," the voice responded, this time with chilling finality. "All will be revealed soon enough."

Suddenly, Vincent heard the unmistakable sound of rushing water—growing louder and closer. It started as a soft trickle, then quickly became a thundering crash. From his left to his right, he could hear the distinct sound of pipes being turned on, water gushing out in floods, echoing around the room. He took a stammering breath, anticipating as if it might be his last.

"Help! Please! Help me!" Vincent screamed again, his voice cracking with fear. "Help meeee!"

But the voice over the speaker had fallen silent, leaving only the sound of the rushing water, intensifying by the second. Vincent's confusion mounted. He had expected to feel the water by now, but the floor beneath him remained dry—unchanged, as if nothing at all was happening.

His mind raced, trying to process the reality of his situation, but all he could focus on was the uncertainty surrounding him. Was the water even real? Was the sound all in his head?

In the chaos of sound and emotion, Vincent found only one thing certain: he was entirely at the mercy of the unseen figure controlling it all. And with every passing second, the grip of fear tightened.

Charles awoke the next morning with a thundering headache from the night before to the sound of his alarm clock, it read;

5:15 a.m.

He went through his usual morning routine with the precision of a man who found comfort in order. He brushed his teeth with meticulous care, the bristles moving in rhythmic strokes across his teeth, as he focused on the task at hand. Next, he moved to the dry-cleaning bag labeled 'Wei's Wash and Press', carefully peeling back the plastic that encased his suit. It was a crisp, freshly pressed outfit, and he hung it on the rack—his rack—neatly arranged by day and color, an organizational system that allowed him to choose his clothing without the slightest hesitation. As he reached for his suit, his fingers gently pulled it off the hanger, feeling the texture of the fabric, taking a moment to inspect it for any imperfections.

However, as always, there was something else to contend with. He had noticed it the night before—the persistent presence of hair from the neighbor's cat, a feline that seemed to take a particular interest in his wardrobe. Charles spent the next fifteen minutes, focused and patient, using a lint roller to remove the wandering cat hairs that had somehow made their way through the walls and into his home, ensuring his suit was spotless for the day ahead.

Just as he was about to put the finishing touches on his Windsor knot, a knock at the door upset his early morning regime.

"Knock, knock..." The voice of Mac called through the door, muffled but unmistakable. "Hey, Charlie boy, you in there? Come on, we're gonna be late!"

Charles' frustration flared instantly at Mac's premature arrival. His eyes narrowed as he took in a deep breath.

The door opened, and as soon as Mac saw Charles' stiff posture, he recognized that he had hit a nerve. Mac was well aware of his partner's fixation around punctuality and order.

Charles' lips pressed into a thin line, trying to maintain his composure. "Well, we better get going," he muttered, forcing his annoyance down.

He locked the door behind him, as was his custom, but did so with a precise series of three turns, ensuring the lock was secure. It was a small act, but it mattered. Everything in his life had its place, its purpose.

Together, Charles and Mac made their way to the precinct, the sounds of the busy city morning echoing around them. Once they arrived at the station, Mac made his way up the stairs to the office, while Charles took an unexpected and out of the ordinary detour toward the missing persons section. It was a stop he never looked forward to, but it was necessary, and today, it meant visiting the one and only "Looney Lyle," a man who's time in Vietnam did more damage than good.

Lyle Duggard was once a highly respected officer, known for his exceptional service in both the military and on the police force. He had earned several commendations for his bravery during the Vietnam War, and his reputation as a dedicated cop continued to grow in the late 70's and early 80's. His contributions to the force were recognized, and he was decorated for his courage and professionalism.

However, in the fall of 1984, everything changed during what was meant to be just another routine beat. As Lyle walked his usual patrol route, he stumbled upon a violent robbery in progress at a local convenience store. The assailant burst out of the store, brandishing a weapon, and immediately began firing indiscriminately at anyone in the area. Lyle, ever the protector, sprang into action, rushing towards a young woman who had been caught in the line of fire. He threw himself in front of her, attempting to shield her from the gunfire, but tragically, the bullets struck him. He was hit in the head, and the officers on the scene, believing he was dead, began to prepare for the worst.

But against all odds, Lyle's body took a shallow breath, defying the expectations of the first responders. In a frantic scramble, he was rushed to Mount Sinai Hospital, where surgeons immediately began working to save his life. Though his survival was nothing short of miraculous, the damage was extensive. The bullet had left him partially paralyzed on the left side of his body, affecting his motor skills and his ability to speak clearly. His once-strong, vibrant presence had been reduced to someone bound to a wheelchair, struggling with every movement and every word.

Confined to the basement of the precinct, Lyle's once promising career had been transformed into a shadow of its former self. He spent his days surrounded by dusty case files and old paperwork, sifting through them in search of anything that might give him purpose or a sense of accomplishment. Cataloging missing persons reports and combing through cold cases had become his life, a way to stay connected to the work he loved, even if he couldn't physically participate in the same way.

"Good morning, Lyle!" Charles greeted, his voice bright and upbeat, hoping to inject some positivity into the day.

Lyle's response was far from warm. "What the hell is so good about it, Mr. Coffey? Care to enlighten me? I'd love to hear your take on it," Lyle snapped, his voice dripping with sarcasm as he maneuvered his wheelchair towards the counter.

Charles, ever the professional, simply shook his head, brushing off the grumpy reception. "Never mind, Lyle," he said with a quick wave of his hand. "We've got a victim on the Doc's table, but no ID on him. Can I give you a description, and you can check your files to see if you have any missing persons reports that match?"

Lyle scoffed, clearly annoyed. "That's all you blues ever come down here for, huh? No donuts, no coffee, no friendly chit-chat with your old pal, Lyle? Fine, whatever... Just give me the description already, would ya?"

Charles, undeterred, began. "Caucasian male. About 35 years old. Roughly 210 pounds. Sandy blonde hair. Blue eyes."

Lyle muttered under his breath, clearly unimpressed. "Jeez, you'd think you were in love with the guy, Charles, the way you're describing him."

"Just being thorough, Lyle," Charles said, his tone now tinged with authority. He had learned over the years not to engage with Lyle's sarcastic remarks. Arguing was pointless—plus, they needed him.

Lyle grumbled but reluctantly agreed. "Alright, I'll check for you. But remember, I only have access to missing persons within the Manhattan area. All the damn paperwork is being transferred to those newfangled computers—hell if I know how to work those things. If your John Doe came from another borough, you're out of luck."

Charles nodded, grateful for whatever help Lyle could offer. He turned to leave the basement office, but Lyle's voice trailed off behind him, still muttering under his breath, as usual.

As Charles made his way back to the main office, he spotted Mac moving toward him at a brisk pace, his expression tense and his body language urgent. Whatever was going on, it seemed like something big was unfolding.

"We gotta go Charles, the Doc has something for us!"

Charles spun around quickly, his footsteps deliberate as he headed toward the car, Mac just a step behind him, his breath coming in quick, shallow bursts as he tried to catch up.

"Doc didn't say much, Charlie boy, but he sounded confused," Mac remarked, the words heavy with anticipation, knowing that whatever they were about to hear could turn their whole case upside down.

The drive to the OCME was consumed by an eerie, almost suffocating silence between the two detectives. The tension hung thick in the air as both men kept their thoughts to themselves, each lost in speculation about what the good doctor might reveal. Charles' mind, consumed by the case, wandered momentarily to the past—his childhood, a subject that always stirred a tangled mixture of joy and pain within him. His thoughts swirled in a maze of bittersweet memories, uninvited yet persistent, before he was sharply jolted back into the present.

Mac slammed the brakes as they came to an abrasive stop, causing Charles to tense up in the passenger seat as they parked the vehicle at the Medical Examiner's office.

Without missing a beat, Mac rushed into the cold, sterile room of the ME's office, his urgency obvious. "What have you got for us, Doc?" he asked, his voice cutting through the air as he addressed Dr. Bullard, who had been waiting anxiously for the detectives to arrive.

"Gentlemen," Dr. Bullard began, his voice grim and heavy, "What we have here is an absolute mystery."

Both Charles and Mac leaned in closer to the covered body on the table, their gazes locked onto the victim as the white shroud was gently pulled back.

Dr. Bullard pointed to the victim's severed hand. "Take a look at where the hand was removed. There's an abrasion here—about two or three months old. It suggests that at some point, the victim was restrained, but that restraint was released a few weeks ago. The other hand, however, is completely clean, indicating he was only bound by one hand. My assumption is that the other hand was left free for a reason."

Charles, eyes narrowing with focus, asked, "Doc, can you tell us if the hand was removed before or after death?"

Dr. Bullard's face hardened with the weight of his answer. "Unfortunately, gentlemen, the hand was removed perimortem. The victim suffered greatly, but based on the blood flow and coagulation, it's clear the victim died shortly after the appendage was severed."

Mac's face twisted in disgust. "So, the sick bastard cut off his hand and then sewed a fake one on after the victim died?"

Dr. Bullard shook his head, a sad frown tugging at his lips. "Not quite, gentlemen. The blood indicates that the artificial hand was sewn on while the victim was still alive. He endured the pain of this procedure, and death occurred shortly after or during that time."

Both detectives exchanged a glance, the horror of the details slowly sinking in.

"We're far from finished, gentlemen," Dr. Bullard continued, holding up his hand as if to halt their thoughts. "I couldn't find anything on the artificial limbs to indicate where they came from. They're made from a silicone base, wrapped in latex to give the wearer the feel of skin over the now replaced appendage. No further clues there, I'm afraid."

Charles, leaning in even closer, not wanting to miss a single detail. "Anything else, Doc?" he asked softly, his voice steady despite the growing sense of unease within him.

Dr. Bullard sighed and continued. "I found slight bruising around the mouth, particularly at the corners of the lips. This suggests that the victim's mouth was forcefully opened before death, which likely caused the bruising."

Charles' eyes widened as he processed the information. "And the fibers?" he asked, his mind already making connections.

Dr. Bullard nodded. "Yes, there were several fine fibers around the lips, likely from a metallic object. Unfortunately, they're not traceable."

"You mean like a metal pipe?" Charles ventured, a sickening thought already creeping into his mind.

"Exactly," Dr. Bullard confirmed, "with an outside diameter of about three to five inches."

The detective's stomach churned as he absorbed the details, but there was more to come.

"Upon further inspection of the mouth and nasal cavity, gentlemen, I then determined the most likely cause of death was suffocation," Dr. Bullard added, his voice taking on a heavier tone.

Charles braced himself for the next revelation. "Great, so he was suffocated?"

"In a manner of speaking, yes," Dr. Bullard replied cryptically.

Charles' voice tightened with suspicion. "What do you mean 'in a manner of speaking'?"

"Well, gentlemen, your victim suffocated to death not from lack of air," Dr. Bullard said slowly, as if weighing each word carefully, "but from soil consumption."

Charles' heart skipped a beat. "Soil? You mean as in dirt?"

"Yes," Dr. Bullard confirmed, his expression grave. "It seems the victim ingested a large amount of soil—enough to fill the stomach and make its way up the esophagus until it eventually blocked his throat."

Charles froze, the room feeling suddenly colder. His breath caught in his throat as his mind snapped back to the small mound of soil placed outside his door the previous night. The realization sent a chill running down his spine, and he could hardly bring himself to speak. "What?!" he whispered, his voice trembling slightly as the weight of the words sank in.

Dr. Bullard's voice took on an even darker note. "What's even more troubling, gentlemen, is that there's no indication the victim resisted the ingestion of the soil. There's no sign that it was forced down his throat."

Charles' stomach turned, and he could hardly speak through the growing horror. "In other words, he chose to eat the soil himself?" he murmured, the words almost impossible to believe.

"Exactly," Dr. Bullard said softly, his tone filled with a grim finality. "He ingested the soil willingly."

Chapter 2

The Good Host

As Charles and Mac continued to mull over the sparse and unsettling evidence Dr. Bullard had provided, they left the Medical Examiner's office. Both men were left in a daze, struggling to process the strange and terrifying case that was unfolding in front of them. For Charles in particular, the weight of the situation was heavy on his stomach, and he could feel the queasy sensation rising. "I think I'm going to throw up, Mac," he muttered, his face contorting in discomfort as he staggered towards the nearest trash bin outside the office.

Mac, trying to maintain a guise of support, placed a hand on Charles' back. "That's it, Charlie boy, get it all out," he said with as much compassion as he could muster, although the oddness of the case was clearly weighing on both of them.

After Charles had wiped his mouth with a handkerchief, both detectives made their way back to the car. Mac, still rattled by what they had just heard, slid into the driver's seat, strapping himself

in with a look of genuine concern on his face. "Charles, what is going on here?" he asked, breathing deeply before continuing. "We've never had to deal with something like this before? We better report this to the Captain."

Charles' mind was distant as he sat beside his partner, trying to shake the gnawing sense of dread that had settled in his gut. His partner's voice became little more than white noise in the background as his thoughts spiraled. This didn't feel like just another murder case. No, this was something much darker, and Charles could feel it deep in his bones. His gut was telling him this wasn't the end—it was only the beginning. The beginning of something far worse.

He thought about the small mound of soil outside his apartment. His chest tightened. Should he tell Mac about it? Should he even speak to anyone about it? He was already questioning his own sanity for even considering it. What would Mac think? What would anyone think if he mentioned it?

Choosing to keep his uneasy secret, Charles snapped back to reality as

Mac continued to speak, his voice growing louder with each passing second. "Charles!" he called, trying to break through his partner's mental fog.

"Enough!" Charles suddenly barked, his frustration bubbling over. "Let's just go already!"

Mac gave Charles a questioning look, but he didn't argue. The tension between them thickened as they began their drive toward the precinct. But just as they were making their way down the street, Charles, unable to suppress his anxiety any longer, shouted, "Stop the car!"

Mac slammed on the brakes, the car screeching to a halt just in time to avoid crashing into the traffic that had suddenly backed up on 5th Avenue. "What the hell, man?" Mac yelled.

"I gotta go, Mac!" Charles snapped, his voice urgent.

"Go where?" Mac shot back, his tone skeptical.

"I'll catch up with you later, okay?" Charles said quickly, already opening the door.

"No, Charles, not okay," Mac countered, his voice rising in frustration. "What about the Captain?"

Charles didn't hesitate, his face set in determination. "Screw the Captain! He can wait a day. I need time to think." Without another word, he yanked the door open, stepped out onto the sidewalk near Central Park, and slammed the door behind him. Finally being able to break free from the confinement of the vehicle.

Mac, not even waiting for a response, revved the engine and sped off with a screech of tires, leaving Charles standing in the street. Mac wasn't impressed by his partner's behavior. He was frustrated, and he knew that while he wasn't usually one to take charge, it looked like he'd have to step up this time—whether Charles was ready to or not.

Charles needed space to think. He had always found his best moments of clarity during long walks, especially when the evening air was cool and the streets were quieter. He'd wander along the boardwalks or city sidewalks, a hotdog in one hand and a cigarette in the other, the familiar rhythm of each step allowing his mind to unravel the complexities of the world. But, he had kicked the habit some time back. The turning point had come during a scene that haunted him to this day—the case of an elderly man gasping for breath, unable to call for help after a break-in at his apartment. The man had suffered from emphysema and collapsed on the floor, unable to reach the phone in time. Charles had witnessed his final moments, and the sound of the man's desperate gasps still echoed in his mind. After that, Charles had walked out of the old man's apartment building, crushed the pack of Texan cigarettes in his hand, and threw them into the trash. It had been the last pack he ever touched.

Now, as he stood on the sidewalk, the weight of the case pressing on him, Charles found himself in need of another escape. He walked over to a nearby park bench, which, judging by the state of it, appeared to have been used as a public toilet by the local pigeons. With a look of disgust, he pulled out his handkerchief and wiped off as much of the grime as he could, before carefully sitting down. He faced the heavy traffic buildup on 5th Avenue, the roar of cars, a distant hum against the stillness of his thoughts. He stared straight ahead, trying to make sense of the knot in his chest. The connection between the mound of soil outside his apartment and the soil ingested by the victim continued to gnaw at him. It felt too much like a sign, something personal, something he should understand. However, despite his best efforts, he couldn't put his finger on it. They had no leads, no answers, and it was all beginning to weigh heavily on Charles.

As he lost himself in thought, trying to silence the questions swirling in his mind, a sudden, unexpected sound cut through the noise in his head. It was soft and melodic, almost angelic, captivating in a sense. Charles' gaze shifted to his left, and there, standing on the corner, was a street performer. He was strumming a vintage Les Paul guitar, its deep, warm tones resonating with a timeless quality, amplified by a matching vintage amplifier that looked as though it belonged to a different era. Charles watched, enchanted, as the music flowed from the performer's hands.

The sound brought with it an unexpected flood of memories. He found himself transported back to his childhood in Great Kills, watching his father on the back porch of their home, strumming away on his old, fifties-style Spanish acoustic guitar. His father's voice, full of warmth and nostalgia, sang along with the melodies of the classics, songs from a time long gone. Charles would sit for hours, mesmerized by the music, admiring his father's talent and the joy he radiated while playing.

It had been so long since Charles had touched a guitar himself. That instrument, once such a source of joy in his life, had long since disappeared. He remembered the day it was sold at a garage sale, never to be seen again.

The memory hit him like a wave, a bitter reminder of all the things he had lost along the way. The music, the memories, and the emptiness left in their wake lingered in his heart, mixing with the unease he felt about the case at hand.

As Charles listened to the woman's voice blending harmoniously with the legendary guitar player beside her, he found a rare moment of serenity. The music wrapped around him like a warm embrace, and for a brief moment, he was transported away from the turmoil of the case. Even after all these years, the rhythm still had the power to move him—without thinking, his foot began tapping along to the beat, the sound sinking deep into his soul. But then, the sharp call of the hotdog vendor broke through the peaceful moment, pulling Charles back to reality. "Fresh dogs here, get ya fresh dogs here!" The words seemed to echo through the air, and before he realized it, his stomach rumbled in response. It had been hours since he had eaten, and his body was suddenly reminded of its need.

Charles stood up from the bench, the street performer's music still playing in the background, his feet carrying him toward the vendor. He passed by the musician, still enjoying the melodies as he moved. The solitary moment of reflection was brief but meaningful—he knew he needed the distraction.

"One hotdog, please," Charles said, his voice low as he approached the vendor's cart.

"Coming right up!" The man replied with a polite enthusiasm, his gaze fixed on the ingredients he was preparing. His navy blue cap obscured his face, making it impossible for Charles to catch a glimpse of his features. The vendor continued to prepare the hotdog, attempting to make small talk as he worked.

"Nice day we're having, eh? You think the weather's gonna turn?"

Charles was caught off guard by the question. He wasn't in the mood for small talk, and his response was clipped, "I don't think so."

As he waited, a vague sense of unease settled in his chest. The conversation felt oddly invasive, like the man was trying to pull him out of his own thoughts. It was unsettling, but Charles didn't know why. "Things can change at any given time, though. My daddy always used to say, "you never know what's gonna happen next." The vendor slapped together the hotdog, still speaking in a calm, offhanded tone.

As he handed Charles the hotdog, the man added, "It's on the house, Detective."

A chill ran down Charles' spine at the unexpected words, his heart skipping a beat as he looked up at the man. "How do you know I'm a detective?" The question slipped out almost automatically, his voice taking on the sharpness of someone who had spent too much time questioning suspects.

The vendor looked up, smiling as he pointed toward Charles's belt. "It says it right there on your badge."

For the first time, Charles's gaze dropped to his waist, where his badge—almost hidden beneath his jacket—was faintly visible. Realization hit, and a flush of embarrassment washed over him. "Ah, right. Thanks!" he muttered, a bit self-conscious.

The vendor simply nodded. "Anytime! Keep up the good work." He grinned, and with a slight nod, he pushed his cart away, wheeling it toward the winding paths of Central Park.

Charles stood there for a moment, watching the vendor disappear among the trees. There was something about the man's demeanor—his calmness, his sense of peace—that made Charles feel a sense of longing. The vendor seemed unaffected by anything around him, his day unfolding in perfect simplicity.

Charles couldn't help but feel a deep, almost jealous yearning to experience that same unshakable tranquility. Watching the man's figure disappear around a corner, the last trace of him fading into the park, Charles found himself wishing he could share that same carefree approach to life. Instead, the burden of his thoughts, his responsibilities, and the case weighed heavily on him, amplifying the sense of emptiness that had taken root in his chest.

Charles began strolling through the park, taking in the tranquil surroundings, the lush greenery, the soft rustle of leaves in the breeze, and the distant sounds of city life blending with the serenity of nature. He allowed himself a few moments to appreciate the beauty of the place—the vibrant flowers, the joggers moving along the paths, the peaceful scene in stark contrast to the chaos he'd left behind, albeit briefly. Yet, his thoughts quickly shifted back to the case, and the weight of the investigation began to creep back into his mind.

He replayed the details of the crime scene in his head. *What about the crime scene?* He mentally asked himself. A busy intersection, smack in the middle of the city—an area teeming with people, yet no one seemed to know anything.

Why was the body left right in the middle of the street?

Did anyone see anything? The thought of witnesses crossed his mind, but he couldn't shake the nagging question—*what was the killer's motive for staging the body in such a public place?* Charles wiped his hands on his handkerchief after finishing his hotdog, and then pulled out his notebook from his shirt pocket, flicking it open with a practiced motion. He scribbled down his first thoughts: *Check for CCTV in the area and interview possible witnesses in the surrounding buildings!*

With his notebook in hand, he let his mind wander, trying to piece together what he knew. *But why leave the body there?* It made no sense. *Was there something about the location that had personal significance? Was the street, or even the specific intersection, meaningful to the victim or the killer or even to me?*

His inner monologue continued to swirl as he walked. Every thought seemed to contradict the next, each possible explanation feeling like a dead end. The truth was, murder investigations were still foreign territory for Charles. He was a burglary and larceny detective—murders were out of his usual scope, and the weight of the unfamiliarity pressed heavily on him.

He spent over an hour walking. Finally, the most logical course of action struck him: the crime scene itself was the key. He needed to go back, see it again, and approach it with fresh eyes. A familiar practice to him just as he would have revisited a scene in his previous cases. There had to be something he had missed, something that would finally make everything click.

Making his decision, Charles turned and headed back toward the street where he'd entered the park, scanning the area for the nearest public phone booth. Once he spotted it, he rushed over, dialing the number for precinct without wasting another second.

"Dispatch, Doris speaking!" came the familiar voice on the other end of the line. "Doris, it's Charles! Is Mac there?" he asked impatiently.

"No, I haven't seen him!" Doris responded.

"Can you get a message to him on the radio?" Charles pressed. "Tell him to meet me on the corner of John & William Street, Financial District. It's urgent, Doris."

"Yeah, yeah, sure, sure!" she replied quickly, and Charles hung up without waiting for further confirmation.

Before he could even fully process the exchange, a cabbie pulled up to the curb, almost as if he'd been waiting for Charles all along.

The cabbie rolled down his window and spoke in his thick Brooklyn accent. "Where are you headed?"

"Corner of John & William Street, Financial District." Charles ordered, his impatience growing. He needed to get there fast.

In the bustling heart of the city, Mac found himself once again at Fraunces Tavern, a place he frequented for what he fondly called his "beer-flavored early dinners." The bar was dimly lit, the sound of clinking glasses and murmured conversations filling the air. Mac leaned back in his seat, swirling his beer in a glass as he spoke to Billy, a regular who had seen him through many a rough day.

"I don't know what to do with this guy," Mac muttered, frustration creeping into his voice as he gestured vaguely toward his troubled partnership with Charles.

Billy, always quick with an answer and a drink in hand, took a hearty gulp of his fourth beer. "I don't know, Mac, get rid of him!"

he suggested nonchalantly, his voice slurring slightly from the alcohol.

Mac frowned as he reached into his top pocket, pulling out a crumpled $5 bill and placing it on the counter. He gave Mike, the bartender, a nod. "Keep the change, Mike," he said, his tone barely masking the tension simmering beneath the surface. He pushed himself up from the bar and moved towards the door.

As Mac stepped outside, the familiar screech of tires echoed in the street as he climbed into his Gran Fury. Before he could settle into the car, a voice crackled through the radio.

"Unit 34, come in."

Mac sighed, rolling his eyes as he grabbed the mic. "Yeah, Doris, what is it? Shouldn't you be off duty?"

"Mac, you are requested to meet Detective Coffey on the corner of John & William Street."

Mac muttered under his breath, his impatience growing as he started the engine and drove towards the Financial District.

Meanwhile, Charles stood on the sidewalk, his eyes scanning the scene in front of him. The street stretched out, the tall, imposing skyscrapers on both sides creating a canyon of steel and glass. His gaze lingered on a

CCTV camera mounted high on a building across the street, its unblinking eye silently watching over the intersection. As he took in the surroundings, Charles couldn't ignore how dim the streetlights were. The shadows seemed to dance at the edges of the pavement, giving the area an almost sinister feel. He began walking towards the building, his mind already racing with possibilities, when the sound of screeching tires pulled his focus back to the present. Mac had finally arrived.

"It's been an hour since I called you, Mac!" Charles snapped, irritation evident in his voice.

"I was busy," Mac responded, his tone casual as he stepped out of the car.

"Too busy for the investigation?" Charles shot back, still fuming.

"At least I didn't wander off!" Mac said smugly, a grin tugging at the corners of his mouth.

Charles, though still irritated, waved it off. "Never mind that, Mac. Look up there, fourth floor."

Mac followed Charles' gaze. "I see it. You think it's real? These things are pretty expensive these days," he said, his skepticism evident.

"We're about to find out," Charles said, his voice carrying a hint of confidence.

With purpose, both detectives approached the front of the building, walking towards the security guard stationed just inside. The guard looked young, his posture stiff and his expression one of discomfort, as though he weren't entirely suited to his job.

"Good afternoon, Detectives Coffey and Mackenzie," Charles said, offering the young man a polite nod. The security guard looked up nervously. "How can I help you, Detectives?"

"We're investigating the homicide—the body that was discovered on the street outside this building on Monday morning ," Charles explained. "Were you on duty that morning?"

The guard scratched his head before answering, "Well, I was on the night shift that evening, and just as I was getting ready to leave, it was about 3:30 a.m., I heard screeching tires. I went to check, but by the time I got there, there was nothing. I just assumed it was a joyrider or something."

Charles frowned. "And the camera on the fourth floor? Can we see the footage?"

The guard's expression grew sheepish. "I'm sorry, Detectives. That camera's a dummy. The owner of the investment firm comes from a long line of tightwads. That's why I'm getting paid 50 cents an hour," he added with a crooked grin.

Charles' frustration flared, but he kept it in check. "Thanks," he said courteously, turning to leave the building. But, as they walked toward the door, the guard's voice stopped them in their tracks.

"Did you speak to Mason?" the guard called out.

"Mason? Who the hell is Mason?" Charles asked, pausing and turning back to the guard.

"Mayhem Mason," the guard clarified, gesturing vaguely towards an alleyway across the street. "The homeless guy who lives there. He's a real character." Charles' curiosity piqued. "No, we haven't. Thanks for the tip," he said, though his tone was more puzzled than grateful.

The guard, eager to share more, leaned in slightly. "But you should know, Mason's not your average homeless guy. He was a POW during Vietnam, only getting out when the war ended. Left him a little... off, if you catch my drift."

Charles exchanged a glance with Mac. "Is he dangerous?" he asked, his skepticism evident.

"Nah, he's harmless. Just a little, uh, eccentric."

Just then, Charles' attention was drawn to a figure sitting across the street on a paint can, shouting incoherently at passersby. His wild eyes and unkempt appearance were unmistakable.

"Is that him?" Charles queried, his voice low.

"Yeah, that's him," the guard confirmed.

Both detectives studied the figure for a moment before Charles nodded, a potential lead forming in his mind. They had to speak to this "Mayhem" Mason.

Charles and Mac made their way over to the homeless man who was still shouting curses at passersby, his voice rising above the city noise. "TEA COFFEE...TEA COFFEE...TEA COFFEE!" he repeated, as if in some kind of twisted chant, his eyes wild and unfocused.

"Mason," Charles called out, his voice firm but measured, trying to reach the man who appeared to be in his early fifties. His face was weathered and rough, skin as worn as leather, his hair and beard was a disheveled mix of grey with a faint greenish tint at the ends. His hair was held back with a faded Americana bandanna. His feet were barely contained in his worn All-Star shoes, the soles worn down to the bare minimum. The smell of body odor clung to his army surplus jacket and pants, overpowering in the closed air of the alleyway.

"Yeah, who wants to know?" Mason's voice was raspy from all the shouting.

"My name is Charles, I'm a detective," Charles said, maintaining a calm demeanor as he stood a few feet away from Mason.

"What do you want? Are you spying on me?" Mason snapped, his eyes narrowing suspiciously. "Your badges, your badges, let me see your badges!"

"Okay, Mason," Charles replied, his tone softening slightly as he and Mac both reached for their badges. Charles handed his badge over to Mason.

Mason took the badge, squinting at it as he traced the letters with his finger, reading out loud. "D-E-T-E-C-T-I-V-E..." His voice trailed off as he stared at it for a moment longer. "Yeah, Detective..." he muttered, his eyes darting nervously from Charles to Mac.

"What do you want? Just leave me alone!" Mason suddenly wailed, his voice cracking as he dropped his head. "They hurt me, they hurt me!" His shoulders hunched in an almost instinctual way, as if bracing for some unseen assault.

"Mason, calm down," Charles said gently, trying to de-escalate the situation. "We just want to ask you a few questions."

Mason recoiled, his hands gripping the air as if trying to ward off an invisible threat. "That's what they said before," he mumbled, his voice trembling. He crouched down as if anticipating a beating, a haunted and submissive look in his eyes.

"No, Mason, we're not here to hurt you," Charles said, his tone reassuring. "Did you see something a few nights ago? Something happened here on this street."

Mason's eyes suddenly widened, and he turned his head to look at Charles. "Yes, I did... yes I did," he replied with a sudden intensity in his voice.

"What did you see, Mason?" Charles asked, leaning in, his curiosity piqued.

"Mrs. Crowley... Yes, Mrs. Crowley..." Mason's voice shifted to a frantic pitch, his gaze growing distant. "Her dog was barking again, yes, barking at me again."

At this point, Mac, who had been standing slightly off to the side, interjected. He gave Charles a pointed look. "We're wasting our time here, Charlie boy. He doesn't know anything."

Charles didn't immediately respond. Instead, he took a step closer to Mason, whose eyes seemed lost in some distant memory. The man's once-vibrant spirit now seemed shattered, pieces scattered in time and place. "Mason," Charles said again, his voice softer this time, "Are you sure you didn't see anything else?"

Mason's eyes glazed over as a strange grin spread across his face. "Ten bucks," he said suddenly, his voice almost childlike. "He gave me ten bucks. Said it was from Jeremy. He said, "If anyone asks, it was from Johnny... No wait, Jimmy! Yes... It was definitely Johnny!"

Charles raised an eyebrow, confused by Mason's ramblings. He glanced down at the man's face, which was now smiling faintly.

"Well, enjoy the ten bucks, Mason," Charles muttered, feeling both sympathy and frustration toward the man.

Charles stood up and glanced at Mac. "I think you're right, Mac. We're wasting our time here."

The two detectives turned and began walking back toward the car, Mason's voice rising behind them, still screaming out his profanity-laden rants into the air. As they walked, Charles couldn't help but feel sorry for the man. Mason had served his country, but society had failed to serve him in return. The thought lingered in his mind.

As they arrived back at the precinct, the weary detectives made their way through the bustling bullpen toward their desks. Charles noticed a pack of files waiting for him. A note was scrawled across the top: Possible matches, three boroughs, Lyle. PS waiting on Brooklyn and Staten!

"What's that?" Mac asked, glancing at the files. "Lyle's brought us ten files that match the description of our victim in the morgue," Charles said, his voice tinged with a mix of hope and frustration. "You take five, and I'll take five."

Charles and Mac then set to work, sifting through the missing persons cases. Some descriptions matched the victim but didn't align with the timeline, while others had timelines that seemed to fit but lacked matching descriptions.

"Mac," Charles said, his voice growing with excitement as he flipped through the files. "I think I've found a few possible matches. Caucasian males, approximately 35 years old, some are from Queens, The Bronx and Manhattan. These four files are all we got to go on Mac. We need to follow up on these leads."

Mac, who had been poring over his own set of files, looked up and nodded. "The rest of my files also fit that profile, Charles, but for now, let's call it a day."

Charles hesitated for a moment, glancing at the clock on the wall. The time had gotten away from him. With a reluctant sigh, he glanced down at his watch. "11:45 p.m.," he muttered under his breath.

"Yeah, we'll pick it up in the morning," Mac said, clearly ready to call it quits for the night.

As Charles and Mac made their way home, the grim fate of Vincent Childs continued to unfold...

"Wake up, Vincent," a distorted voice crackled over the loudspeaker, cutting through the haze of unconsciousness. As Vincent slowly stirred, his blurred vision gradually cleared.

For the first time, he realized that the blindfold had been removed, and he could see the room around him.

He immediately became aware of his nakedness, the chilling touch of chains biting into his wrists. He tried to move his arms but felt the unyielding steel that restrained him. Looking around, Vincent began to understand why he felt so cold. The walls of the room were made of brushed steel, not polished but instead deliberately distorted, as though they were meant to reflect nothing clearly, only distorting whatever light made contact with them.

The air around him was thick with a mist, heavy with water vapor that seemed to coat the walls and ceiling. Thick steel pipes ran along the room, their ominous hum echoing through the space. From the sound and the way the pipes seemed to snake through the room and disappear into the walls, Vincent assumed that he was being held beneath the city, possibly beneath the main water supply. The pipes appeared deliberately modified, their high-pressure mist saturating the room and making the air feel heavy and damp. Vincent's skin was slick, his body clammy, as if drenched in sweat, though he realized it was just the thick moisture filling the air.

The room felt eerie and was empty, apart from the loudspeaker mounted in the top left corner, encased in a metal box. Wires twisted and turned
across the ceiling, disappearing into a wall above the only steel door in the
room. The door had no visible lock or handle, only a small hatch in the
center, almost like the kind seen in prison cells. The chair he was strapped
to was bolted to the floor, his back to the wall, preventing him from seeing
behind him. Every few minutes, he heard a faint clicking sound, raising his
anxiety and the fear of the unknown. Vincent knew he had lived a life full
of choices that would eventually catch up to him, but he never imagined it
would culminate in such a horrific nightmare.

"Are you awake, Vincent?" The voice crackled again, this time closer, as if
mocking him. "I trust you enjoyed your rest."

"Why am I here?" Vincent asked, his voice hoarse, his senses still reeling
from the disorienting situation.

"Now, Vincent," the voice responded smoothly, "before we dive into that,
let's take a moment for proper introductions."

There was a clicking noise, followed by the sound of bolts unlocking one
by one on the opposite side of the door. With a loud thud, the door swung
open, revealing the shadowy silhouette of a man standing in the threshold.

"Hello, Vincent," the man greeted, his voice calm but chilling. "Nice to
finally meet you face-to-face. My name is Michael. The silhouette of the man
faded as he came into view. Would you like some water?" He raised a glass
to Vincent's lips. "You must be thirsty?"

Vincent, still in a daze, nodded faintly, his dry throat barely allowing him
to speak. "Yes, please."

Michael carefully tipped the glass to Vincent's lips, slowly pouring the
cool water into his mouth, ensuring every drop was consumed. The refreshing sensation of the water soothed Vincent's throat, momentarily grounding
him in reality. "Now wasn't that refreshing?" Michael asked, his eyes studying Vincent, who was still lost in the surreal nature of his predicament.

"What have you done to me?" Vincent croaked, his mind still trying to
process the situation.

"It's just a mild sedative to help you relax," Michael explained casually.
"Now, back to your earlier question—'Why are you here?' Well, Vincent, this
is how things will go. I'm going to get to know you, and in turn, you'll get
to know me. And over time, we can hopefully become friends. What do you

think of that?"

Vincent stared at him, confusion and fear clouding his thoughts.

"Why can't you just let me go?" Vincent's voice was shaking, his desperation rising.

Michael's smile didn't falter. "Now, Vincent, don't spoil the fun. Give it time, and you'll see." With that, he moved closer to Vincent. "Now rest. We've got a lot of work ahead, you and I."

Without another word, Michael pulled a syringe from his right trouser pocket and swiftly injected it into Vincent's neck. As the darkness took hold, Vincent could only hear the persistent rush of water and Michael's voice drifting into the distance. "Good night, Vincent. Sweet dreams."

The world around Vincent swirled between consciousness and unconsciousness, his mind drifting in and out of reality. The next time Vincent regained any sense of awareness, he found himself lying down. He stared at the ceiling above him, feeling oddly comfortable. For the first time in what felt like ages, the room didn't seem cold anymore. He sat up, realizing he had been moved from the chair to a bed, positioned directly opposite the steel door.

The back wall of the room, previously unseen, now had two fans mounted on it, circulating warm air to counter the coldness he had once felt.

Vincent swung his legs over the bed and noticed, to his surprise, that he was now clothed. The sensation of clothing, especially after being naked for so long, felt almost unnatural to him. He had always lived his life wrapped in the finest Armani suits and designer shoes, yet now he was dressed simply—something that, in this strange new reality, felt oddly comforting.

His eyes drifted across the room, now noticing a small metal table beneath the loudspeaker. On the table was a pitcher of water, glistening with ice, lemon and mint floating on top. The water looked refreshing, inviting even, and the sight of it made Vincent's dry throat ache.

Without a second thought, Vincent reached for the glass, pouring himself a drink. The cool water, tinged with the hint of lemon and mint, slid down his throat, leaving a refreshing chill. He drank it all in one gulp, the sensation flooding him with relief.

Just as Vincent was about to pour himself another glass, the sound of bolts being undone echoed through the room. The door swung open, and

Michael's booming voice filled the space. "Good morning, Vincent! How did you sleep?"

Vincent froze, glass still in hand, paralyzed by a mix of fear and confusion. He managed to mutter, "I slept well, thank you."

"Sit down, Vincent," Michael instructed, gesturing toward the bed. Vincent obeyed quickly, moving toward Michael, who stood framed in the doorway.

"Enjoying your water?" Michael asked, his smile unchanging. "Refreshing, isn't it? I made sure to use only the finest ingredients and the purest water I could find."

Vincent didn't know how to respond. He only sat silently, staring at Michael, trying to make sense of his situation. Michael then set a steel chair opposite Vincent, sitting down with an air of calm authority.

"So, Vince!" Michael began, his voice light. "Can I call you Vince? I've heard quite a bit about you. You're quite the artist, aren't you? My mother was an artist too. She used to teach me how to turn something ordinary into something beautiful with just a few strokes."

Vincent looked at Michael in confusion. "I do enjoy drawing," he replied, unsure of where Micheal was going with these questions.

"Come on, Vince, don't be modest," Michael continued, his voice full of praise. "Who would you say your influences are? Monet? Turner? Perhaps Cassatt? I've seen your work. Your copy of Monet's Bridge Over a Pond of Water Lilies was flawless. You have talent, Vince." Vincent's eyes widened with fear. Panic rose within him as tears welled up in his eyes. Deep inside, he knew this was the reason for him being here.

"Shhh..." Michael soothed, his tone gentle. "Calm down, Vincent. Here, let me give you some more water."

Michael poured more water into the glass and handed it to Vincent. He grabbed it with both hands, gulping it down eagerly, feeling his breath return to normal as the cool liquid soothed his throat.

"Do you feel better?" Michael asked, his voice filled with false concern.

"I do, thank you," said Vincent, trying to steady his breathing.

"I tell you what, Vince," Michael said, his tone shifting to something more sinister, "I'm going to make sure you get the finest canvas and watercolors. I want you to create something truly inspired, an impressionistic view of the world for this room, it's missing something; don't you agree?".

"Yeah, sure," Vincent replied, believing that this strange new reality was about creating art for Michael's benefit. Little did he know, Michael had darker plans in store.

Over the next weeks, Vincent and Michael spent every day together. Vincent poured more of himself into his artwork, and Michael offered endless praise for his "talent." Vincent started to grow comfortable with Michael as his fear began to dissipate, even finding an odd attraction to him, though he couldn't quite explain why. Each day, Vincent was treated to a new water flavor—aloe and thistle, pineapple and watermelon, and so on. He drank water by the gallon, often relieving himself into a bucket in the corner of the room. He didn't notice, but the temperature in the room slowly began to rise, a half-degree at a time.

He was fed thick, buttered ciabatta bread every day, but the real excitement came with the anticipation of what new, exotic water flavor would await him. It became an obsession.

One day, Vincent woke up to find himself in the chair again, but this time, the room was unbearably hot. The heat was unlike anything he had felt before, radiating through his skin and searing his body. "Michael! Michael!" Vincent screamed, frantic and disoriented. "What's going on? Help me!"

But there was no answer. Only the soft buzzing of the speaker. Hours passed, and the heat grew more intense. Vincent cried and screamed for help, but nothing came. As the days dragged on, the room became a furnace, and his skin began to blister, the boils creeping up his back, legs, and neck.

Vincent's screams grew more desperate, but the silence remained. Eventually, dehydration and exhaustion took its toll, and he passed out.

Then, Michael's voice returned, cold and final. "Vincent... Vincent... wake up!"

Startled, Vincent jolted awake, realizing quickly that he was free of his restraints, only to be greeted by a new torment. Michael's voice filled the room with scorn. "You disgust me, Vincent". "You took something beautiful and turned it into something vile. You destroyed works of art—replacing them with fakes and selling them to the highest bidder. You ruined lives with your greed, Vincent. But now it's time for justice. The scales have tipped, but no more. I am balance. I am reason. I am liberty."

Vincent screamed, his mind unraveling as he realized the full extent of Michael's twisted reasoning.

The speaker went silent.

Days bled into each other, and Vincent's body continued to degrade, his strength waning as dehydration escalated. The once refreshing water now seemed like a distant memory, and his cries became hoarse and desperate.

Then, without warning. The pipes above his head rumbled with the force of incoming pressure. The water gushed through the pipe in the ceiling, hitting Vincent with immense force, ripping open the boils on his body. But Vincent didn't care anymore. He ran toward the water, pressing his mouth against the pipe, desperate for relief.

The water came in waves, slamming into him. Vincent felt himself being torn apart as the water surged down his throat, forcing him to swallow faster than he could process. The pressure was overwhelming.

With his last breath, Vincent held on, feeling the water overwhelm him, flooding his body with a sense of finality. The pressure increased, his body becoming limp, and with one last gasp, he drowned. Vincent Childs, once a man of greed, was gone. His victims had finally been liberated...

On a bustling street in The Bronx downtown, Charles and Mac had just finished an interview with the family of a missing person who seemed to match the description of the victim in the morgue. After weeks of chasing leads, it was another dead end.

"Where to from here, Charlie boy? This nonsense has been going on for weeks. It's really starting to get to me," Mac grumbled, wiping mustard off his already shabby tie, which had seen better days.

Charles, however, kept his gaze straight ahead, his attention focused on the task at hand. He ignored his partner's feeble complaints, as his mind was elsewhere.

"Let's head over to the 122nd," Charles suggested, his voice growing more impatient. "If we wait any longer for their file to arrive, we'll both be retiring before we get any answers."

The two detectives made their way toward the 122nd precinct in Staten Island, driving past the 68th and 72nd precincts along the way. As they crossed the Narrows Bridge and passed South and Midland Beach, Charles took a more scenic route down Father Capodanno Boulevard. The sight of people leisurely strolling along the beach, laughing and enjoying each other's company, caused Charles to momentarily reflect. He could not help but think, if only life could be that simple.

Finally, they arrived at the precinct. As they stepped inside, they were greeted by the duty officer, who had a grin on his face, clearly not expecting any serious business. "Yeah! How can I help you two fine gentlemen today?" the officer asked with a smirk, glancing up from the front desk.

"Detectives Coffey and Mackenzie," Charles replied as he and Mac flashed their badges. "We're here about a file that was supposed to be sent by Lyle Duggard to the Police Plaza. You know anything about that?"

The officer paused for a moment, seemingly recalling something. "Yeah, yeah, I remember. That was about three weeks ago, right?"

"Yeah, three weeks ago," Charles repeated, his frustration mounting. "Can you just check and see if it's ready?"

The officer sighed and put down his sandwich before walking over to the pigeonholes behind the desk. He rummaged through the papers, taking his sweet time. "Here you go, Detectives," he said, finally pulling out a file and handing it over with a cocky grin. "We couldn't deliver it before, due to... let's just say, 'ethical conflicts'."

"Ethical conflicts?" Charles asked, his eyebrows raised.

The officer smirked. "We've been waiting for a transcript from the plaza for over a month. You don't give us what we want, we don't give you what you want," he said, leaning back with a defiant look on his face.

Charles leaned in, clearly agitated, but Mac placed a hand on his shoulder, guiding him back. "It's not worth it, Charlie boy. Let's go." With a frustrated sigh, Charles turned his back on the officer, and they left the precinct. Once they were outside, Charles opened the file and began reading. It was a missing person's report for Jeremy Wilkins, who had been reported missing on March 5th, 1987.

"Jeremy Wilkins," Charles muttered. "I've heard that name before, Mac."

"Don't ring a bell," Mac replied, distracted as he absentmindedly stuffed his face with another snack.

Charles read through the report: Jeremy Wilkins, a 34-year-old man, Caucasian with blonde hair and blue eyes. He stood 5'9" and weighed 205 pounds. The report also listed his last known contact: Mrs. Adele Wilkins, living at 33 Poi Crescent, Staten Island.

"That's pretty close, Mac," Charles said, his eyes narrowing. "We better get over there and interview the wife."

On the drive to Poi Crescent, Charles couldn't shake the feeling that something was off. The name "Jeremy Wilkins" seemed to linger in his mind, but he couldn't quite place it.

As they arrived at the house, Mac commented, "Nice place."

Charles, still deep in thought, asked, "You got the photograph of the victim from the morgue?"

"Yeah, I got it, Charlie boy," Mac replied, barely looking up as he grabbed the photo from the glove compartment.

The house was a well-maintained two-story building, with a beautiful garden out front. The door was white, hidden behind a mesh security door. Charles rang the doorbell, and after a moment, a figure peered through the lace curtain that hung over the glass of the front door.

"Can I help you?" the woman asked, her tone uncertain.

"Mrs. Adele Wilkins? asked Charles

"Yes," she replied.

"Detectives Coffey and Mackenzie, Ma'am, we're here about the missing person's report you filed."

The woman hesitated for a moment, then unlocked the door and opened it. "May we come inside, Ma'am?" Charles asked politely.

Without a word, the woman stepped aside, gesturing for them to enter. Inside, the house was immaculately clean and modern. The furniture looked brand new, and everything had a polished, almost sterile feel. Mrs. Wilkins offered the detectives to take a seat as she gestured for them to move into the living room. above the fireplace, very proudly displayed hung a family portrait, showing the husband, wife, and their son.

Charles and Mac knew that they had entered the home of the man lying in the morgue.

"Is that your husband, Ma'am?" Charles asked, gesturing to the portrait that hung on the wall.

"Yes, it is," the woman replied, her voice wavering. "Why? Have you found him?" Charles' expression softened. "Mrs. Wilkins, we regret to inform you that your husband has been found. He is deceased. I'm so sorry for your loss."

The woman's face crumpled, she collapsed into tears, her hands trembling as she covered her eyes. After a few moments, she wiped her tears with a kitchen towel from her apron and looked back at them, trying to compose herself.

"What happened to him?" she asked in a muffled voice, barely able to speak through her sobs.

"Mrs. Wilkins, he was found in the financial district in Manhattan," Charles said gently. "Does he work near there?"

"No, not at all," Mrs. Wilkins replied, shaking her head. "My husband is a used car salesman in Richmond. He would make trips to the city every so often to meet with 'clients,' as he called them."

"Clients?" Charles repeated.

"Yeah, these rich wannabes who want to live the high life. He would rent sports cars for the weekend and meet with these 'clients' who own their own sports cars, take trips on their boats, or fly out to Vegas every now and then. My husband always lived beyond his means. We cannot afford all this stuff in the house. The credit cards are maxed out, and we are buried in mortgages. He even cashed in his life insurance to pay for a trip to some exotic island."

At that moment, a small boy came running down the stairs and peeked into the sitting area. He smiled brightly at Charles, who gave him a small wave. "Come downstairs, honey," Mrs. Wilkins called. "Say hello to the nice men."

The little boy, no older than four or five, greeted them with a wide smile. Charles could not help but feel sympathy for the boy, unaware of the pain that was to come.

"Go upstairs and play now, okay?" Mrs. Wilkins said gently, watching the boy race back up the stairs before turning her attention back to the detectives.

"So, Ma'am," Charles began, "When was the last time you saw him?"

"It was February 27th," Mrs. Wilkins answered, seeing Charles looking at the report. "I think I wrote that down."

"That's right," Charles said, his eyes lingering on the date for a moment. It struck him briefly that the victim had gone missing on his own birthday. Was there any connection? Could it be a coincidence?

Shaking himself out of his thoughts, Charles asked, "What happened the day you last saw him?"

Mrs. Wilkins looked down, her voice cracking slightly. "He left to spend the weekend with his clients. I was busy trying to find shoes for our son, whose old ones were falling apart. He wouldn't buy him a new pair. He said, 'Let them stretch'."

"When he didn't come home after six days, I knew something was wrong. Where has he been all this time?" she added, her voice barely a whisper. "We're trying to find that out, Ma'am," Charles replied. "We'll need you to come downtown to formally identify your husband. We may also need to question you further."

Before they left, Charles handed her his business card. "If you think of anything else, please don't hesitate to contact us."

Once outside, Charles sighed, a sense of unease settling over him. "You know, Charlie boy, something's off here." Mac added.

"How does a used car salesman from Staten Island end up dead, with soil in his mouth, in the middle of the street, in one of the busiest places in the world?" Mac asked, still chewing on his snack. "And to top it all off, he's been missing for four months?"

"I'm thinking 'money' is the key here," Charles said, his voice low and thoughtful. "The financial district, his obsession with money, everything tied to it."

"Could be the Mob," Mac suggested. "What about these 'clients' his wife speaks of? Maybe they are more than just wealthy customers. Could they be part of something bigger?"

Charles, pondering the possibilities, looked over to his partner. "Let's dig deeper, Mac. There's more to this than meets the eye." he said as they reversed out of the drive of Mrs. Wilkins and headed back to Manhattan.

That evening, when Charles arrived home, a nagging feeling about the case continued to haunt him. There was something about it that he couldn't shake off, something that lingered in the back of his mind. Moving cautiously, he approached his front door, aware of the strange unease creeping up on him. He placed the key into the lock, proceeding with his usual routine as he turned it and stepped forward—but as he did, something felt off.

His front door mat was soaking wet. Charles lifted his foot, surprised to find water dripping from the soles of his shoes. He paused, scanning the area for any explanation. Was there a spill, perhaps something from a neighbor watering plants or some sort of mess? But no—everything was perfectly normal. No plants, no signs of water, nothing that would explain why his mat was soaked.

Charles stood there for a moment, confused and unsettled. He couldn't make sense of it. Skipping dinner, he went straight to bed, hoping to find some peace. But sleep eluded him. Tossing and turning, his thoughts kept drifting back to the little boy he had met earlier in the day. The image of his innocent face haunted Charles, knowing the kind of pain that awaited him.

The grief of losing his own father resurfaced. He had been older, but the pain was just as sharp, though clouded with anger. His feelings had never been simple—anger at his father's choices, at the way he had left things unresolved between them. That anger had fueled his sleepless nights, and now, it was the same feeling that kept him tossing in bed, unable to escape the growing sickness he felt about the victim's selfishness. His actions, his disregard for his family, made Charlie feel sick to his stomach.

By morning, Charles knew he couldn't stay cooped up any longer. He called Mac, telling him he would meet him at the station later on. He needed to be alone for a while—to digest everything that had happened, to try and make sense of the case, and to understand the twisted motivations behind taking a father away from his son.

Charles took the bus into work, trying to clear his mind. As he walked into the precinct, he could feel the tension in the air. There was a buzz of commotion that immediately caught his attention. Before he could make sense of it, Mac came sprinting down the hallway toward him, his face pale, his eyes wide with panic, as if he had seen a ghost.

"What the hell is going on, Mac?" Charles asked, his tone sharp with concern. "We have another one, Charles!" Mac said, out of breath, clearly shaken.

"We have another *what*, Mac?!" Charles demanded, his impatience growing.

"Another victim, Charlie boy," Mac replied, his voice trembling. "Same MO as the first one—middle of the street, hand removed... and there's another note on the body... it's addressed to you!"

Chapter 3

The Voice of Reason

The Hunt

Judith Barlow was as beautiful and manipulative as they come, a woman whose charm was as potent as it was dangerous. With nothing more than a soft smile and a simple "Hello", she had the power to ensnare even the most devoted of husbands, drawing them irresistibly to her side. Professionally, she was a highly regarded hypnotherapist, practicing in the bustling heart of Lower Manhattan at 476 Broadway. Her personal life mirrored the same high-class allure, as she resided on the Upper West Side at The Langham, occupying a luxurious penthouse with panoramic views stretching across Central Park West.

I can still vividly recall the first time I laid eyes on her—a frozen moment in time that has remained etched in my memory. I knew I had to have her. She was the epitome of everything Manhattan represented: a city that thrived on the combination of finance, art, fashion, and design. She was the very picture of perfection—her 36-24-36 frame made her seem almost unreal, as if she had stepped right out of a dream.

It was a breezy Tuesday afternoon in June of '86, the kind of day that felt like it was designed to be remembered. A light, gentle rain fell from the sky, just enough to refresh the air without being substantial enough to require an umbrella or to seek shelter under a bridge. The temperature hovered around 62 degrees in the shade, a crisp and cool Summer day. She was strolling through Central Park, nibbling on dry cracker bread while cradling a steaming cup of coffee in her hands.

I, too, had just picked up my morning coffee from a stand just outside the park before heading out for a walk. She wore a beige V-neck blouse, its soft fabric fluttering in the breeze as it draped gently down her torso, falling just below her waistline. Her outfit was completed with a dark brown pencil skirt that hugged her figure, reaching just below the knee, and a grey double-breasted lapel overcoat that cascaded over her shoulders, flowing to meet her ivory-colored calves. Her black high-heeled shoes, with a strap that wrapped around her ankles, added an air of sophistication, making her the epitome of elegance.

Her dark brown, full-bodied hair tumbled in waves around her shoulders, dancing with the playful wind that day; it seemed to be in sync with every movement she made. She was on display for all to see. As she walked past me, I couldn't help but notice the meticulous attention to detail in her make-up. Her mascara was perfectly applied, giving her lashes an almost hypnotic effect. Her eyeshadow was gently brushed just below her eyes, accentuating her already striking features. The eyeliner, bold yet alluring, was expertly drawn on her eyelids—like war paint, yet somehow inviting, as if daring you to come closer.

Her lips were painted the brightest red, a shade so vivid and deep, it resembled the color of blood—a hue that was both dark and brilliantly intense, mesmerizing her audience. And the coup de gras, her perfume: The gentle fragrances of wild flowers seemingly the middle notes of the scent, ultimately pushing through a sweetness that resonated behind her as she moved.

I stood frozen, watching her as she walked further into the distance, my gaze lingering on every graceful step she took. Everything about her was captivating, but it was her eyes that brought me to my conclusion: *"She will do nicely."*

Up until that moment, I had only encountered Judith Barlow through the pages of the newspaper, where her name had recently made front-page news in The New York Times. She was at the top of her field and respected across several. Over the past week, I had also noticed her face on the side of a bus or two, which only deepened my curiosity about her.

Judith Barlow was the one who had conducted the infamous interview with Richard Ramirez, also known as "The Night Stalker." The article I had previously read detailed Judith's determination to meet with Ramirez, who had been sentenced two years prior. The piece I was now reading was a first-hand account of her experience with him—her time spent speaking and connecting with the notorious figure, delving into his dark world. Judith had become a figure of notoriety herself, forever linked to the Satanic Ramirez. As I sat there, I found myself wondering how she felt being in the presence of such a chilling figure. She had conducted four taped interviews with him, an act that seemed almost sacrificial in nature—like a lamb walking willingly to the slaughter, but all in the name of advancing her career. Judith was in such high demand that I had to wait four months to secure an appointment with her. Clients sought her out from all corners, and I could only imagine her to be almost unattainable in her personal life for friends and lovers.

The anticipation of finally meeting her was both thrilling and surreal. Judith glanced up from her notepad as the door creaked open. A tall, well-dressed man stepped inside, hesitating for just a fraction of a second before making his way toward the chair opposite her. She gestured toward it with a slight nod.

"Mr. Radford, won't you take a seat, please?"

He gave a small chuckle, shaking his head as he sat down. "Michael, please. Mr. Radford was my father."

Judith acknowledged his preference with a subtle smile. "Very well, Michael. Did you find the place okay?"

"I did indeed, thank you." He shifted slightly, as if adjusting to the atmosphere of the room, his fingers fidgeting against the armrest.

"So, how can I help you today? Why are you here?"

Michael exhaled, running a hand through his hair before speaking. "Well, firstly, I just want to say thank you for squeezing me in today. I know you're a very busy and successful woman, and I appreciate you making time for me."

Judith offered a small nod of acknowledgment. "You're welcome, Michael. Cheryl informed me of a cancellation, and I thought it would be best to offer you the slot sooner rather than later."

Michael hesitated, his gaze dropping to his hands for a moment before he continued. "When I saw you on television last month, I knew you were the person I needed to see. But I was nervous about coming in today. I nearly told your receptionist that I couldn't make it." He exhaled sharply, a half-hearted smile tugging at the corners of his lips. "But, here I am."

Judith gave him a reassuring smile but remained silent, allowing the moment to settle.

Michael shifted in his seat again, as if trying to find comfort in the unfamiliar setting. "Would I be able to get your autograph, Ms. Barlow? Maybe before I leave?"

She raised an eyebrow, amused. "How about you sign for the consultation, and I'll have Cheryl type up a letter for your employer confirming you were here? I'll sign that instead. How does that sound?"

Michael chuckled softly, nodding. "That would be lovely. Thank you."

"You got it," she said, leaning forward slightly. "But first, I need to make sure I earn the right to give you my autograph. Will that be fine, Michael?"

"That's perfectly fine," he said, folding his arms.

Judith shifted in her chair, crossing her legs. She clicked her pen as if ready to start the session. "Speaking of work, Michael, what do you do?"

His expression darkened slightly. "Why does everyone always ask that?"

She tilted her head slightly. "Pardon me?"

"Why does everyone always ask, 'So, what do you do for a living?' Why don't people ask, 'Are you happy?'"

She leaned back in her chair, considering his words. "Interesting perspective. Are you unhappy, Michael?"

His response was immediate, raw. "Very. Very unhappy. I also can't sleep. My mind won't switch off. And then there's also..."

Judith lifted a hand slightly. "Michael, just breathe. Let's take it one step at a time. Why don't we start with something simple? Tell me—who is Michael Radford?"

He let out a soft chuckle, though there was little humor in it. "Well, I love my job—if that's where you want to start. I'm recently single. My girl and I were together for about two years, but it was a mutual break-up." He paused, running a hand over his face. "And I'm an artist in my spare time."

"Painting or drawing?" Judith asked.

"Those and more."

Judith waited for him to elaborate but she was met with an uncomfortable silence and a blank stare.

"I'm sorry to hear about the break-up." she stated, hoping to break the silence.

"Thank you," he responded.

"What was her name?"

Michael's eyes flickered with something unreadable. "What was her name? She's still alive, Judith."

"Yes, but you broke up. Fine, what is her name?"

"Emily."

"How long were you together?"

"About two and a half years."

"And when did you break up?"

"Two weeks ago."

Judith folded her hands in her lap. "It's interesting that you referred to her as 'my girl' just now."

Michael frowned. "Sorry?"

"When you mentioned her earlier, you said 'my girl'."

His brows knitted together. "Did I? I didn't realize."

"You did," she confirmed. "Perhaps you still think of her as yours, even though you've broken up?"

Michael let out a small, dry laugh. "Are you saying I'm a bit possessive or something like that?"

Judith remained neutral. "No not at all, but are you, perhaps?"

Michael smirked, shaking his head. "Little early to jump to conclusions, don't you think, Doc?"

"My apologies, Michael."

"That's okay, Judy. Listen, can we maybe circle back to Emily when I'm feeling more comfortable? It's still quite fresh, and I'm feeling a bit overwhelmed."

"Of course, Michael." Judith nodded. "So, let's go back to your work. The work you claim to 'love' so much. What do you do?"

"I'm a neuroscientist, and I also own a company called MR Investments. It's more of a side-hustle—something I work on after hours."

Judith smiled. "Impressive, Michael. It's nice to have someone on an intellectual level I can connect with. Sometimes, I have to deal with some real 'basic brains' in this office." she chuckled quite condescendingly.

Michael smiled. "I can only imagine, Judy."

Her expression turned serious. "Judith, please, Michael. Or Miss Barlow. I won't insist you call me 'Doctor', but let's keep this professional."

"Sure. My apologies this time around, Miss Barlow."

She gave a small nod. "Would you prefer to discuss the present—your relationship, your work, your art—or would you rather start at the beginning?"

Michael exhaled. "You're the expert, Doctor. I trust you."

"Very well, Michael. Then, why don't you tell me about your childhood?"

Michael met her question with reluctance. Once again the room fell victim to the uncomfortable silence as Michael sat staring down at the floor, his foot beginning to tap vigorously. Judith knew she had hit a nerve.

"My apologies, Michael, but you did say you trust me. And in order for me to help you to the best of my ability, I need to understand who Michael Radford is. Where did he come from?

How was he molded? What makes him tick? Will you allow me to step into your world, tell you what I see, and, God willing, maybe even become a part of it?"

Michael smirked and simply responded, "Sure."

Judith gave a small, approving nod. "Alright then. So, your childhood…"

Michael's expression darkened, his demeanor shifting as a shadow flickered across his face. His jaw tightened, and for a brief moment, his gaze seemed distant, as though he were staring past Judith and into some long-buried memory.

"Well, my father was in the military—" he began, but his words faltered mid-sentence. A sudden change overtook his face, a mixture of anger and sorrow settling into his features.

For Michael, whose Father was indoctrinated in the military, life was tough. A memory flooded to the forefront of his consciousness, he blurted out at Judith;

"My father and I were meeting the train coming into Grand Central Station one morning in '75. One of his Army buddies was coming home and Father wanted to meet him there with open arms. The feeling I got when they embraced was chilling, I didn't understand it as he had never treated me like that, with love. I will never forget his words that followed on the drive home after dropping his buddy off, 'They promised us all a home fit for heroes once the war was over, what we got was heroes fit for homes'."

A tense silence followed before he exhaled sharply, shaking his head as if physically pushing the thought away.

"You know what? I'm feeling a bit overwhelmed talking about all this so quickly," he admitted, his voice carrying a slight edge. "Let's save the childhood conversations for another time, shall we, Doc?"

Judith met his gaze with an understanding nod, her tone calm and measured. "Of course, Michael. There's no need to rush these things. Healing is a process, and it cannot be forced. It must be respected."

Michael considered her words for a moment before giving a slight smirk.

"Fair enough."

The conversation then shifted to more ordinary topics, with Michael recounting the mundane tribulations of his daily life. As he spoke, he observed Judith closely—her subtle reactions, the way her body language shifted with each of his words, the nuances in her expressions. He wasn't just answering her questions; he was studying her, analyzing her, committing her every movement to memory. After Judith concluded their session and discussed a follow-up appointment with him, Michael then stood up, offered a polite nod before exiting Judith Barlow's office.

The moment he stepped outside, his entire demeanor changed. His measured politeness dissolved into something darker, something raw and possessive. A wicked grin played at the corners of his lips as his mind whirled with a singular, consuming thought.

What a bitch. What a prize.

His pulse quickened with the realization.

I have to have her.

The Connection

A few months later, Judith Barlow found herself in Philadelphia, preparing to take the stage at a prestigious mental health conference. But she wasn't just another speaker—she was the keynote. The main event.

Her voice was her instrument, smooth and commanding, capable of entrancing an audience whether she was addressing a packed auditorium or an intimate room. This conference was the former. The hall was filled with mental health professionals, doctors, and researchers, all eager to hear Judith Barlow's groundbreaking approach to treating mental illness.

Her method was deceptively simple—almost too good to be true. "By silencing the ego," she explained, "we bypass the mind's defenses and tap directly into the heart of a patient's struggles. Where there is truth, there is healing. Where there is truth, there is freedom."

Michael looked up. He was sitting toward the back of the auditorium, watching her with a detached amusement. He knew the truth: Judith Barlow was a liar to her very core. Yet, here she was, standing before a room full of highly educated professionals, lecturing on trust and transformation—at

$150 per person. She was doing to them exactly what she did to her clients in Manhattan: weaving a careful illusion, selling a sense of security they didn't realize was false. And, they worshiped her for it.

Judith charged double what a family doctor's house call would cost, yet her clients lined up willingly, paying for their weekly hour in her presence. And why wouldn't they? She was just that good. Michael had sat across from Judith before, seen her up close. But tonight, he chose to observe her from a distance, concealed in the sea of faces. She didn't know he was here. Not yet.

He glanced at the woman seated a few rows ahead—Heather. He had known her before she started seeing Judith. She'd once been a woman with mild anxiety, perhaps a little lonely on weekends, nothing unusual. Then, after just a handful of sessions, something changed.

Heather ended her seven-year relationship with a man who had adored her. She sold her home, the one she had once loved. She publicly confronted her boss, humiliating them in front of an entire team, and was subsequently fired. A stable relationship, a home, a career—none of it mattered to her anymore. But missing a session with Judith? That was unthinkable. "Judith helped me see the truth," Heather had said. "Henry was cheating on me at every opportunity. I had to stand up for myself at work. And thank God I sold that house before the market crashed. I owe Judith my life."

Michael smirked bitterly. Judith's only weakness was music, which was ironic for a woman who seemed to lack a soul.

The audience erupted into applause, rising to their feet in unison, like obedient sheep following a cue. They clapped for her as if she were an Olympic athlete who had just taken home the gold for her country.

Judith Barlow smiled—perfect, poised, and utterly insincere. She blew two kisses into the crowd, a theatrical display of gratitude not just for their presence, but for the money they had willingly parted with to hear her speak.

She exited the stage and returned to her table, where an elderly man and a woman—perhaps a year or two older than Judith, with an extra fifteen pounds to her frame—were seated. A plump older sister, perhaps? The type who hid behind the veil of sisterly

support but was really just there for a free dinner and to bask in the reflected glow of her younger, more glamorous celebrity sibling.

Even as the night wore on and the room began to empty, a small group of sycophants still lingered near Judith's table—well-dressed professionals, eager to be seen in her orbit.

One by one, they drifted away. The elderly man and the sister eventually bid her goodnight, leaving together. The last hanger-on, a middle-aged man in a suit two sizes too small, hovered a little longer, desperate to impress Judith with every trick in the book. One could see he was a parasite, a skid mark on the undergarments of Philadelphia. But, even he eventually slithered away back into the hole from which he came—most likely given a subtle but firm dismissal from the infamous Dr. Barlow.

Michael checked his watch—11:03 p.m.

Finally, she was alone.

Judith stared down at her half-empty wine glass, no longer performing for cameras or important guests. The manipulator had stepped off her stage. She was vulnerable now.

Michael seized the moment, making his way toward her as she sat seated in the bar of the hotel lobby. She didn't see him coming.

"Can I buy you a drink, Ms. Barlow?"

As she looked up, he caught the subtle shift in her expression—the flicker of surprise, the moment of exposure. Then, just as quickly, she recovered, slipping effortlessly into one of her public masks.

At first, she wore a generic expression of polite reception, the kind designed to accommodate any stranger. But then, recognition dawned on her. And with it, something else—confusion.

It wasn't a look Judith Barlow was used to wearing.

"Michael? she paused, retrieving his last name... Michael Radford? Is that you?"

Judith's voice carried a note of surprise as she looked up, her expression momentarily unguarded.

"Hello, Dr. Barlow. We meet again."

Her eyes narrowed slightly, as if trying to process the coincidence—or determine if it was one at all. "What are you doing here?"

Michael smiled faintly. "I attended the conference."

She blinked. "But you live in Manhattan, Michael."

"And so do you, Judith," he countered smoothly.

Her lips curled into something between amusement and suspicion. "Are you stalking me, Dr. Radford?"

Michael leaned in slightly, his tone mischievous. "That depends."

She had been serious, but he was playful. She didn't like that. Judith preferred control.

With a soft, practiced laugh, she shifted in her seat, regaining composure. "Michael, my private clients and my professional colleagues should never overlap. They belong to two separate worlds—worlds that simply cannot coexist."

Michael noted the way her fingers tightened around the stem of her wine glass. He hadn't planned on it, but somehow, he had stumbled upon an insecurity of Judith's.

He raised his hands in a gesture of sincerity. "I do apologize, Ms. Barlow. That was not my intention. Did I overstep a boundary?

Judith hesitated for the briefest moment before waving it off. "No, not at all. It's just... how I prefer things. It's safer for everyone that way."

Michael's eyes sharpened. "Safer—I can respect that."

She met his gaze, unreadable for a moment, then exhaled. "It's a personal preference. My work life and my personal life need to stay separate."

Michael nodded, the glint in his eyes fading just slightly. "Understood."

A beat of silence passed between them. Then, Judith's expression softened. "But, you're here now, and so am I. So, how about that drink?"

Michael tilted his head. "What can I get you, Judith?"

As the evening wore on, they talked over several glasses of wine, conversation flowing more easily than either had anticipated. The walls between them, while not completely lowered, had thinned enough for glimpses of something more—curiosity, intrigue, maybe even something neither of them was willing to name just yet.

Eventually, Michael glanced at his watch and sighed. "Well, Judith, it's getting late. I already traveled over two hours just to watch you from a distance." His lips quirked in amusement. "Can I call you a cab?"

Judith let out a quiet chuckle, shaking her head. "Thank you, Michael, but no. I think I'll sit here a little longer. Just rest my feet. It's been... quite a day."

Michael gave a small nod, acknowledging something unspoken. He stood, ready to leave, when Judith suddenly looked up at him. Her next words caught him off guard.

"I hope to see you again, Michael."

His gaze held hers for a moment before he responded. "Me too, Judith."

With that, he turned and walked away, heading toward the hotel's lobby entrance, Leaving the atmosphere open-ended and uncertain for a now almost lonely Judith Barlow.

As Michael stepped outside and hailed a cab, instinct made him glance back through the hotel's glass doors.

Judith was still at the table, staring directly at him. Their eyes locked, and for the first time that night, she didn't mask her expression. There was no calculated smile, no poised indifference. Just something raw. Something uncertain.

Michael climbed into the cab, and as the vehicle pulled away, Judith remained seated, wine glass in hand, lost in thought.

Had something happened here tonight?

The sensation in her stomach—was it the wine? Or was it something else? Something unexpected? She found herself hoping, just for a moment, that he would call.

The Courting

Judith had fully expected a call the following Monday morning. But, as the hours stretched on, her phone remained silent.

Page five of the dating playbook.

A few days turned into a week. Then, nearly two and a half weeks had passed. More than a fortnight had gone by, and Judith found herself increasingly unsettled. Maybe Michael wasn't going to call her after all.

And yet, she couldn't stop thinking about him.

There was something about him that intrigued her—an intellectual and professional fascination, certainly, but also an undeniable personal connection. A chemistry she had never experienced with a patient before.

A simple conference—one like so many others she had spoken at—had unexpectedly led to an encounter that refused to leave her thoughts. It gnawed at her, crept into her mind at odd moments, and now, she couldn't stand it any longer.

"Maybe I should just reach out to him," she muttered to herself, pacing around her office, waiting for her next client.

At that moment, a soft double-knock on the door interrupted her thoughts. Cheryl stepped inside hesitantly. "Sorry to disturb you, Ms. Barlow, but Mr.

Radford called earlier. He said he's been held up at work and wanted to let you know that he'll call you in the next couple of days."

Judith froze.

Then, unexpectedly, she lashed out.

"If a patient calls, Cheryl, I want to know about it immediately! Do you understand me!?"

Cheryl's eyes widened as she scrambled to hold back tears, hastily grabbing a tissue to dab at her nose. "I'm sorry, Ms. Barlow. It won't happen again," she mumbled before quickly exiting and shutting the door behind her with a soft thud.

Judith sank into her chair, her mind racing.

Why now?

Why wait over two weeks to reach out?

Had she not been clear enough that evening? Had she been too subtle in her approach? She needed answers.

As the days dragged on, Judith found herself waiting—anxiously anticipating Michael's call.

On Tuesday evenings, she always had a ritual: stopping by the local newsstand to pick up the latest issue of Vogue. Keeping up with fashion trends was a small but important pleasure in her life.

That evening, as she left her office, she took her usual route—walking up Broadway, turning onto Spring Street, and heading toward Uncle Tony's, where she often stopped for a late coffee and a bit of conversation.

But, as she approached, something caught her eye. There standing on the corner was the man she had been waiting to hear from—Michael.

He was standing outside, chatting with Tony, a cup of coffee in his hand, casually enjoying the evening—just as she did every Tuesday.

Her heart skipped a beat.

"Michael?" she said, her voice calm but laced with curiosity.

He turned, surprised. "Judith? What are you doing here?"

"I visit Tony every Tuesday," she replied, as Tony handed her the usual— her coffee and her Vogue magazine—without her even needing to ask. He gave her a knowing wink.

"And what about you?" she asked, tilting her head suspiciously.

Michael grinned. "Can't a guy grab a bite to eat from his favorite news stand?" He turned to Tony. "Where's my sub, old man?"

Tony waved him off dismissively. "I've never seen this guy in my life," making them both laugh.

Michael turned back to Judith. "You working late tonight, Dr. Barlow?"

She nodded. "Tuesdays are report nights, so I always grab a coffee from Tony on my way home."

Judith studied him for a moment. "Don't you work on the other side of town, Michael?"

"Yeah, but I happened to be in the neighborhood," he said smoothly. "Figured I'd stop by and see an old friend, we go way back."

"Old friend?" Tony snorted.

Judith smiled as Michael laughed it off.

Then, unexpectedly, he asked, "Would you like some company on your walk home, Ms. Barlow?"

She hesitated for just a moment—just long enough to take in his deep ocean-blue eyes, the sharp cut of his jawline, the five o'clock shadow that made him look effortlessly rugged.

She couldn't resist him.

"That would be lovely, Michael—if it's not too much trouble," she said softly.

As they said their goodbyes to Tony and strolled away, Judith could feel it—the shift.

Michael was no longer her patient. And, she was no longer his doctor.

Something was happening and there was nothing she could do to stop it.

As they walked, Michael glanced over at her. "So, where did you grow up, are you from around here?"

"No, originally from Chicago. Old Edgebrook," she said. "Do you know it?"

Michael shook his head. "Never heard of it. Sounds nice enough."

She smiled. "It's a great place to raise a family."

They continued down toward the intersection, the streetlights casting a soft glow around them.

"My sister and I had a wonderful childhood there," she continued. "Beautiful gardens, friendly neighbors—the typical American dream."

She paused, then added thoughtfully, "Come to think of it, if I hadn't grown up in Edgebrook, I might never have ended up in this profession."

Michael raised an eyebrow. "Oh? How so?"

"Well, Edgebrook is close to Norwood Park—where John Wayne Gacy lived." Her voice lowered slightly, as if the name itself carried weight. "I remember, as a child, hearing stories about the boys he hurt. I remember my parents whispering in the kitchen, talking about how unsafe the world was. Even back then, I knew—I needed to understand the mind. I needed to know what made people like that tick."

Michael studied her carefully. "Is that why you worked with Ramirez?"

She nodded. "When the opportunity came up, I didn't hesitate."

Michael's expression darkened slightly. "What was it like? Were you scared?"

Judith hesitated, then exhaled. "Terrified. Sitting across from The Night Stalker gave me chills. But my goal wasn't just to get him to talk about the crimes. I wanted to go deeper. Why was he this way? What kind of trauma created a man like that?"

Michael listened intently.

"One of the things I found fascinating was how casual he was about it all," she continued. "He would just walk into homes in broad daylight and—" She stopped herself. "Anyway. I tried hypnosis to tap into his thought process."

"Did it work?" Michael asked.

She shook her head. "Not really. Just screams and cries. But after speaking with his family, I confirmed what I suspected—his upbringing was... traumatic, to say the least."

Michael's expression was unreadable. "Did you interview the families of his victims?"

Judith stiffened slightly.

She turned to look at him. "Michael, can we change the subject? I've done enough work for today."

Michael nodded slowly. "Of course, Judith. Another time."

Something flickered in his gaze—satisfaction, perhaps.

Judith didn't notice.

As they made their way through Central Park, their conversation turned lighter. They spoke of their dreams, their interests, their ambitions. Eventually, they reached a park bench and sat down.

Michael looked out at the skyline of the big apple in the distance. "What a view!" he exclaimed.

Judith smiled. "That's why I have an apartment overlooking this park.

Every morning, I wake up, look outside, and remind myself—there's no other city I'd rather live in."

Michael turned to her. "That's how you know something is right. When it feels natural. Like writing a song. Like falling in love."

Judith's breath hitched slightly.

"You're right," she said. "For the first time in a long time, I feel free."

She placed a hand on his leg.

Michael met her gaze.

"Judith," he said, his voice low. "Would you have dinner with me tomorrow night?"

"I'd love to." she said. As Michael smiled, she ran her fingers along his cheek.

Michael Radford had conquered one of the most important tasks he had to complete: Getting Judith Barlow to trust him.

She had no idea what she was walking into. And she never could have anticipated what would happen next.

At approximately 7:45 p.m. the following evening, a sleek black cab pulled up just outside the theater. The rain-soaked pavement shimmered beneath the glow of the streetlights as Michael stepped out, his long black suede overcoat swaying slightly in the evening breeze. Beneath it, he wore a sharp Armani tuxedo, the crisp white of his dress shirt accentuated by a perfectly tied jet-black bow tie.

Spotting Judith, he straightened his posture and approached her with a confident stride.

"Judy, I'm so sorry I'm late. Traffic was backed up all the way down Seventh Avenue," he said apologetically.

Judith looked up at him, her dark lashes fluttering as she batted her eyes with innocent charm. "All is forgiven, Michael. Really."

Michael took a step closer, his gaze sweeping over her. "You look absolutely stunning this evening," he proclaimed.

Judith smiled, tilting her head slightly. "Thank you, Michael. You clean up quite well yourself, if I may say so."

His eyes flickered to the ornate brooch pinned delicately to the fabric of her dress—a golden butterfly, its wings adorned with tiny sapphire gems. "What a striking brooch," he remarked, his tone shifting ever so slightly. His expression, once filled with admiration, darkened into something unreadable.

Judith noticed the change instantly. "Thank you," she said softly. "It was my mother's. She adored butterflies..." She trailed off, watching his face closely. "Michael, are you okay?"

His jaw tensed. His hands curled into tight fists.

"I... I don't know," he muttered. Without another word, he turned away, striding toward the curb.

Raindrops trickled down his face as he stared into the gutter, watching his own distorted reflection ripple in the water flowing toward the drain. The city lights bounced off the wet pavement, warping his features until they became something unrecognizable.

His breath grew uneven. His chest tightened. His eyes now closed, a childhood memory surged forward, shutting out everything around him...

It was Summer. The air was thick with heat, clinging to my skin as I walked home from school, sweat soaking into my clothes.

"Mom? Mom!" I called, as I stepped inside.

No answer.

Then—a sound.

Singing. A soft, melodic voice drifted from upstairs, calling me toward my mother's art studio.

Slowly, I ascended the stairs, my small fingers grazing the banister. As I reached the door, I hesitated before pushing it open—just an inch.

Inside, my mother sat at her desk, completely immersed in her work. She was my inspiration, my muse. I loved watching her create beautiful things.

And oh, how beautiful they were.

Butterflies.

Majestic, delicate creatures fluttered about the room in every imaginable hue. It was magical, like stepping into a dream.

She was in the closet, organizing them by color. I remember the process so vividly—how she would let a butterfly land gently on her hand, waiting patiently for just the right one. And then, with meticulous precision, she would slide a thin needle into its thorax.

It would struggle. Its wings would beat desperately.

And then—stillness.

She would hand me the next one. Coaching and guiding me, her hands soft, moving slowly with mine.

I always got it right on the first try.

Years later, I would realize that my mind had rewritten the truth.

The elegant butterflies dancing in the air had never existed. They were a lie—a mental shield against a much darker reality.

My mother's singing?

Not a lullaby.

Not a song, but blood curdling screams.

The butterflies had been trapped. Stuffed into glass jars, their fragile wings fluttering frantically against the glass as they suffocated. She would pull their wings off slowly.

And she... she relished in their suffering.

I could still see it. The way she would pin them down while they were still alive, mutilating them, watching as the scales flaked off their wings like dust.

She was an abuser of things and yet adored me endlessly. She could create anything from nothing, she possessed a rare gift, the ability to bring beauty into existence. However, like most artists, the world was too heavy for her fragile spirit to bear.

Michael's breathing grew ragged. His fists clenched so tightly that his fingernails bit into his palms, drawing blood.

A hand touched his shoulder.

"Michael?" Judith's voice was gentle, concerned. He whirled around, his expression contorted. His knuckles were white, his body rigid.

"I have to go!" he barked, his voice raw and unsteady.

Before she could say another word, he turned and sprinted into the rain, leaving Judith standing there, stunned and bewildered.

His mind raced as he ran through the streets, the city blurring around him.

He had let himself get too close.

"Emotions are for the weak," he muttered under his breath. "Emotions are for the weak!"

He turned down a narrow alleyway, panting, his heart hammering against his ribs.

This had gone on long enough.

No more pretending. No more games.

It had to be now.

Slamming his fist into a nearby dumpster, he sent it crashing against the brick wall. His pulse thundered in his ears as he tilted his head back, rain streaming down his face.

The decision had been made:

It had to be now. The butterfly memory coursed through his very being and fueled what he had to do next...

Nearly a week had passed since Michael had abandoned Judith outside the theater. The memory of that night still lingered in her mind, raising questions she couldn't quite answer. Then, returning home late one evening, she noticed the red light on her answering machine blinking, signaling a new message.

She pressed 'Play'.

Beep...

"Hey, Judy... It's Mike. Listen, I just wanted to say how sorry I am about the other night. I—I don't know what came over me. Things at work have been overwhelming lately, and I guess the stress just got to me. But, I want to make it up to you. I've reserved a table for two at The Oak Room tomorrow night. It would mean a lot if you joined me. Please, meet me there at 8:00 p.m. sharp. I truly hope to see you... and again, I'm so sorry."

Beep.

Judith leaned back, the corners of her lips curling ever so slightly.

The following evening, Michael arrived at The Oak Room fifteen minutes early. He had planned everything down to the last detail—this was his chance, perhaps his final opportunity, to pull Judith into his grasp for good. His reflection stared back at him from the darkened restaurant window, distorted slightly by the light drizzle falling from the sky. He adjusted the cuffs of his suit, exhaling slowly as he rehearsed his next moves in his mind. Then, precisely at 7:50 p.m., a taxi pulled up to the curb. The door opened, and Judith stepped out, draped in an evening gown somehow more breathtaking than before.

Michael's lips curled into a smirk as he stepped forward. "Hey, Judy. You look absolutely beautiful," he said, his voice dripping with charm.

She flashed him a knowing grin. "Thank you, Mike. But tell me... you're not going to run off on me again, are you?"

"Never again," he swore, reaching for her hands and holding them gently in his. "I was a fool. Can you forgive me?" His dark eyes locked onto hers, studying every shift in her expression.

Judith hesitated for only a moment before offering a soft nod. "Let's see if you can make it up to me."

With that, they stepped inside, the warm glow of the restaurant surrounding them. The evening unfolded effortlessly—conversation flowed once again, laughter came easily and for a brief moment, it was as if their last encounter had never happened.

Then, Michael snapped his fingers.

"Waiter," he called, his tone commanding yet smooth.

A suited gentleman promptly arrived at their table.

"I'll have the wine I requested earlier. Chilled, of course," Michael stated with quiet authority. His gaze flickered toward Judith, gauging her reaction. Moments later, as the waiter returned, presenting the bottle, Judith's eyes widened slightly.

"Michael! That's the—"

"Yes," he interrupted, leaning forward slightly. "The same wine you were drinking the night we met at the conference. I took note and ordered a special bottle just for tonight."

Judith let out a soft, approving laugh, shaking her head in disbelief. "That's very thoughtful of you, Mike. Thank you."

Michael raised his glass. "To us."

Judith clinked her glass against his. "To a new chapter," she added before taking a sip.

As she placed her glass back on the table, she fixed her gaze on him, studying him as if he were a specimen under a microscope.

"Tell me, Dr. Radford," she said, a slow smile playing on her lips, "What is your take on the meaning of life? I'd love to hear your thoughts."

Michael recognized the game she was playing. He had seen it before—this was a test. She was calling checkmate.

But Michael was always three moves ahead.

He leaned back slightly, running a hand through his hair as if considering his words carefully. "Well," he began, "fluidity has its place in life, but structure and order... they have their advantages. Even the most abstract minds can benefit from a bit of discipline—it teaches restraint, organization, purpose."

Judith tilted her head. "Purpose?"

"A free spirit, bound yet liberated," Michael continued, his voice measured. "A prison, in a way, but one that provides focus. Absolute, unrestricted liberty is too heavy for a single soul. It leaves one incapable of making an effective choice, paralyzed by endless possibility. But too much control—" he paused, fingers tapping against the stem of his wine glass, "—and you risk compromising the most valuable elements of human existence."

"And what would those be?" Judith asked intrigued.

"Freedom, creativity and play, in my opinion." he responded.

Judith's eyes gleamed with fascination. She could not comprehend that he was the same man who had entered her practice and felt overwhelmed to discuss a break-up.

Michael continued, his voice weaving an intellectual web around her. "We attach so much meaning to life and death," he mused. "But the truth? Human physiology mirrors the cycle of life in a microcosm. A perfect ecosystem of interconnectedness, scaled down to the individual. Only the living can speak of death—but they know nothing of it."

Judith exhaled, shaking her head in awe. "Michael... you astound me. Your theories, your ideology... you truly are a gift to society."

Conversely, Michael studied her and was intrigued. *Who had raised this woman? A stepfather? A distant relative perhaps?* Her coldness was unprecedented, an emotional detachment that intrigued him. She was perceptive, yet disconnected. A sexual being, but without true intimacy. Depth without soul. Perhaps that's what fascinated him. Perhaps that's what he recognized in himself.

"Just last week," Michael said suddenly, shifting the conversation, "I was sitting by the lake over on Fifth Avenue, watching the trees swaying in the wind."

His voice faltered. His eyes welled up with emotion.

Judith caught the shift instantly. "Michael," she said softly, leaning in. "Are you okay?"

Michael exhaled sharply. "Yes," he said reassuringly. "I just became overwhelmingly aware of how everything is connected. We're all one."

Hook, line and sinker.

Judith's breath hitched, emotion welling up in her eyes now. "Michael," she whispered, "that's... beautiful."

Michael fought the urge to smile. She was his.

Moments later, he paid the bill, leaving a generous tip before leading Judith outside. The night air was crisp, the rain now just a faint drizzle.

"Michael," Judith said, hesitating under the restaurant's awning. He turned to her, expecting the moment he had been waiting for.

"Once in a while," she began, tucking a strand of hair behind her ear, "I gather some of my colleagues to review psychological cases—studies of various personalities we encounter in our work. We analyze them, exchange insights. I'd love you to join us, share your perspective. I'm certain they'd be just as fascinated by you as I am."

Michael held back a smirk.

He nodded smoothly. "Of course, Judy. I'd be honored. I'd also love to meet your colleagues."

As the cab pulled up and Judith climbed inside, she turned to wave, her mind already spinning with ideas.

This was it...

Over the next few days, she meticulously planned their next meeting. She would let her guard down completely—at least, that's what she wanted him to believe. She paced up and down her office, scribbling notes, constructing the perfect approach.

Michael Radford was unlike any specimen she had ever encountered. He would be her greatest challenge yet.

And this time... she would win.

The Seduction

Michael arrived at Judith's office promptly at 6:00 p.m. on September 9th, just as she had instructed. Though she had framed their meeting as a simple "working session", he knew better. Judith had an agenda. But, so did he.

He knocked once. A pause. Then her voice—soft, yet piercing—drifted through the door.

"Come in."

As Michael stepped inside, he immediately sensed the weight in the air, thick with an unspoken tension. The dimly lit room was an extension of Judith herself—calculated, deliberate, shrouded in mystery. Darkness pooled around her desk like an unseen presence, while the glow from a nearby lamp illuminated only the space where she would sit, the very place from which she would delve into the human mind. A faint melody played in the background, its eerie notes a curious mix of serenity and unease.

She was waiting for him.

"Michael," she said, stretching out a slender arm toward the luxurious two-seater sofa opposite her. The gesture was subtle but intentional—a silent invitation for him to relax, to lower his guard.

He accepted, sinking into the plush cushions with a slow, measured movement. He appeared almost awkward—his hands cupped downward, resting on his knees, as if consciously resisting the temptation to sprawl comfortably. Judith noticed.

"You seem... uneasy," she said, her lips curving into a playful smile.

Michael met her gaze, expression unreadable. "Judy... are we alone this evening?"

"Yes, Michael, I apologize for the deception. I know I said that we would be joined by my colleagues, but that is not the case."

Michael Radford had her exactly where he wanted her—she just didn't know it yet. Judith rose from her chair with a slow, deliberate grace and ascended the single step that led to the cabinet at the back of her office. Without a word, she reached for the tape deck, pressing 'Stop'. The room fell into silence for a brief moment before she removed the cassette and replaced it with another. A flick of her manicured fingers, and the new tape began to play.

The violinist's notes drifted through the speakers—soft at first, melodic, almost hypnotic. But then, without warning, a dissonant screech shattered the harmony. The melody fluctuated, dipped off-key, then found its footing once more, only to spiral back into discord. It was unsettling, yet strangely captivating. Every element, carefully orchestrated.

Judith returned to her chair, the warm light catching the subtle imperfections in her otherwise flawless façade. She leaned forward slightly, her eyes locked onto his.

"How are you feeling now, Mike?" she poised.

Michael exhaled, his voice low and steady. "I can't quite put it into words, Judy... but being here, with you, it just feels right."

Slowly, he rose to his feet. His movements were fluid, almost trance-like, as he circled behind her chair. His gaze never wavered from hers, even as he reached out—his fingers barely grazing the smooth skin of her forearm.

Judith didn't flinch. She wore a soft smile as anticipation flickered in her eyes.

His touch grew firmer, tracing a slow, deliberate path up her arm to her shoulder. With his other hand, he mirrored the motion, his fingertips pressing gently against her skin. Judith responded instinctively, tilting her head back, her thick curls cascaded and tickled his hands.

She let out a soft, satisfied chuckle.

"Michael... you know you want me."

"Yes, Judy." His voice was a whisper, a promise. "But let's take our time."

She turned her head slightly, lips parting. "You can have me. All of me. Right here. Right now."

Michael's hands moved in unison, kneading the tension from her shoulders with calculated precision. His grip was firm, commanding, yet never rough. His fingers traveled up either side of her neck, searching for the tense muscles to ease that would make her melt beneath his touch. He spread his fingers wider, running them through her hair, inhaling deeply as he took in the intoxicating blend of her perfume and the faint scent of hairspray.

He understood now. Understood why people gravitated toward her, why she commanded the confidence of so many. She was magnetic. Hypnotic.

Michael felt a rush of adrenaline, a sharp spike of exhilaration coursing through him. But he remained in control. He always remained in control.

He moved his hands again, this time delicately cupping her earlobes between his thumbs and forefingers, massaging them with slow, circular motions. Judith's breathing deepened, her body responding instinctively. Her eyes fluttered with arousal.

And then—

His fingers shifted.

Just slightly.

His index fingers slid away, his thumbs pressing down—firmly now—against the soft area just behind her earlobes, where the vagus nerve lay beneath the skin.

Judith's body tensed.

Her eyes opened, hazy with pleasure, then flickered with something else. Confusion.

Michael's breathing slowed. He was motionless now, his thumbs unmoving, exerting just enough pressure to be felt, but not yet understood.

Judith swallowed. A ripple of unease passed through her, dull at first, like a whisper in the back of her mind. She reached behind her, fingers grazing the back of his neck, an attempt to pull him closer—to reestablish the rhythm, to ground herself.

But, he did not move.

He stood there, a sculpted figure of unrelenting stillness, elbows bent outward, hands fixed in place.

The moment stretched. Judith's breath hitched again, but this time, it was not from pleasure.

The atmosphere had changed. The balance had shifted.

"Michael..." Her voice was softer now, uncertain. She tried to lift a hand to push him away, but her body wasn't responding the way she expected it to. A faint dizziness crept into her mind.

Michael's grip did not tighten, but it did not lessen either.

Her pulse quickened, but the adrenaline that once fueled her excitement was now turning cold, curdling into something else. Her muscles, once flexible, felt heavy. Uncooperative.

The realization struck her with the force of a crashing wave.

Panic set in.

She tried to move again—nothing. Her limbs refused to obey.

The edges of her vision blurred. The darkness at the corners of the room seemed to creep forward, swallowing her whole.

Her lips parted, perhaps to protest, perhaps to plead, but no sound came.

And then—

Her world went dark.

The Capture

Judith stirred at the low hum of an engine and the subtle rocking motion beneath her. The sensation was disorienting, as though she were adrift in a fog. Her mind struggled to pull itself from the depths of unconsciousness, her senses sluggishly catching up. The surface beneath her was not her familiar leather armchair, nor was she reclining in the comfort of her apartment. No, this was something else. Something foreign.

As her awareness sharpened, she realized she was lying down in the backseat of a moving vehicle. The air inside was thick, slightly stale, carrying the faint scent of leather and something metallic. The radio was on, but instead of music or conversation, it emitted only a soft, hissing white noise—static, relentless and oppressive.

A dull heaviness settled over her limbs, as if she had been sedated. Her muscles felt weak, her thoughts clouded. She attempted to move but quickly discovered that her wrists and ankles were tightly bound. A sharp panic shot through her, but she forced herself to remain composed. Swallowing hard, she noted the dryness in her throat—it was parched, but thankfully, her mouth was not gagged.

As her eyes adjusted to the dimly lit interior, she made out a shadowy figure in the driver's seat. His silhouette was unmistakable. The passenger seat beside him was empty, the vehicle's interior eerily still apart from the rhythmic vibrations of the tires against the road. Her breathing quickened as fragmented memories flickered through her mind—the last thing she recalled was being in her office, locked in a game of seduction and hypnosis with Michael. And then... darkness.

A whisper was all she could manage, though in her mind, she had intended to scream.

"Where...?"

The driver, sensing her awakening, spoke before she could find the strength to say more.

"How are you feeling now, Judith?"

His voice was calm, almost amused. It was the same voice she had come to know over the past few weeks, yet something about it now sent a chill down her spine. He reveled in all of this—her disoriented state, her powerlessness.

She recognized him instantly.

"Michael," she croaked, trying to mask the tremor in her voice. "What the hell is going on? Where am I?"

She wanted to sound assertive, to command control of the situation, but even as she spoke, she knew the power dynamic had shifted beyond her reach. The leverage to be had was not hers.

Michael chuckled softly. "I knew you'd react like this. That's exactly why I chose you, Judy. It's just who you are."

"*Chose* me?" Her thoughts slow to form. "What are you talking about?"

"I'm not angry with you, you know. Quite the opposite. You didn't disappoint me in the slightest." His tone was almost complimentary, as if he were proud of her.

"Michael, where are we? Where are you taking me?"

"We just crossed the East River," he answered nonchalantly. "We're heading toward Queens. Just a few more miles, and then we'll turn around."

Judith's pulse quickened. "Michael, this isn't funny. Untie me. Now."

A pause.

"Oh, Judy," he said, his voice shifting to something colder. "My name's not Michael."

Silence hung between them. A dreadful, suffocating silence.

A fresh wave of panic crashed over her. "What...? Then who the hell are you?"

"All in good time," he replied, his focus fixed on the road ahead.

Judith clenched her fists, the rope digging into her skin. She twisted her wrists and ankles, testing for even the slightest bit of slack, but the knots were expertly tied—unyielding.

She took a sharp breath, trying to regain composure. "Listen to me. You do realize that I'm very well known around New York, right? People are going to start looking for me. If you think you can just—"

Michael let out a quiet chuckle.

"A queen in Queens," he mused to himself, ignoring her words. "It's almost poetic." She could hear him drumming his fingers on the steering wheel, as if this was nothing more than an evening drive through the city.

"Judith," he continued, "I know exactly who you are. And you... You seem to have forgotten how we met. How we reconnected."

Judith's mind raced. How *we reconnected?*

Her breath shuddered.

"Just relax," he said smoothly. "If you're tired, feel free to take a nap."

She scoffed. "I just woke up in the backseat of your goddamn vehicle, tied up like an animal. Do you really think I'm going to just doze off?"

Michael sighed, shaking his head. "Judith, you of all people should understand the power of the mind. You wield it better than most."

Her gaze darted to the rearview mirror, where something caught her eye—a dreamcatcher dangled from the mirror, its black and gold web threaded with white and brown beads, soft feathers swaying with the motion of the vehicle.

Something about it unsettled her.

"I'm not a bad person, Michael," she said quietly. "Why are you doing this?"

"On the contrary; you're extraordinary, Judith!" he proclaimed. "That's why I chose you."

"Again with 'the choosing'!" she snapped.

"You're part of something greater," he continued, his voice almost reverent. "And you're the first special one."

Her stomach twisted. "Michael, you're scaring me."

"You're safe with me," he assured her. "You know that."

Then, with an almost playful tone in his voice, he added, "This is a safe space. Isn't that what you always say to your clients?"

Judith remained silent.

No further words exchanged, not even a throat clearing.

Minutes passed, the atmosphere in the vehicle growing heavier. The city lights blurred as they drove deeper into Queens, the night seemed to envelop them.

And then, without warning, Michael spoke again.

"Oh, this will do nicely."

Judith snapped to attention.

"Where are we now?" she asked, her voice barely above a whisper.

Michael answered her quite proudly, "Queens Judy, I told you this already!"

He slowed the vehicle to a stop in the middle of an empty street. He leaned slightly, peering out the driver's side window, scanning the road below.

"Corner of Britton Ave and Judge Street," he stated. "Yes, it will be here."

She considered screaming. Every muscle in her body tensed in preparation—but something in her gut told her not to.

Michael then turned to her, meeting her gaze through the rearview mirror. His eyes were warm. Familiar.

"This will do," he muttered. "Let's head back."

Judith exhaled, relief flooding through her. Maybe... Maybe this was just some elaborate game. A test of control. Maybe they would go back to her office, pick up where they left off.

Maybe he wasn't a monster.

The vehicle rumbled to life again.

But then he spoke once more, his voice quiet.

"We're headed to Staten Island now, Dr. Judith Barlow, famous hypnotherapist."

Judith's stomach dropped.

"What's in Staten Island?" she asked, barely able to keep her voice steady.

Michael didn't answer.

Instead, his hands tightened around the wheel. The vehicle sped forward, the city lights disappearing behind them.

Judith swallowed hard, sinking into silence. She retreated into the depths of her own mind, desperately seeking refuge from the terrifying reality unfolding around her. She traced back the events of the day, recalling how it had begun in the comfort of her routine—her morning coffee, the familiar hum of city life outside her office window. Now, she was bound in the backseat of a vehicle, hurtling toward an unknown fate. The contrast was staggering.

Her thoughts drifted to her mother in Oklahoma, a woman who had always worried about her being so far from home. And then there was her sister, somewhere in Africa, undoubtedly on another humanitarian mission, dedicating herself to saving lives—one starving orphan at a time. The thought of them brought a brief moment of solace, but it was fleeting. She closed her eyes and willed her mind to wander—away from the dimly lit streets of Queens, away from the oppressive reality of her confinement.

She understood the power of the mind better than most. If she allowed herself to succumb to fear, to panic, she would lose what little control she had left. So, she focused on her breath, inhaling deeply through her nose, holding it for five slow seconds before exhaling through her mouth. She repeated the process, centering herself, refusing to let fear dictate her next move.

Michael's voice suddenly broke through the silence.

"That's it, Judith. I'm so proud of you!"

Her eyes opened slightly, startled by his words. She hadn't expected him to speak, let alone acknowledge what she was doing. But, she didn't respond. Not yet. If this was a game, she would play it too—on her terms. She closed her eyes again, redirecting her thoughts to something more tangible, more grounding. Her cat, Chloe. *Was she hungry? Had the doorman, Mr. De Santos, noticed her absence? Would he think to check on her apartment if she didn't return soon?* The thought of Chloe pacing by the empty food bowl filled her with guilt, but at least it gave her something to hold onto.

The hum of the vehicle's engine blended with the distant sounds of traffic. The ride had become smoother, and she surmised they

were now on a freeway. The rhythmic motion threatened to lull her into sleep when Michael spoke again, his voice tinged with a disturbing cheerfulness.

"We're almost there, Judith."

Still lying down, she forced her eyes open and turned her head toward the front of the vehicle. She felt it slow down—not for a stoplight, but for something else. A turn signal clicked, and soon, the vehicle veered off the paved road onto what felt like a rough, unpaved dirt road.

The glow of city street lights faded behind them, replaced by darkness. The road beneath them became uneven. Trees flanked both sides of the vehicle now, their looming silhouettes barely visible in the dim light. Instinct urged Judith to sit up, to see where they were going.

Michael's voice cut through the tension. "Alright, Judith. It's been a hell of a day. I'm a bit tired. I'm sure you are too. We're here now."

The vehicle came to a halt. Michael climbed out of the front seat, the sound of his door shutting sliced through the still night. A few seconds later, the rear door beside her swung open. He was standing there, his expression eerily calm as he held a pair of scissors in his hand.

Without a word, he leaned forward and carefully cut the ropes binding her wrists. His touch was strangely gentle. Then, kneeling beside the vehicle, he severed the restraints around her ankles.

Michael looked up at her and smiled. "Now, Judith. I trust you not to scream, and I trust you not to run."

He stepped back, giving her space—an unspoken invitation to step out.

Judith hesitated, then slowly moved, her white high heels sinking into the damp grass as she climbed out. The pristine shoes she had so carefully chosen that morning were now soiled, a stark contrast to the manicured world she had left behind. She stood beside Michael, scanning her surroundings. They were in the middle of nowhere—no buildings, no lights, no signs of life. Just the two of them.

Michael's voice broke the silence once more. "Kick off your shoes, Judy. Your expensive shoes hold no value or beauty here."

He crouched again, this time collecting her discarded heels as she nudged them off with her toes. Rising to his full height, he held them in one hand while his other hand trailed down her forearm, fingers weaving into hers.

Judith tensed at his touch, but she didn't pull away. With a soft chuckle, Michael began walking, leading her forward. His grip wasn't forceful or aggressive; she could not say that. It was assertive, it was romantic and taking charge like "the man of the house" and this scared her, but not in the same way it had in the past few weeks she had come to know Michael.

"It's almost like we're heading to a beautiful cabin in the woods for the weekend, isn't it? Like a couple of newlyweds."

His voice was warm, almost affectionate.

Judith Barlow was walking to her death. And, she was doing it willingly, hand in hand with her killer.

Chapter 4

Dirty the Colors

Arriving at the scene of the latest victim, Charles found the streets teeming with people, their anxious mutters blending into the chaotic hum. Uniformed officers struggled to hold back the growing crowd, their efforts barely containing the onlookers desperate for a glimpse of the crime scene. As Charles scanned the faces in the crowd, he could see the unmistakable look of fear and unease etched into their expressions.

Moving toward the taped-off area, Charles carefully lifted the yellow crime scene tape over his head, stepping onto the restricted ground. Dr. Bullard was already kneeling beside the lifeless body, his gloved hands methodically examining the victim.

"What do we have here, Doc? Do you think we're looking at the same MO as the first victim?" Charles queried, crouching down beside him.

Dr. Bullard glanced at him briefly before turning his attention back to the body. "I'm not sure yet, Detective. Let me take a closer look." He then pried open the victim's mouth and shone a small flashlight inside, scrutinizing the throat. "I don't see anything unusual. It looks clean, but I won't be certain until I have him on the slab," he added.

Dr. Bullard shifted his focus to the victim's hands. "We have a Caucasian male, approximately 20 to 25 years old. Just like the first victim, one of his hands has been removed—this time, it's his left. The cut is flawless, executed with the same precision as before. No immediate cause of death is apparent. However, unlike the previous case, the right hand remains intact, fingerprints untouched."

Detective Coffey's attention sharpened as Dr. Bullard continued. "And, just like the first victim, there was an envelope left on the body. It's addressed to you."

Slipping on a pair of gloves, Charles reached for the envelope which Dr. Bullard handed him. The paper felt identical to the first one—thick, slightly textured. A sinking feeling settled in his chest as he carefully opened it, already suspecting what he would find.

As he pulled it from the envelope, his assumption was confirmed. It was a birthday card, nearly identical to the one from the previous crime scene. The front featured well-known Sesame Street characters—Big Bird, Elmo, and the Cookie Monster—cheerfully gathered around a large blue number "2," accompanied by colorful balloons on either side. The words on the front read:

Hooray!
Woo-Hoo!
So glad you are Two!

With his palms slick with sweat, Charles carefully opened the card, his fingers trembling slightly. As he parted the edges, a small object nearly slipped from within—his reflexes kicking in just in time to catch it. Facing him was a driver's license, its glossy surface reflecting the dim crime scene lighting. His eyes quickly scanned the details printed on it, and it read:

NEW YORK STATE
*****DRIVER LICENSE*****
CHILDS, VINCENT
APARTMENT 3A, 1111 LAFAYETTE AVE
BROOKLYN, NY 11221

Charles stared at the driver's license, a growing sense of unease settling in his chest. It didn't make sense. The first victim had been a complete mystery—no ID, no fingerprints, nothing to reveal his identity. Yet now, with this second victim, they suddenly had a name, home address and fingerprints handed to them on a silver platter. It felt too easy, almost deliberate, as if someone wanted them to find this information.

"His name is Vincent Childs," Charles announced, his voice laced with suspicion as he turned to Mac and Dr. Bullard.

He handed the license over to Dr. Bullard, who examined it briefly before shaking his head. "Well, gentlemen, I suppose you won't need my help identifying the victim this time. I'll get him transported to the morgue and let you know what I find." Dr. Bullard returned the license to Charles, who carefully bagged it for evidence. As the forensic pathologist prepared to leave, one of his assistants approached, ready to move the body.

"Are you finished with the victim, Sir?" the assistant asked, waiting for permission to proceed.

Charles let out a frustrated sigh. "Just give me a minute, will ya?" he snapped, irritation seeping into his tone.

Something didn't quite seem to fit. He flipped the card open again, half-expecting to find another cryptic message, a poem, or a taunting note from the killer. But, there was nothing—just the license. That was it.

"Mac, this doesn't sit right with me," Charles said. "The rest of the card is empty. No message, no taunts. Just his license."

He stood up, adjusting his flannel pants where they had bunched up at the knee. His gaze scanned across the scene as he tried to absorb every detail, searching for something—anything—that might give them something else to work with.

He was standing at the intersection of Vesey and Church Street, deep in the heart of downtown Manhattan. Only half a mile separated this crime scene from the first.

Charles fell into deep thought. What was the connection? Could the two victims have known each other? And why was the killer choosing intersections? Was there significance to the locations?

His eyes flicked back to the street signs. A sudden realization hit him. "Church and Vesey," he said aloud, testing the names on his tongue.

"What about the streets?" Mac asked, quite puzzled.

Charles' heartbeat quickened and his mind raced, subsequently locking eyes with Mac.

"The first letters of the victim's name match the first letters of the streets."

Mac narrowed his eyes. "What are you getting at?"

Charles spoke out loud with confidence. "Vincent Childs—Vesey and Church," he stated, excitement creeping into his voice. "Our first victim, Jeremy Wilkins, was found at the intersection of John and William Street."

Mac's expression shifted as the connection became clear.

"The victims' initials match the street names where they were found," Charles stated, almost breathless with revelation. Finally, a pattern was emerging. Something was starting to make sense.

His eyes darted to the buildings surrounding them—the federal building on one side, an apartment complex on the other. If the killer had been precise enough to choose locations based on initials, he had to be calculating in other ways as well.

"Do you see any surveillance cameras, Mac?" Charles asked, scanning the area.

Mac squinted and shook his head. "Nothing from here, Charlie boy."

Charles exhaled sharply. "Let's get back to the precinct and start piecing this together."

As they walked back to their vehicle, Charles felt something he hadn't allowed himself to feel in days—a glimmer of hope.

The pieces were starting to fall into place. They had more information now than they did with the first victim. Maybe, just maybe, they were getting closer to solving the crime.

But then, a darker thought crept into his mind. Why now? Why give us this much information?

He gripped the steering wheel as they drove away, his mind racing. *Is he getting sloppy? Or does he want to be caught?*

The ride back to the station was silent. Charles was lost in the intricacies of the case, while Mac, as always, was preoccupied with something far more pressing—figuring out where he'd get his next meal. Mac had lost his passion for the job long ago, but Charles on the other hand, had never wanted to solve a case more than he did now.

Finally back at the station, Charles wasted no time pinning the latest pieces of evidence onto the board. Crime scene photos of both victims were now displayed side by side, a grim reminder of the case that was beginning to take shape. He rifled through the Wilkins case file, searching for a specific photograph—the one capturing the street sign from the first crime scene. As soon as he found it, he grabbed a red marker and circled the name in bold strokes, a sense of satisfaction washing over him. This had to be a significant connection.

Moving to the top of the evidence board, he carefully drew another red circle around the letters "J" and "W," reinforcing the link between Jeremy Wilkins and the location of his murder. Drawing a clean arrow from the victim's name down to the name of the street, he repeated the process for Vincent Childs, methodically marking "Vesey and Church" in the same bold red. Before leaving the scene earlier, he had instructed the crime scene techs to capture a close-up shot of the street sign.

Satisfied with his work, Charles turned on his heel and strode toward Captain Stevens' office. He pushed the door open without hesitation.

"Captain!" he called. "We've found a link!"

Captain Stevens barely looked up from his desk, his fingers wrapped around a cup of coffee so dark and thick it resembled tar. "This better be good," he muttered before taking a sip.

Charles took a deep breath, knowing how this conversation was likely to go. "Both victims were found at intersections where the street names match the first letters of their names. It's a pattern, Captain."

The Captain frowned, unimpressed. "And what exactly does that mean, Detective? Do you have the killer's name?"

"No, Sir," Charles admitted.

Captain Stevens set his coffee down with a loud thud. "Then get out of my office and don't come back until you have something more concrete!" he barked.

Charles clenched his jaw but knew better than to argue. He left the office and made his way back to where Mac was stationed, who was now devouring a greasy New York slice they'd picked up on the way back to the precinct. A long string of melted cheese stretched from the pizza to Mac's mouth as he looked up at Charles.

"What did the Captain say?" Mac asked, chewing with little regard for manners.

"Nothing of significance," Charles grumbled. He wasn't about to let the Captain's attitude get in the way of their momentum. "Let's head over to Childs' apartment—see if we can find anything useful."

After a frustrating back-and-forth to secure the spare key with the building maintenance manager, Charles and Mac finally entered Apartment 3A at 1111 Lafayette Avenue.

The hardwood floors gleamed beneath the soft glow of the skylight overhead, the rich grain and knots catching the light beautifully. It was an open-concept space, seamlessly blending the kitchen and sitting area, while the bedroom was enclosed by a sleek brushed-steel partition. The whole place had an air of sophistication—modern, yet timeless.

Mac let out a low whistle as he surveyed the apartment. "Nice place," he said. Then, with a shake of his head, he added, "This is old money, Charlie boy. I can smell it a mile away. A rich kid using Daddy's fortune to play house, with no real appreciation for what he's got." His voice carried a note of irritation, as if the very idea offended him.

The walls were adorned with a collection of artwork—everything from impressionism to deco, from expressionism to abstract. It was as if Vincent Childs had curated his own private gallery. Charles moved slowly through the room, studying the pieces with interest. Some were signed by Vincent himself, while others bore the names of artists he didn't recognize, at least not initially.

"Looks like he was an artist," Charles noted, running a gloved finger lightly over the frame of one of Vincent's paintings.

Mac then seemed to wander off and Charles' gaze shifted toward the office, tucked beside the sitting area. A desk sat neatly arranged, papers scattered across its surface.

Charles approached it and lowered himself into the chair. He subsequently began sifting through the documents when something caught his eye—a business card placed in the corner sleeve of a desk pad.

He pulled it out and read aloud:

Lumain Gallery
101 Pearl Street Manhattan, NY
Vincent Childs – Gallery Assistant

Charles felt a flicker of understanding. *It's making sense now; Vincent worked at an art gallery!*

Mac's voice then echoed from the loft above, "Charlie, get up here!"

Charles climbed the wooden staircase, his thoughts briefly drifting to the cost of this place. *How does a gallery assistant afford such a high-end apartment?* Maybe Mac had a point—*old money.*

Reaching the loft, he found Mac standing in front of a stack of canvases, each wrapped in protective bubble wrap and carefully lined up as if awaiting shipment. "Take a look at these," Mac said, gesturing to the collection.

Charles unwrapped a few, revealing paintings in a variety of styles, signed by different artists.

"Maybe he was an art dealer on the side," Charles pondered curiously, carefully stacking the pieces back in order. "Would explain how he could afford this place."

A thought struck him. "Mac," he said, straightening up. "Let's get the techs in here to dust for fingerprints. If our killer was here, we need to know. In the meantime, let's head over to the gallery and see what we can dig up."

As they left the apartment, Charles couldn't shake the feeling that they were getting closer—closer to understanding Vincent Childs, closer to unraveling this killer's intent. And with that came an even more unsettling thought: *If the killer wanted us to see this connection, where is he leading us next?*

When the duo arrived at the Lumain Gallery on Pearl Street, Charles felt a growing sense of urgency. Someone here must have surely noticed that Vincent was missing.

As they stepped inside, they were greeted by a well-dressed man with slicked-back silver hair and a warm, yet professional demeanor.

"Good morning. Welcome to Lumain," the man said with a practiced smile. "My name is Franc Du Moore, Gallery Curator. How may we assist you today?"

Charles flashed his badge. "Good morning, Mr. Du Moore. We are Detectives Coffey and Mackenzie."

Before either of them could explain the reason for their presence, the curator's face fell, his expression shifting from polite interest to immediate concern.

"Oh no... You're not here about Vincent, are you?" Du Moore's voice wavered as he spoke.

Charles exchanged a glance with Mac before responding. "So Vincent was an employee here?"

Du Moore's eyes darted between them, his expression growing more desperate. "*Was?* Detectives... what do you mean—*was?*" His voice cracked with dread.

Charles sighed. Delivering this kind of news never got easier. "I'm sorry to inform you, Mr. Du Moore, but Vincent was found dead two days ago."

The color drained from the curator's face instantly. His breath hitched, his body swayed, and before he could react, his legs buckled beneath him. His eyes rolled back as he collapsed.

A nearby gallery assistant gasped and lunged forward just in time, catching Du Moore before he hit the polished marble floor.

The news sent a visible ripple of distress through the gallery staff. A hushed murmur filled the room as employees exchanged stunned glances, some wiping away tears, others whispering in shock.

A little while later, after composing himself with the help of his colleagues, Du Moore sat down, dabbing at his reddened eyes with a silk handkerchief. "I... I apologize, Detectives. This is quite a shock!" His voice trembled as he spoke.

"We understand, Mr. Du Moore," Charles said, his tone softer now. "But we need to ask you a few questions."

Mac, on the other hand, remained unmoved, his expression making it clear that he had little patience for dramatics.

"When was the last time you saw Vincent?" Charles asked.

Du Moore sighed. "It was May 29th, a Friday. We were preparing for the La Fue Exhibit set to open the next evening. La Fue is...

He is meticulous about how his paintings are displayed. Vincent and I spent the entire day carefully arranging the pieces."

He swallowed hard before continuing. "I arrived at the gallery at 5 a.m. the next morning to ensure everything was perfect. We were ready—entrees prepared, lighting adjusted—but by 8 a.m., Vincent still hadn't shown up. I called him. No answer. Straight to his answering machine. You can check that, right?"

"Yes, we can," Charles assured him. "And what happened next?"

Du Moore's expression darkened. "To be blunt, Detectives, I was furious! La Fue arrived at exactly 8:46 a.m., already displeased with the setup. I had to deal with him, the art critics, and a catering disaster—it was an absolute mess. I tried calling Vincent again around 3:30 p.m., but still, nothing, and again, straight to his answering machine."

Du Moore paused, hesitating before adding, "Vincent wasn't exactly... a good boy, Detectives, if you catch my meaning."

Charles looked on curiously. "You'll have to be more specific, Mr. Du Moore. We know almost nothing about Vincent—except that he's now lying in the morgue. Anything you can tell us would be helpful."

Du Moore sighed, leaning back in his chair. "What I mean is... Vincent didn't live cautiously. Unlike the rest of us who have found love with the men of our dreams, Vincent... played a different game. A dangerous one. He had a taste for the underground scene—the kind of places most wouldn't dare step foot in..."

Charles and Mac waited for Du Moore to elaborate further.

Hesitatingly, he continued, "On Friday nights, Vincent frequented the old theaters where they played gay pornographic films, places where men could indulge freely without shame or consequence. Vincent loved his freedom. He lived for the thrill. I assumed that night was like any other—that he got caught up in his usual Friday night escapades, maybe took something he shouldn't have and ended up lost in some drug-fueled daze. But, if I had known he was in danger..."

Du Moore's voice broke. He turned away, pressing his hands to his face, shoulders shaking with silent sobs. "I just... need a moment," he whispered, walking away to compose himself.

Charles watched him carefully, a thought forming in the back of his mind. *How did Mr. Du Moore know so much about Vincent's personal life? Were they close?* More than just colleagues? Before he could dwell on it, something else caught his eye.

A painting—hanging prominently in the front lobby of the gallery.

It wasn't flashy or immediately captivating, but Charles recognized it. He had seen this painting before.

This same painting was in Vincent's apartment.

"Mr. Du Moore," Charles called, motioning toward the artwork. The curator lifted his head, eyes still red from crying.

"What can you tell me about this painting?"

Du Moore sniffled and turned to face it. "That is *Desconsuelo* by Eduardo Kingman—also known as *Grief.* A magnificent piece. Wouldn't you agree?"

Charles took a step closer, studying the fine details—the bold, sorrowful lines, the deep, mournful hues. The artist had captured emotion so vividly that anyone looking at it could feel the subject's pain.

It was the same feeling he had when he saw it in Vincent's home.

It has to be the same one.

"What about the artist himself?" Charles asked. "What do you know about him?"

Du Moore seemed confused by the sudden shift in questioning but answered nonetheless. "Kingman moved to the U.S. in 1945 from Bolivia. He's been working out of California ever since. Why do you ask?"

Charles exhaled, his instincts sharpening. Something about this painting mattered.

He turned back to Du Moore. "Mr. Du Moore, I need you to come with us. We need your assistance in our investigation."

The curator's face paled once more. "But... I haven't done anything wrong," he stammered, his voice tinged with fear.

Charles didn't answer. Instead, he and Mac escorted Du Moore out of the gallery and into the waiting Gran Fury, its engine rumbling as they drove off.

As Charles and Mac drove toward Vincent's apartment, Charles turned slightly in his seat to face Mr. Du Moore, who sat in the back of the vehicle, visibly shaken. His hands were trembling, and his eyes remained fixed on the floor.

"Mr. Du Moore, I want to assure you that you are not under investigation," Charles said in a steady voice. "But I have to be honest—I don't believe you're telling us the whole truth."

Du Moore flinched but quickly composed himself. "I've told you everything I know," he insisted. "We worked closely together at the gallery. He was a great friend."

Charles studied him carefully, his gut telling him otherwise. "You know," he said, his voice firmer now, "I don't think you're being completely honest with us. I think you knew Vincent more intimately than you're letting on."

Du Moore's posture stiffened. "We were close, like I said!" His voice rose with frustration. "We knew each other well! We both loved art—it was our life, our passion."

His breathing became shallow, his eyes darting between Charles and Mac. "We were kindred spirits," he continued, his tone inherent with pain. "I wouldn't have reported him missing if I didn't care!"

He exchanged a quick glance with Mac before turning back to the curator. "Wait—what? When did you report him missing?"

Du Moore blinked as if realizing his mistake. He swallowed hard before answering. "Two months ago," he admitted. "I assumed he had run off with one of his... 'friends.' That's why I was so angry, Detectives." His voice faltered. "He truly hurt me..."

His shoulders slumped, and without warning, he lowered his head between his knees, his body shaking as he let out a wailing sob—the kind of cry that could only come from losing someone you deeply loved or cared about.

"I'm sorry," he whispered, his voice barely audible over the hum of the vehicle's engine. "He was my lover. Once. He was my everything."

Charles noticed the tremor in his hands. His suspicions had been correct—Du Moore hadn't just been Vincent's boss or friend; he had loved him.

"I need you to tell me everything," Charles said gently.

Mac, on the other hand, rolled his eyes, for he was becoming impatient with Mr. Du Moore's antics.

Du Moore wiped his eyes, took a deep breath, and nodded.

"We were very close," he began. "One night, after working late at the gallery, one thing led to another... and suddenly, we weren't just colleagues anymore. It felt like we were made for each other. Every day with him felt like a dream I never wanted to wake up from."

A smile flickered across his face before it quickly faded.

"We even talked about opening our own gallery one day. It was going to be our future, our legacy."

His fingers curled into fists. "And then—just like that—it was over."

His voice grew distant, haunted. "He started pulling away. He became... withdrawn. Almost shy. He wouldn't talk to me the way he used to. He shut me out completely."

Du Moore exhaled sharply, his eyes darkening as he recalled the night everything changed.

"About three months ago, I asked him to come over to my place. I realized we never stayed at his—he always called it his 'sanctuary,' but I never believed that.

"That night, as soon as he walked through the door, I knew something was wrong. His mood was dark. He barely looked at me."

Du Moore clenched his jaw. "Then he told me... he didn't feel comfortable around me anymore. That we had grown apart." "I was devastated. Furious. We screamed at each other. And then—just like that—he stormed out. After that, everything changed. It was only about work and art. Nothing more."

Silence filled the car.

Charles studied him carefully. "Why didn't you tell us this before?"

Du Moore straightened his posture, shaking his head. "I didn't want to raise any suspicion. We were just colleagues now. That's all."

Charles didn't respond, but his expression made it clear he wasn't entirely convinced.

"Well," he finally said, "we're on our way to his apartment. I guess you're finally going to see what was inside his *sanctuary*."

When they arrived, the forensics team was still processing the scene, their equipment set up across the apartment. Yellow tape blocked off certain areas, and flashes from cameras illuminated the dimly lit space.

Charles led Du Moore inside, his eyes scanning the room.

"Wow," Du Moore exclaimed in disbelief, taking in the luxurious surroundings. He ran a hand over the polished wood flooring and examined the intricate wall finishes. "This place is breathtaking. But... how could he afford this?" He turned to Charles, bewildered. "He didn't make much at the gallery, and his family wasn't wealthy."

Charles glanced at Mac, who had previously speculated that Vincent might have come from 'old money'.

Mac sighed, throwing up his hands. "Alright, so I was wrong," he grumbled.

But Du Moore's attention had already shifted to something else.

"Look at this," he said, stepping closer to a painting hanging on the wall. His fingers hovered just above the canvas, his expression a mixture of awe and confusion.

"This is an original Du Pont." His voice was reverent. "The linework, the depth of color—it's absolutely magnificent!"

He turned back to Charles and Mac. "Alfred Du Pont passed away in '82, I think. This piece must have cost a fortune."

Charles raised an eyebrow. "How much are we talking about?"

"I have a Du Pont in my gallery that sold for $250,000," Du Moore said. He shook his head in disbelief. "How on earth did Vincent afford this?"

A troubled look crossed his face. Nothing was adding up.

Charles studied the painting, stepping closer. Something wasn't right.

"I don't think it's an original, Mr. Du Moore," he said quietly.

Du Moore scoffed. "Of course it's original. He signed it, Detective. Look—right there."

He pointed to the lower left corner, where a signature read "Du Pont" in flowing script.

Charles frowned. "I think you should come with me to the loft," he said, motioning toward the staircase.

As Charles and Du Moore ascended the stairs, Mac lingered in the office area, his eyes scanning the desk. Something caught his attention.

An answering machine.

It sat beside an old Rolodex, its small red light blinking. The forensics team hadn't gotten to it yet.

Mac smirked, stretching as he leaned back in the office chair.

"Hey, Harry!" he called out.

A muffled response came from across the apartment. "I'm working here, Mac! What do you want?"

Mac grinned. "Relax, I'm just gonna check out the answering machine. Not gonna touch anything, I promise."

He tugged on a pair of gloves, eyes glinting with curiosity as he reached for the 'Play' button.

The message waiting inside could be the key to everything. As Mac pressed the button on the answering machine, a robotic voice announced:

"You have three new messages."

A faint crackle followed before the first recording began to play.

"First message. Time: 8:15 p.m. Date: February 24th."

A harsh **beep** filled the room, followed by an angry, breathless voice.

"Childs! This is Jeremy… You screwed me, man! You really screwed me!"

The voice trembled with fury.

"The wife is breathing down my neck about this damn painting! I spent over a hundred grand with you, and you sold me a fake? My buyer is furious!"

There was a sharp intake of breath before the voice—Jeremy—continued, his tone now venomous.

"You're going to pay me back, every single cent you owe me! Who the hell do you think you are, man? You think you can just get away with this?"

A tense silence followed, then the final, chilling words:

"You're really gonna pay for this. I'll make sure the last name you ever remember is Jeremy Wilkins! Got it?"

Beep.

Mac stood speechless as the message ended.

He took a slow step back, his mind racing. Jeremy Wilkins… Vincent Childs… There was a connection between the two victims. This was the break they had been waiting for.

Before he could process further, the machine moved on.

"Second message. Time: 8:12 a.m. Date: May 30th."
Beep.
This time, the voice was different—frantic, desperate.
"Vince! Where are you??"
There was a muffled rustling in the background, followed by a sigh.
"La Fue will be here any minute! I hope the reason you're not answering is because you're already on your way to the gallery!"
The voice softened, almost pleading now.
"Please don't let me down, Vince... Please."
Beep.
Mac knew the voice of the man on the second message, it was Mr. Du Moore, who at that very moment was upstairs in the loft with his partner.
The machine clicked again.

"Third message. Time: 3:38 p.m. Date: May 30th."
Beep.
This time, the voice was filled with raw anger and heartbreak.
"Vince! I cannot believe you've done this to me!"
"You've let me down too many times—in more ways than one!"
"It's over, Vince. You hear me? It's over!"
The voice grew colder.
"You can come collect your things during the week. You're through at this gallery."
Beep.
Silence.
Mac remained frozen, staring at the machine as the weight of the messages sank in.
"They knew each other... the victims had a connection!" he muttered under his breath.
His pulse quickened. If these messages were any indication, Vincent had been in serious trouble.
Without wasting another second, Mac turned and bolted up the stairs to find Charles and Mr. Du Moore.

While Mac had been downstairs listening to the messages on the answering machine, Charles had carefully picked up one of the paintings stored in the loft, having turned it slightly to examine the intricate brushwork. He glanced at Mr. Du Moore, curiosity flashing in his eyes. "What do you make of these?" he asked, holding the artwork out for the curator to inspect.

Mr. Du Moore took the painting in his hands, tilting it toward the dim loft light. His eyes narrowed as he traced the strokes with a practiced gaze.

"Well... that's very interesting," he said, his voice laced with intrigue.

Raising the canvas closer, he studied the technique with growing intensity.

"The brushwork is flawless... just like the one downstairs. Are you telling me, Detective, that these are fake? That these stunning pieces of art—these works that mimic the masters so perfectly—are nothing more than counterfeits?" The realization of the deception became more apparent to the curator.

His voice trembled slightly as he turned to face Charles.

A flicker of raw emotion crossed his face, and for the first time since arriving at the apartment, the weight of the truth seemed to crash down on him. His lip quivered, his fingers tightening around the frame.

The realization was undeniable now. Vincent had lived a double life.

A choking sound escaped him—half a laugh, half a sob—as he stared at the stack of paintings Vincent had created, each one a deception.

"This is... unbelievable. And unbearable both at the same time." He took a shaky step back, as though physically recoiling from the betrayal unfolding before him. His sorrow quickly hardened into anger.

"This is a disgrace! He was so talented!"

His voice cracked.

"If only he had come to me... If only he had let me see what he was capable of! And now? Now I stand here, left to witness his brilliance after he's already gone—what a devastating loss to the art world."

He swallowed hard, rage and sorrow warring in his expression.

"But what he did is unforgivable! These masters—these visionaries—spend their entire lives honing their craft, perfecting their art. And then, someone like Vincent comes along and takes it all away in an instant."

He exhaled sharply, shaking his head in disgust. Finally, he shoved the painting toward Charles.

"I assume this is evidence, Detective?"

Charles gave a slow nod.

"Yes, Mr. Du Moore."

A fire burned in the curator's eyes as he straightened his posture.

"Then get it out of my sight! Burn them, destroy them, throw them into an incinerator—I don't care! These forgeries should never see the light of day." Without another word, he turned sharply on his heel and made his way down the stairs.

As Mr Du Moore descended, Mac was on his way up, excitement brimming in his expression.

He barely registered the curator brushing past him, his head down, silent tears trailing down his cheeks.

Mac didn't wait. He hurried to Charles, nearly tripping over himself in his eagerness.

"Charles, you gotta hear this!" he exclaimed, his voice thick with urgency.

Charles raised a brow, intrigued.

"The two men knew each other! Jeremy Wilkins left a message on Vincent's answering machine!"

Mac was practically buzzing with energy—something Charles never thought he'd witness from the grizzled detective. It was a rare sight to see the old dog genuinely excited about catching a break.

Moments later, after listening to the recordings and ensuring that Mr. Du Moore was safely sent home in a taxi, Charles and Mac exchanged a knowing glance.

There was only one place left to go: The Wilkins residence.

They had a strong feeling that this time they would find out more about the connection between Vincent and Jeremy; Mrs. Wilkins would be the key to unlocking the mystery.

Charles and Mac navigated through the thick congestion of rush hour traffic, the Gran Fury inching forward as they made their way across town to the home of the deceased Jeremy Wilkins, his widow and their son. The streets were packed with honking vehicles and impatient drivers, but the detectives remained focused on their destination.

As they finally pulled up to the house, something felt off. The home looked different—almost as if it had been drained of life.

The once-pristine walls now appeared darker, possibly stained from neglect and some passing time. The front lawn, which had previously been well-kept, was now overgrown, with tall grass spilling onto the walkway leading to the entrance. Exchanging a knowing glance, Charles and Mac stepped out of the vehicle and approached the front door.

Their knock was quickly answered by Mrs. Wilkins, who stood in the doorway with a weary expression.

"Detectives, can I help you?" she asked, exhaustion evident in her voice.

"Mrs. Wilkins, may we come in? We need to ask you a few more questions," Charles requested politely.

Without hesitation, she stepped aside, allowing them to enter. As they walked into the house, the changes became even more apparent. The interior was nearly bare. The furniture was gone, as were the decorative tables, wooden art pieces, and paintings that had once adorned the walls. The living room—where they had previously sat to discuss the case—was now stripped of everything but a single woolen blanket on the floor, the only thing left to sit on.

"I apologize, Detectives," Mrs. Wilkins said with a heavy sigh. "I can't offer you any water or coffee. They shut off the water about a week ago, and I can no longer afford coffee."

A look of despair flickered across her face before she continued.

"You see, Jeremy left us drowning in debt. I've had to sell almost everything to cover what he owed, and yet we've barely made a dent. He was a burden when he was alive, and in death, he's proven to be even worse," she said bitterly, shaking her head.

Charles and Mac exchanged glances before Charles cleared his throat. "We appreciate your time, Mrs. Wilkins. We were hoping you could help us with something. Do you by any chance recognize the name, Vincent Childs?"

Mrs. Wilkins looked at the detectives puzzled, considering the name for a moment before nodding. "Yes, I've heard that name before. I believe he was a friend of Jeremy's," she said with a hint of recollection.

Her eyes widened slightly as more memories resurfaced. "Actually, I remember now. One night, Jeremy asked me to prepare for a guest. He told me to set up platters of food for himself and his visitor. I'm almost certain that man was Vincent." A pause. "Yes—come to think of it, it was Vincent. He's the one who painted the portrait." She gestured toward the object sitting beside the fireplace. "Why do you ask, Detectives?"

Charles hesitated before delivering the news. "Mrs. Wilkins, I'm sorry to inform you, but Vincent was found dead two days ago.

Mrs. Wilkins gasped, her hand flying to her mouth. "That's terrible! What happened to him? Is his death connected to Jeremy's case?"

"I'm sorry, Ma'am, but we can't disclose any details of an ongoing investigation," Mac said apologetically.

Mrs. Wilkins exhaled sharply, nodding in understanding. "I don't know much about their relationship, Detectives. They weren't exactly close friends—more like acquaintances. But, I can show you the painting he made for us."

She walked over to the sitting area, pulling back a piece of builder's cloth to reveal a large family portrait.

"There," she said, pointing to the bottom left corner.

Sure enough, at the very edge of the painting, a signature stood out—"V. Childs."

Charles leaned in for a closer look. "Did Jeremy ever mention any bad blood between them?"

Mrs. Wilkins shook her head. "Not that I'm aware of. Though, shortly before he went missing, he did say he needed to meet an old friend. But it couldn't have been Vincent... could it?"

She hesitated before continuing. "What I do know is that, right after that meeting, Jeremy took out another loan—one of many. He assured me it would be settled quickly, but, as usual, it wasn't. That debt, a hundred thousand dollars, was just added to the mountain of money we already owed."

Charles frowned. "Did he ever say what the loan was for? Or who it was for?"

Mrs. Wilkins let out a bitter laugh. "Jeremy never told me anything. Everything was always a secret. He had this way of making me believe he had it all under control. But look at us now!" she cried, her voice rising with frustration. Her hands clenched into fists so tightly that her knuckles turned white.

Regaining her composure, she took a deep breath and gestured toward the nearly empty house. "Everything you see here, Detectives, has to be auctioned off. Everything except this painting." Her lips quivered as she added, "And that's the strange part."

Charles raised an eyebrow. "What do you mean?"

"A few days ago, I got a call about it. Someone was asking specifically about this painting," she explained. "I told them it was going to auction, but they immediately made me a private offer for it. I have no idea why anyone would want a family portrait of strangers, but... I'm desperate for money. So I accepted without hesitation."

Mac's interest piqued. "Did the buyer give you a name?"

Mrs. Wilkins pouted her lips in thought. "I don't recall if he did. But I do have the delivery address." She disappeared into the kitchen for a moment before returning with a folded piece of paper, handing it to Charles.

He unfolded it and read the words aloud: M.R. Investments, Corner of John and William Street, Manhattan.

As soon as he read the address, the words jumped off the page and his grip on the paper tightened.

"Mrs. Wilkins, may I keep this?" he asked, his tone now one of urgency.

"Of course, Detective. The shipping company already has the details," she assured him.

"Thank you for your time, Ma'am," Charles said before turning toward the door.

As he left the room, Mac followed, a puzzled expression on his face.

"What's going on, Charlie boy? You look like you've seen a ghost!" Mac exclaimed as he slid into the driver's seat and reversed the Gran Fury out of the driveway.

Charles exhaled sharply. "Mac, that painting—it's being delivered to the exact same location where Jeremy's body was found!"

Mac's hands tightened on the wheel. "You think it's connected?"

Charles nodded. "Absolutely. We're missing something, and I have a feeling M.R. Investments is where we need to start looking. Let's call it a night. First thing in the morning, we head there."

As Charles made his way home that evening, he couldn't shake the feeling that he was finally onto something. He had never been one for high-profile cases, nor had he sought out media attention. But, for the first time in a long while, he felt like he was making real progress—like he was finally proving himself. He found himself often wondering if his father would have been proud.

That evening, as Charles arrived at his apartment, he followed his usual routine. He ascended the stairs, counting each step as he always did, a habit that had become second nature over the years. The rhythmic pattern of his footsteps against the worn steps brought him a strange sense of familiarity, a small moment of order in an otherwise chaotic life. When he reached his landing, he instinctively reached for his keys and approached his front door.

Just as he was about to slide the key into the lock, something made him pause. A small but significant change caught his attention, and for Charles, unexpected changes were rarely a good sign.

His eyes drifted to the wall between his apartment and his neighbor's. About three feet from his door, a hanging pot plant had always been mounted there—a subtle, but permanent fixture that marked the division between the two living spaces.

But now, the plant was missing. In its place hung a Native American dreamcatcher, roughly six inches in diameter, its delicate webbing and feathers swaying ever so slightly in the evening breeze.

His first thought was of the building's maintenance man—a self-proclaimed druid who had an odd habit of leaving symbolic trinkets around the complex. Charles had learned about the man's spiritual inclinations one Sunday afternoon when he had unexpectedly cornered him at his apartment door, rambling about energy flows and protective charms.

Shaking his head, he dismissed the thought. It was just another one of the maintenance man's quirks. Nothing to be concerned about. With a shrug, he turned back to his door, unlocked it, and stepped inside, pushing the dreamcatcher from his mind.

The next morning, Charles and Mac drove toward the corner of John and William Street, a silent tension filling the Gran Fury as they anticipated what they might uncover. Something about this case felt different—tangled in a way that neither of them had quite unraveled yet.

When they arrived, it felt like déjà vu. Stepping into the investment firm once again, they were greeted by the same security guard standing by the entrance.

"Good morning," Charles said, nodding in greeting.

The guard smirked. "Good morning, Detectives. Back again so soon?"

As Charles walked further into the building, his gaze landed on the large, polished sign displayed proudly above the reception desk. He frowned.

"Has the name of this firm always been Skylark Investments?" he asked the guard, a note of curiosity in his voice.

The security guard shrugged. "As far as I know, yeah. Been working here for 18 months, and it's always been Skylark Investments."

Charles exchanged a glance with Mac before asking, "Does the name M.R. Investments mean anything to you?"

The guard shook his head. "Nope, don't ring a bell. But, if you're looking for someone who might know, you should talk to Mason."

"Mason?" Mac asked.

The guard nodded. "Yeah. That old fool has been in that alley for years. If anyone remembers anything about the history of this place, it's him."

Mac shot Charles a look, his expression filled with disbelief. "No way," he muttered under his breath.

Charles thanked the security guard, and the two detectives exited the building. Before they even stepped fully onto the sidewalk, they could already hear Mason's voice. His shouting carried across the street, a familiar, erratic sound as he ranted at the passing pedestrians.

Mason was in full swing—waving his arms and muttering half-formed phrases to himself, his eyes darting wildly from one person to another.

Charles approached him cautiously. "Mason," he called.

For a moment, everything went silent. Mason's glazed eyes locked onto Charles, his head tilting slightly as he processed the familiar face and voice.

Charles took a step closer. "Do you remember me? My name is Charles. I'm a detective."

Mason blinked. Then, slowly, he repeated the word. "D-E-T-E-C-T-I-V-E?" He stretched each syllable out, as if testing the weight of the word on his tongue.

"Yes," Charles confirmed, keeping his voice calm. "Do you remember me?"

A flicker of recognition passed through Mason's eyes. Then, seemingly out of nowhere, he muttered, "Jeremy. Yes, Jeremy. He gave me ten bucks. Ten bucks, yes." His voice wavered, his manner unfocused.

Charles exchanged a look with Mac before pressing further. "What about Jeremy, Mason?"

Before Mason could answer, Mac placed a firm hand on Charles' shoulder, his tone more serious than usual. "Should we really be doing this here? The man is clearly confused, Charles; we need him to be calm."

Charles hesitated. Mac had a point—Mason wasn't in the right state to be questioned properly.

If they wanted to get any useful information out of him, they needed to bring him somewhere safe, somewhere quiet.

He turned back to Mason, speaking gently. "Mason, would you like to go for a ride with us? We have a nice car—and we'll get you a hot meal."

Mason's eyes brightened, childlike in nature, his cracked lips stretching into a wide, almost innocent smile. "Food?" Charles nodded. "That's right. A warm plate of food. Come with us."

Without hesitation, Mason agreed. The detectives carefully escorted him back across the street and into the backseat of the Gran Fury. As the car doors shut, Charles leaned back in his seat, pausing for a moment to catch his breath. The duo proceeded to the precinct where they would attempt to move the case forward with the help of Mason.

He knew something about Jeremy. He knew what had happened to him.

The question was, would Charles be able to get the truth out of him?

Charles leaned in slightly, lowering his voice as he spoke directly into Mason's ear. "Did you have enough to eat, Mason?" His tone was gentle, almost reassuring, as he sat across from the unkept man in Interview Room 3.

Mason, still chewing on the last bits of his meal, looked up at Charles with wide, childlike eyes and gave a slow, exaggerated nod, a small, satisfied smile stretching across his face.

Charles offered a warm smile in return before continuing, "Mason, do you mind if we record this conversation? It's just so we can remember exactly what you say. Is that okay with you?"

Mason blinked a few times, processing the question, before his head bobbed up and down again in acknowledgment.

A sharp beep filled the room as the recorder was switched on. "This is the official questioning of Corporal David Mason," Charles stated clearly for the record. "Present in the interview room are Detective Charles Coffey and Detective Peter Mackenzie. The time is 16:00, and the date is September 9th, 1987."

Charles glanced at Mac before focusing back on Mason. He kept his voice steady, careful not to startle or agitate him. "Mason, how long have you been living in the alleyway at the corner of John and William Street?"

Mason hunched his shoulders slightly, his fingers tapping randomly against the edge of the table. "Long time... long time," he muttered under his breath, his voice distant, as if speaking more to himself than to the detectives.

Charles exchanged a quick glance with Mac before pressing on. "Were you there in the early hours of the morning on May 31st of this year?"

Mason's eyes flickered with recognition. He nodded slowly. "Always there, always there... always watching." His voice was barely above a whisper, yet there was an eerie certainty in the way he spoke.

Charles leaned forward. "Did you see anything that night, Mason?"

Mason's expression shifted, he raised a trembling hand to his forehead. "Bright light... hurt my eyes," he muttered, shielding his face as if the memory of it still burned.

Charles narrowed his eyes. "What light, Mason? What did you see?" Mason hesitated for a moment before breaking into a wide grin. "He walked in front of the light... came to my tent... gave me money." His words came slowly, his gaze unfocused, as if he were recalling a dream rather than a memory.

Charles' pulse quickened. "Who, Mason? Who gave you money?"

Mason's fingers drummed against the table again, his lips parting slightly before he finally spoke. "A man... said it was from Jeremy. Yes... from Jeremy."

Charles felt a shift in the room. He exchanged another glance with Mac, who gave a subtle nod, urging him to keep going.

"Was the man's name Jeremy?" Charles asked, standing up now, his voice firm, yet patient.

Mason's expression changed. His grin faded and was replaced by a blank stare as he looked past Charles, his eyes unfocused. He simply shrugged, the silence stretching uncomfortably between them. His train of thought had been completely derailed.

For the next few hours, Charles and Mac continued their questioning, trying every approach they could think of to break through Mason's scattered thoughts. They circled back, rephrased their questions, even tried to jog his memory with leading details, but it was no use.

Eventually, Mac leaned back in his chair and let out a quiet sigh, shaking his head. He gave Charles a subtle but clear signal—it was time to wrap this up. Charles clenched his jaw in frustration, rubbing a hand over his face before finally switching off the recorder. "Interview concluded," he muttered.

He gestured to one of the officers outside the room. "Take Mason back to the alleyway," he instructed.

As Mason was led out, Charles remained seated for a moment, staring at the empty chair across from him. He knew Mason had seen something. He knew the answer was buried somewhere inside the man's fractured mind.

The problem was—how were they going to retrieve it?

As the days of frustration turned into weeks, Charles and Mac worked tirelessly, sifting through evidence, revisiting crime scenes, and searching for any clue that could bring them closer to identifying their elusive suspect. They had brought Mason in for questioning half a dozen times, but each interrogation yielded the same frustrating result—muddled half-truths, incoherent ramblings, and a dead end every time.

Charles was convinced that Mason held the key to unlocking the mystery.

The morning of November 6th, 1987, started like any other for Charles. At the time, he had no idea it would be a day he would remember for the rest of his life.

As he drove toward the precinct, the hum of the car radio filled the silence.

"Good morning, Manhattan! You're listening to WMCA-AM, and I'm your host, Kenny Collins, bringing you the latest on this chilly Friday morning. The weekend is almost here, folks, but for some, it's not a time of celebration—it's a time of mourning and heartbreak. I'm talking, of course, about the families of the victims—two tragic murders that have plagued our city these past few weeks!

Joining me in the studio is none other than Joan Gibbs, our very own human rights activist. Good morning, Joan."

"Good morning, Kenny."

"Joan, what's your take on these killings? Are they premeditated? Calculated?"

"That, I can't say for certain, Kenny. But what I do know is that yet another gay man has been brutally murdered, his life cut short, and the police are doing absolutely nothing about it. I'm convinced these crimes will go unpunished. The detectives handling this case are biased—when it comes to anything outside of heterosexual relationships, they turn a blind eye. It's *disgusting and immoral..."*

Charles exhaled sharply and switched off the radio. He shook his head as he pulled into the precinct parking lot. *These people have no idea what we're up against.*

Activists were always quick to frame it as a 'hate crime', always eager to push an agenda—without any concrete proof. It frustrated him, not just because it was unfair, but because it saddened him to see what the city had become.

As he walked into the precinct, he spotted Mac at their shared desk, hunched over his usual breakfast, chewing with a level of dedication that would put most men to shame. A stray piece of food clung stubbornly to his beard while his jaw worked tirelessly, his lower lip bouncing like a piston.

"Eating again?" snapped Charles in frustration, stemming from the lack of progress on the case.

"Gotta get sustenance from somewhere, Charlie boy," Mac grinned, crumbs spilling from the corner of his mouth. "And there ain't no better place than George's." Another unidentifiable piece of food slid from his sandwich and landed on the floor next to him.

Charles shook his head. "The 'Cap' wants to see us this morning," Mac continued between bites. "Said something about Behavioral Sciences, Profiler and the FBI but I wasn't really paying attention."

Charles ignored him. His mind was still fixated on Mason. "I want one more crack at him, Mac." He leaned over the desk, locking eyes with his partner.

Mac sighed, wiping his mouth with the back of his hand. "No, Charlie boy. We're done with that washed-up old has-been. He doesn't know anything. And even if he did, what kind of useful information do you think we're gonna get out of him? The guy's a waste of time." He leaned back in his chair, shaking his head. "I say we go see the 'Cap' and take it from there. It's been almost two months now. Let it go. Let the pros take over."

But, Charles wasn't listening.

Without breaking eye contact with Mac, he turned slightly and called out across the room, "Officer!" A rookie standing near the water cooler snapped to attention.

"Go pick up Mason. Corner of John and William, downtown," Charles ordered.

The officer hesitated for a brief moment, as if registering the command, then nodded and rushed off.

Mac let out an exasperated sigh, shaking his head once more. "You just don't know when to quit, do you?"

Charles didn't answer. He didn't need to. Something told him that Mason knew more than he was letting on. And if there was even the slightest chance of cracking him—Charles was damn well going to take it.

Before long, Charles and Mac once again found themselves seated across from Mason in the dimly lit confines of Interview Room 3. This time, however, Mason appeared calmer than usual. His restless energy had settled into an almost eerie stillness. He wore nearly the same tattered clothing as before, but draped around his neck was an assortment of pendants that Charles had never noticed until now.

Charles narrowed his eyes, searching for an opening. "Are those new, Mason?" he asked, his voice steady but probing.

Mason glanced down at the pendants, lifting each one delicately between his fingers, rubbing them as though they held some kind of power. "Not all new," he muttered. "Some old."

Charles leaned forward slightly, his eyes drawn to a particular pendant Mason seemed to favor. A tarnished crucifix, worn from years of handling, hung from an aged leather cord, tied haphazardly at the back with a crude knot.

"This one is special," Mason whispered, his grip tightening around the cross.

Charles studied it carefully. "It looks old, Mason. How long have you had it? Was it a gift?"

Mason's eyes flickered with something—nostalgia, fear, maybe both. "Very old," he muttered. "It was my friend... in that place." His fingers curled tightly around the crucifix, as though shielding it from unseen hands. "I hold onto it tight at night... so nobody can take it."

Charles softened his tone, sensing they were on the brink of something. "No one is going to take it, Mason. It's yours, okay?"

Mason nodded suspiciously, continuing to stroke the pendants, his fingers never still. Across the table, Mac shifted uncomfortably and shot Charles a knowing look—the kind that said *We're wasting our time here.*

But then, Mason's expression shifted. A flicker of excitement lit up his face as he lifted another pendant toward them. "This one is new," said Mason. A two-inch Native American dreamcatcher, its delicate web woven within a wooden hoop—certainly the most noticeable of all of them around his neck.

Charles' breath staggered. His mind flashed back to that night months ago—the pot plant holder outside his apartment, the missing plant, and the dreamcatcher that had mysteriously taken its place. It had to be a coincidence... right? Charles thought to himself.

Mason's voice broke through his thoughts. "He gave this to me... yesterday."

Charles snapped his attention back to him. "Who gave it to you, Mason? A friend?"

"A new friend," Mason replied, his tone laced with something unreadable. He hesitated before adding, "Your friend."

"My friend?" Charles echoed, confused.

Mason nodded. "He said I must give it to Charles. But I don't want to!" His sudden outburst sent a jolt through the room. His face twisted in anger, his hands trembling as he clutched the dreamcatcher tightly.

Charles leaned in. "Who is he, Mason? Who's my friend?" His voice was urgent now, pressing for answers.

Before Mason could respond, a sharp knock echoed through the room. The metal door creaked open, and a uniformed officer stepped inside.

Charles clenched his jaw. "What is it?" he snapped, clearly irritated by the interruption.

"Sir, Captain needs to see you and Detective Mackenzie immediately."

Charles exhaled sharply, trying to contain his frustration. "Just give me a damn minute, will you?" he barked, rolling up his sleeves as he turned back toward Mason. But the officer stood firm.

"Now, Detectives." His voice left no room for negotiation.

Charles exchanged a look with Mac, exasperation etched across his face. Then, with a resigned sigh, he reached over and pressed the stop button on the recorder. "Interview terminated at 17:25."

Turning back to the officer, he gave a quick order. "Take Mason to a holding cell. Make sure he gets whatever he wants—food, coffee, I don't care. I want to speak to him again as soon as we're done with the Captain."

The officer nodded and stepped forward, motioning for Mason to follow.

Mason rose from his chair slowly, that vacant, faraway look settling back over his features. He walked toward the door without protest, without a word.

Charles called after him. "We'll be back to talk to you soon, Mason. Okay?"

Mason didn't respond. He simply disappeared through the doorway, leaving the two detectives alone in the silent room.

As soon as the door clicked shut, Charles slammed his fists against the table. "Dammit!" The sound reverberated off the walls. "We were *getting* somewhere, Mac!"

Mac sighed, shaking his head as he stood up. "He's a loon, Charles. You're not gonna get anything out of him. Mark my words." But Charles wasn't ready to give up. Not yet. Because for the first time in months, he felt it—an unmistakable shift. A crack in the wall Mason had built around his memories.

And Charles was determined to break it wide open.

Charles and Mac walked briskly down the corridor toward Captain Stevens' office, the weight of the investigation pressing heavily on their shoulders. As they stepped inside, they found the captain hunched over his desk in deep concentration as he scanned a file spread open before him. His expression was grim.

Without looking up, he slammed his fist against the desk, causing a few loose papers to flutter. "We have another one, men!" he growled, exasperation evident in every word he uttered.

Charles and Mac exchanged a glance, bracing themselves for the news.

"The reason we didn't know about this one?" Stevens continued, his tone growing sharper. "Because it wasn't found in Manhattan.

It was all the way in *Queens!*" He jabbed a finger at the file in front of him before shaking his head in disbelief.

Then, his voice rose. "Now tell me—why the hell would a killer terrorize Manhattan, practically under our goddamn noses, and then suddenly decide to take a trip to Queens? Can either of you geniuses explain that to me?"

Charles cleared his throat, still absorbing the information. "Are we sure it's the same killer?" he asked.

Stevens let out a bitter laugh before turning his gaze directly towards Charles.

"You want proof, *Detectives?*" He leaned forward, his voice seething with anger. "The body was found dumped in the middle of the street. A body part had been taken." His grip tightened on the file. "Oh, did I forget to mention? The son of a bitch removed her eyes!"

The Captain stood abruptly, snatching up the file and hurling it toward Charles, who barely caught it before it hit the floor.

"The 110th Precinct caught the case," Stevens continued, pacing now. "They had no damn clue we had similar cases here in Manhattan. They tagged the body and sent it straight to the morgue—no ID, no fingerprints. And before you ask, Coffey, no, there wasn't an envelope found on the body."

Charles' stomach tightened. *That had been one of the killer's signatures— leaving behind cryptic, taunting messages with both of the victims, same MO , however no birthday card!? It didn't seem to fit.*

"I've already pulled some strings to have the case and the body transferred to us," Stevens went on. "Dr. Bullard will handle the autopsy. I know the Doc needs time, but I don't give a damn how long it takes—you better solve this thing fast. The FBI is breathing down my damn neck, wanting to send in a profiler, and I swear to God, I will not let those bastards near my crime scenes! Do you understand me!?"

His roar filled the office, and before either detective could respond, he waved them off, muttering curses under his breath.

Charles and Mac didn't need to be told twice. They hurried out, leaving Stevens fuming in his office. They didn't want to admit it but the captain was right—Dr. Bullard would need time with the body before they could get any useful forensic details.

In the meantime, the only logical step was to head to the 110th Precinct and gather everything the original investigating officers had compiled: crime scene photos, witness statements, forensic reports, and any potential evidence collected at the scene.

At the 110th precinct in Queens, Charles and Mac worked methodically, combing through files, speaking to the officers who first arrived at the scene, and reviewing the crime scene photos in gruesome detail.

Then, mid-conversation with one of the detectives, realization hit Charles like a lightning bolt. His body tensed.

"Mac!" he shouted across the room.

Mac, who had been sifting through a different stack of documents, barely looked up.

"Mason! We left him in the holding cells!" Charles blurted. "We were supposed to go back—he's probably climbing the damn walls by now!"

Mac simply shrugged, unconcerned. "Yeah? So what?" His tone was dismissive, his focus still on the case. "It's not like we were gonna get anything useful out of him, Charlie boy."

Charles muttered something under his breath but didn't argue. Mason would have to wait. They had a fresh body and a crime scene to piece together.

Once they were back in the vehicle, Charles turned his attention to the crime scene photographs, flipping through them one by one.

The images were grotesque—the most recent victim's face mutilated, the empty sockets where her eyes should have been sending a shudder through him.

Then, something caught his attention. He stared hard at one of the photos taken by the forensics team, his mind racing.

"There it is, Mac. You see it?" He pointed to a street sign captured in the background of the crime scene photo.

"Cnr of Judge and Britton Street." He exhaled sharply, his pulse quickening. "Look at the name, Mac. It matches the first and last name of our victim."

Mac frowned, glancing between the image and Charles. "You know who the victim is?"

Charles closed the file and leaned back, his expression grim. "Mac, there isn't a city bus or a sidewalk bench in this town that doesn't have her face plastered all over it."

Mac blinked.

"Our third victim is Judith Barlow," Charles said, his voice low but certain. "The world-renowned hypnotherapist."

Mac let out a long breath. "Are you sure? Because if you're right..." He shook his head, his expression darkening. "This case is about to turn into a goddamn media frenzy."

Meanwhile, back at the precinct, Mason had been placed in a secure holding cell, separated from the other detainees due to his erratic behavior and unpredictable psychotic episodes.

The cell, a cramped 3x3 space, was dimly lit, its cold concrete walls offering no comfort. Mason sat hunched in the furthest corner, knees drawn to his chest, his fingers absentmindedly tracing patterns on the filthy floor as he rocked back and forth. His thoughts running rampant, triggers and reminders of his past surrounded him. He felt like a prisoner.

The officer on duty made his routine rounds, stopping momentarily to peer through the narrow slot in Mason's cell door. What he saw was nothing out of the ordinary—Mason, swaying rhythmically, whispering to himself in an incoherent manner.

"Mason, you okay in there?" the officer asked, his voice flat with disinterest.

Mason stilled, his eyes flicking up toward the slot. "What day is it?" he muttered, barely audible.

The officer sighed. "It's Sunday. You should be at church," he added with a smirk, clearly amused by his own sarcasm. Without waiting for a response, he shut the flap with a dull clang and continued on his rounds.

Inside the cell, Mason remained motionless, his head tilting slightly to the side. "Sunday... Sunday," he whispered, his fingers tightening around the dreamcatcher pendant hanging from his neck. "Rest day... sleep day." His voice trembled, barely above a breath.

His grip on the pendant grew firmer as his whispering became more frantic. "Must go to sleep now. He needs me to go to sleep. Need to give Charles the present. They said they would come back.

They said they *would* come back... Must go to sleep now... He will find it..." His words trailed off, his eyes dull with realization.

A slow, eerie calm settled over him. He rose to his feet with an almost unnatural stillness, his fingers moving methodically as he loosened the knot securing the pendant's leather cord around his neck. With delicate precision, he approached the heavy steel door and looped the cord around the handle, tying it carefully, his hands trembling as he completed the knot.

"They never came back," he whispered, a hollow sadness in his voice. "Left me... like my friends did. Must go to sleep now..."

His breathing grew uneven as he slipped the leather cord around his own neck. His hands shaking as he turned once... then again... tightening the makeshift noose with each slow, deliberate movement. The leather bit into his flesh, constricting with an unyielding grip.

Mason turned to face the bed, his entire body rigid. "Must... go... to sleep now," uttered Mason one last time, the words barely escaping his lips as his Adam's apple pressed desperately against the tightening strap.

Then, with one final motion, he let his feet slide forward, his legs stretched out in front of him, allowing the full weight of his body to bear down on his throat. A strangled gasp escaped him as his body instinctively fought for air. His chest shuddered while his muscles were convulsing violently.

His vision blurred and then darkened. A thick string of saliva dripped from the corner of his mouth, splattering onto the cold, concrete floor. His limbs twitched—one final protest from his failing body—before his head lolled to the side, his vacant eyes staring at nothing.

His body slumped against the cell door, lifeless.

Mason was dead.

Chapter 5

Where The Truth Lies

Oblivious to the cataclysmic event that had transpired within the confines of the holding cell back at the precinct, the two detectives pressed on, making their way towards the office of Dr. Bullard, the coroner.

As Charles and Mac navigated through the dimly lit corridor of the coroner's offices, an unusual heaviness permeated the atmosphere.

The duo pushed through the imposing metal doors of the examination room. Inside, they were greeted by the sight of three corpses, each one draped in a pristine white sheet, lying silently upon the cold steel tables, side by side.

"Detectives, I appreciate you giving me some time with this case. It was much needed. What an absolute mess!" Dr. Bullard exclaimed.

"We've seen the crime scene photos, Doc. It was a gruesome sight." Charles responded. "What can you tell us about the victim?" He then asked. His tone was measured, yet eager for answers.

"First and foremost, Detectives, I presume you know the identity of this victim, correct?" Dr. Bullard asked, his gaze shifting between the two men.

"Yes, Doc. It's Judith Barlow," Charles confirmed with a nod.

"Then I'm certain you don't need me to emphasize the gravity of this case. A Caucasian female in her late twenties, a renowned hypnotherapist who has graced the stage of The Oprah Winfrey show! Her death will undoubtedly attract significant media attention in this city," Dr. Bullard remarked as he began to carefully draw back the shroud, revealing Judith's head and stopping just above her chest.

"The condition of her body is horrendous, gentlemen. Initially, I suspected starvation as the cause of death, but the contents of her stomach contradicted that theory," the doctor explained, moving away from the corpse towards a table where a plastic bag containing a mixture of liquid and solid matter rested. "It appears to be a blend of water and cake, only partially digested. I estimate this was consumed between 12 to 24 hours prior to her death."

"When the body arrived here, the coroner in Queens had not yet conducted an examination. Fortunately, he was an old protégé of mine," Dr. Bullard stated with a hint of pride in his voice. "We were incredibly fortunate that all the forensic evidence remained intact. Her lips bore a vivid red lipstick, smudged as though she had been interrupted while applying it. The foundation of her makeup was unusually dark, perhaps an attempt to conceal bruises. However, upon removal, I discovered it was merely makeup, nothing more. The most alarming aspect is the absence of her eyes! Once again, our killer has removed a body part from his victim and substituted them with artificial ones, likely sourced from a doll of some sort in this case. The precision with which the eyes were removed is unfathomable—no bruising around the frontal or zygomatic bones. One cannot help but marvel at the time and effort invested, regardless of the horrific nature of the act. Unlike the previous victims, however, her eyes were removed postmortem. Curiously, she was also wearing an ash blonde wig, which is peculiar given that her natural mousy brown hair is exceptionally well-maintained. Fibers and scrapings have been collected from both the hair and fingernails for further analysis."

Charles and Mac both just stood there, stunned and speechless. They were trying to process everything—from the gruesome sight before them to the coroner's explanations.

Dr Bullard continued, "Now, gentlemen, let us discuss the cause of death. I deliberated on this extensively. Her face exhibits all the classic signs of a beating and starvation—dark rings around her eye sockets, swollen cheeks, and a reddened complexion. Then, I recalled an article I read in a medical journal from the early 1960's about an experiment conducted on Soviet prisoners, testing the limits of sleep deprivation. It was an ingenious, yet undeniably cruel study. The prisoners were allowed to sleep for a few hours before being awakened, only to be put back to sleep again shortly after.

This cycle persisted, with the duration of sleep gradually decreasing until they were forced to remain awake, aided by an aerosol gas containing a stimulating agent that prevented sleep."

"The condition of the men in that experiment was unlike anything previously documented—eleven straight days without sleep—until now. I concluded that Ms. Barlow had been subjected to sleep deprivation and was tortured to death. Her brain had shrunk, her organs had failed, and her heart rate had slowed to a fatal silence, all resulting from the extreme lack of sleep. It is an utterly horrific way to die," Dr. Bullard said, shaking his head in sorrow.

Charles and Mac stood beside Judith Barlow's body, in a state of shock. This was, without a doubt, the most peculiar death they had ever encountered. The sight of one of the city's most stunning women—her face now reduced to leathery skin, broken teeth, and lifeless doll's eyes staring back at them—made them cringe.

"So, gentlemen, regarding your investigation, I have a sinking feeling that we have not seen the last of this monster. The first victim died by consuming soil of his own volition, the second drank water until his stomach could no longer bear the weight and he drowned, and now your third victim— so young and beautiful—succumbed to having her mind shattered through unimaginable pain and torture, her system ultimately shutting down. This is truly sickening!" Dr. Bullard declared, standing beside Judith's body as tears streamed down his face. He was not typically a man of much emotion, but at the sight of Judith's body, all his medical training and logic took a back seat.

Before Charles and Mac could step away to allow the doctor to compose himself, Dr. Bullard uttered one final, chilling statement: "It is official, gentlemen. You now have a serial killer on your hands."

Charles and Mac departed from the coroner's office, their minds reeling with disgust and unease. Even Mac, in the prime of his career, had never witnessed anything as bizarre as what they had encountered that day.

Returning to the police station, another unsettling feeling gnawed at Charles' gut ,though he couldn't quite pinpoint it. The duo walked through the station's entrance and were immediately greeted by the desk sergeant.

"Well, well, look who's back! Boy, do you two have some explaining to do to the Chief," the sergeant remarked with a smirk, clearly relishing the situation.

"What's going on!?" Charles demanded, in no mood to entertain this level of sarcasm after their experience with Dr. Bullard.

"Your guy, Mason—found dead in his cell a few hours ago. The fool must've gotten his necklace tangled in the door or something and was too dim-witted to figure out he just needed to stand up!" the sergeant chuckled, oblivious to the gravity and complexity of the investigation unfolding before them.

Without a word, Charles bolted down the corridor, leaving Mac behind with a smug I told you so expression plastered across his face, as if he had anticipated this turn of events.

When Charles reached the scene, he found Mason still suspended from the cell door. The forensics team was already present, alongside a representative from Dr. Bullard's office, there to officially confirm the death. The Captain stood nearby, gazing down at Mason's corpse with a grim expression.

"The press is going to have a field day with this," he muttered, turning his head just in time to catch sight of Charles standing beside him. "Where the hell have you been!?" the Captain yelled, his voice echoing through the confined space.

"We were at the coroner's office, Sir—you knew that!" Charles shouted back, his frustration boiling over as he matched the Captain's intensity.

"What in God's name do you make of this mess? I've got a homeless man dead in my precinct, a murderer running rampant who's claimed three lives in the past five months, and an incompetent detective with his bumbling sidekick who seems more concerned about where his next pastrami sandwich is coming from than solving this damn case!" the Captain roared, pacing furiously around the holding cell. His face red with anger, the jugular vein in his neck throbbing visibly with every furious word.

Charles stood motionless, his eyes fixed on Mason's body as the Captain's ramblings washed over him. He barely registered the insults hurled at him and Mac. What truly captivated his attention was Mason himself. A lost soul, broken by the horrors of war and abandoned by a country that failed to support him upon his return—that, to Charles, was the real crime. America, the so-called "land of the free and home of the brave," owed its moniker to men like Mason, who had fought and bled so children could sing those words in classrooms. Yet, Mason had been discarded by the world, unable to find the help he so desperately needed. In that way and in that moment, Charles saw a reflection of himself.

Eventually, the Captain stormed off, muttering something incoherently as he disappeared down the corridor. Charles sank to his knees beside Mason's body, his gaze softening with regret.

"I'm sorry we failed you," he said, his voice barely above a whisper, as though speaking directly into Mason's ear. As he pulled back from the body, his eyes caught on the array of pendants dangling from Mason's neck—particularly the one that had served as his noose. There, seared into the skin at the center of his throat, was the unmistakable outline of a dreamcatcher pendant. A memory flickered in Charles' mind, words from Mason's earlier interview replaying like a haunting echo around the unforgiving room:

"Who gave this to you, Mason? A friend?"
"A new friend... your friend..."

Charles had his suspicions about that pendant but had dismissed them, choosing not to dig deeper. Now, that decision fueled a surge of regret within him.

"Well, at least he can ramble on to God now, eh, Charlie boy?" Mac said quite inappropriately as he walked down the corridor toward Mason's lifeless body.

Charles shot to his feet and closed the distance to Mac in an instant. With a surge of fury, he seized Mac by the collar of his shirt and slammed him against the nearest wall.

"Show some respect for the dead, Mac! Respect the dead!" Charles growled, his voice low and commanding.

He released Mac with a shove, sending him stumbling to the side. "We had one witness—one lead—and now he's gone. Our only thread in this case, snuffed out!" Charles spat, his frustration spilling over as he turned and stormed down the corridor, leaving Mac standing there, uncharacteristically speechless. Charles went outside to cool off for a few minutes and settle his emotions.

Once he managed to compose himself to some extent, Charles then went back inside and returned to his desk, pulled out his chair forcefully, and sat down. There resting on top of his desk was a package, neatly wrapped in a simple brown paper. The top of it read:

Charles William Coffey
1 Police Plaza, Police Plaza Path
New York, NY 10038

Charles reached for the package and lifted it—it felt as light as a feather. He determined that it couldn't possibly be a bomb; all incoming packages were thoroughly scanned at the front desk before being distributed. Besides, its light weight suggested it couldn't cause any significant harm, even if it were an explosive device.

With curiosity, Charles began to unwrap the parcel, peeling back the brown paper to reveal a plain, cardboard box beneath. He gave it a gentle shake, detecting the faint sound of something shifting inside. His fingers worked to peel away the tape, securing the top, and then he carefully opened the flaps. What greeted him was all too familiar—yet another birthday card staring up at him!

In shock, Charles let the box slip from his hands—which crashed to the floor. To preserve any potential evidence it might contain he retrieved a pair of gloves. He slid them on, one by one with practiced precision, and then knelt down to retrieve the box from the floor.

Extracting the card, he saw that it was, yet again, a children's birthday card. The front featured a cheerful animated dinosaur, its green scales accented by a row of protruding red spines trailing down its back. In one claw, it clutched a bright yellow balloon; the bold text proclaimed:

Have a ROARSOME birthday!
You're 3 TODAY!

Charles braced himself, fully aware of the pattern these cards seemed to follow, yet he felt an unshakable unease about what might lie within this one. As he opened the card, he found the interior blank once more—no garish illustrations or printed greetings. Tucked inside, however, was a folded piece of papyrus paper, its texture fragile and ancient-looking. Charles unfolded it with the utmost care, mindful of both its delicacy and the significance it held. As he had seen before, the page portrayed perfectly hand-written calligraphy, the ink flowing in elegant, precise strokes. This time, though, it was different—no clues, no driver's license, no taunting poem. Instead, it was a letter, addressed directly to him, penned by the serial killer himself. It read:

My Dearest Charles,

How exhilarating it is that I can finally communicate with you. This moment has been meticulously crafted—a culmination of painstaking effort and patience to reach a point where I can unveil my true self to you.

Have you ever felt the intoxicating urge to create, Charles? To shatter the brittle confines of the mundane and conventional? That, my friend, is my deepest desire for you—a sinister invitation to transcend the ordinary and join me on this journey. The three "gifts" I've bestowed upon you—the lives I've extinguished—are merely the opening notes of our twisted symphony, the prelude to a path we shall walk together.

With each passing day, I unearth more of my own dark essence, peeling back layers of restraint to reveal the artistry of my purpose. My wish is that you too, are evolving alongside me, awakening to the grim beauty of our shared path. After all, every soul must crumble to dust eventually—yet some, like me, achieve greatness on their way down, leaving a legacy etched in blood and terror.

These wretched "people" now cluttering the morgue—those pathetic husks occupying space on those cold steel slabs—don't even deserve that dignity. They belong in the filth of the gutter, their decaying carcasses left to rot and fester, a fitting end for such loathsome creatures. Through their deaths, I've liberated their victims, unshackling the innocent from their torment. You must see it, don't you, Charles? Their demise was necessary. I've purged their transgressions and balance has been restored. It's done now.

For now, I must rest. A season has passed. My hope is that you rise from the ashes of your mundane existence; for mediocrity is a tragedy. Purify yourself of doubt, and rest with me, I will see you soon. I am certain of it, as certain as the darkness that binds us.

Take care, my old friend...

P.S. If you were wondering about Jeremy and Vincent, allow me to elaborate. Mason—poor, broken Mason—was an old comrade of mine, a pliable tool in my hands, an instrument if you will. I offered him to you as a gift, a pawn to aid in your investigation, but sadly, Charles, your time ran out and so did his, what a pity. And with it, so too did any chance of unraveling the threads I'd laid before you. Rest assured though—Jeremy and Vincent will never again prey upon the innocent. I have seen to that.

Charles sat motionless, his eyes locked on the letter before him, staring at the page for what felt like an eternity. He read the words repeatedly in his mind, each phrase looping through his thoughts like a relentless echo.

"Old friend..." the words screamed at him.

The killer's voice seemed to slither through the ink, addressing him with a chilling familiarity. *He speaks as if he knows me—truly knows me!* Charles thought, his pulse quickening. Who is this man? *Could it be someone I've crossed paths with before?* The realization struck him with cold certainty: *They definitely know me—intimately, deliberately.* His mind churned with questions, each more frantic than the last. *What have I done to earn this twisted attention? What sin or oversight has tethered me to this monster's game?* These thoughts raced through Charles' head, as he sat with the letter, desperate to unravel its sinister meaning.

As his gaze drifted from the paper, Charles' eyes fell upon the box, still resting exactly where he'd left it after extracting the letter. Peering inside, he discovered three feathers nestled within. They were striking in their beauty. Each feather gleamed ice-white from the shaft, the pristine hue extending halfway down the posterior vein. There, the color rapidly changed, as though the feathers had been plunged into a vat of vivid red ink. The red blended seamlessly into a deep midnight blue, which then darkened gradually, transitioning into an inky black that consumed the tips of the vexillum. Charles paused, captivated by the creator's craftsmanship—the hues were impeccable, blending with a softness, yet bold, arresting presence.

He couldn't place their origin; they might have belonged to an exotic parrot, flaunting its vibrant plumage, or perhaps a rare species of owl, steeped in nocturnal mystery. Yet, their purpose was unmistakable to Charles. The killer had intended these feathers as a grotesque tribute, a symbolic representation of the three victims—each color a twisted echo of their fates. More disturbingly, they seemed to mirror the dreamcatcher pendant that had been found around Mason's neck, a deliberate and sickening thread woven into the killer's design. This was no random act of violence; the perpetrator was methodical, cunning, and undeniably clever. Charles felt a chill settle into his bones as he realized the truth: this predator was far from finished with his dark mission and it felt personal.

Later, Charles then briefed the Captain on the latest piece of evidence—the letter and the feathers. The Captain's expression hardened as the implications of the investigation sank in, and it became crystal clear to everyone involved that they were no longer chasing a mere murderer; they were hunting a serial killer, a calculating architect of death whose reign of terror had only just begun.

Breaking News: *In our top story tonight... Yet another body was discovered in the early hours of Thursday morning, in the borough of Queens. The victim has been identified as none other than Judith Barlow, a globally celebrated hypnotherapist whose fame skyrocketed following her gripping documentary series detailing the heinous crimes of Richard Ramirez, infamously known as 'The Night Stalker,' the California serial killer. According to our exclusive sources, Ms. Barlow's body bore the same distinctive and gruesome hallmarks as those of the two previous victims found in Manhattan earlier this year, suggesting a horrifying pattern that has gripped the city in fear. Earlier today, Captain Stevens of the New York Police Department addressed the press with an official statement, shedding light on this disturbing case. Here's what he had to say:*

"We extend our deepest gratitude to the dedicated officers of the 110th Precinct, whose swift response brought this case to our attention. They have since relinquished jurisdiction to our department, allowing us to spearhead the ongoing investigation. While formal identification of the victim is still pending, we are highly confident—based on preliminary evidence—that the most recently deceased is indeed Judith Barlow. This remains an active and evolving investigation, but we can now confirm with certainty that these three murders, spanning Queens and Manhattan, were committed by the same individual. At this time, we will not be entertaining any additional questions from the press. We appreciate your cooperation as we continue our around the clock investigation. Thank you."

Charles and Mac stood closely beside Captain Stevens as he addressed the gathered press, delivering his statement with a stern, authoritative tone. Charles' gaze drifted across the sea of reporters before them, their microphones extended to their limits like desperate hands grasping for answers. In their tense expressions and wide eyes, he could understand their fear.

Once Captain Stevens concluded his remarks and dismissed the media, he leaned in close to Charles, his breath hot against Charles' ear. "Get this done, Coffey," he hissed, his voice a low growl seething with barely contained fury. "I don't care how you do it—just get it done!" He took care to keep his outburst discreet, his words sharp but quiet, mindful not to fuel the press with a spectacle of his anger.

By this point, the partnership between Charles and Mac was fraying with each passing minute under the weight of the case. Despite their strained dynamic, duty bound them together—they still had a job to complete, and the stakes were higher than ever.

They had established that the first two victims, Wilkins and Childs, were acquainted with one another, though only on a casual level. What remained uncertain was whether Judith Barlow, the latest victim, shared any connection to either of them—a link that could prove pivotal.

Determined to chase down this lead, the duo set out for Midtown, heading to Judith's professional offices to meet with Ms. Cheryl Barker, her longtime secretary, in hopes of uncovering answers amidst the growing shadow of the killer's spree.

As the detectives stepped into the late Judith Barlow's office waiting room, they were met with an emotional scene. Cheryl Barker stood in front of the desk, locked in a tight embrace with another woman. Tears streamed down her face, her eyes squeezed shut as both women wept uncontrollably.

"Ms. Cheryl Barker?" Charles asked gently.

Cheryl slowly pulled away from the embrace, dabbing at her tear-streaked face with a crumpled tissue. "Yes, I'm Cheryl. Can I help you?"

"I'm Detective Coffey, and this is Detective Mackenzie. Could we have a moment of your time?"

"Of course, Detectives," she replied, composing herself. "We can talk in her office."

Before leading them inside, she turned to the young woman beside her. "Heather, please don't leave, okay?" Heather gave a small nod and took a seat in the waiting area, her expression equally distraught.

Cheryl gestured toward the chairs in Judith's office. "Please, have a seat, Detectives," she said, as she shut the door behind them, still clutching the tear-soaked tissue.

Charles offered a sympathetic nod. "We know this is a difficult time, Ms. Barker."

"Cheryl," she interrupted, shaking her head firmly. "Please, call me Cheryl."

"Alright, Cheryl," Charles continued. "As I was saying, we understand how hard this must be. But we need your help. Could you tell us about the last time you saw Ms. Barlow?"

Cheryl took a deep, shuddering breath. "The last time I saw Judy was on Wednesday, September 9th. She had finished for the day and told me she was hosting a roundtable session that evening with a few colleagues."

"A roundtable session?" Charles queried, inviting her to elaborate further.

Cheryl nodded. "Yes. It's when some of New York's greatest minds in psychology and forensics come together to discuss cases—both current and past—to share insights and learn from them. Judy was passionate about her work and her patients. She was a wonderful person," Cheryl said, her voice breaking as she lifted the tissue to her nose.

Charles gave her a moment before pressing on. "And what happened after that?"

"The next morning, when I arrived at the office, I placed my bag on my desk and noticed faint music coming from inside her office. I assumed she was preparing for a patient, so I didn't disturb her."

"Did she actually have a patient scheduled?" Charles asked.

"That's what was strange," Cheryl said, shaking her head. "I checked her diary, and she had no appointments scheduled for that day or the following one. However, she had occasionally seen people without an appointment, so I didn't think much of it. But after an hour passed with no sign of her, I decided to check in. When I stepped inside, her office was empty. The tape player was still running, and the music was on repeat. It looked like she had been working late, but unlike her usual roundtable sessions, there weren't any signs of multiple people being there. Normally, after those meetings, the office would be littered with glasses, notebooks, and papers. I always made sure to tidy it up before she arrived the next morning."

"Cheryl, can you give us the names of the people who might have attended the meeting that night?"

She sighed. "I'm sorry, Detectives. I wouldn't know. Judith arranged those meetings herself. My job was just to make sure the office was ready and that the coffee was fresh."

Across the room, Mac, who had been quietly taking in the conversation, suddenly interjected, "Hold up!" he called out, his voice booming and his tone sharp. "Are you telling me the last time you saw your boss was in September?"

Cheryl blinked, taken aback. "Yes, Detective."

Mac's expression darkened. "So you didn't think it was strange that she was missing for three months? It didn't occur to you to call someone—like the POLICE?" he demanded, his voice rising.

Cheryl recoiled as fresh tears welled in her eyes. "I did! I did call the police, Detective!" she cried.

"Mac! Enough!" Charles barked, shooting his partner a warning look.

He turned back to Cheryl, his voice softer now. "Let's all take a deep breath. Cheryl, please, continue."

Cheryl wiped at her face before continuing shakily. "As I mentioned, Judith sometimes took a few days off—she'd disappear to some spa upstate for a long weekend. So at first, I didn't think much of it. But by Monday morning, when she missed her first two appointments, I knew something was wrong. And then she missed her afternoon session with Heather." She shook her head. "That's when I really started to panic. Judy would never miss her appointment with Heather."

Charles leaned forward. "What did you do next?"

"I tried calling her at home—no answer. I left messages on her answering machine. I even paged her. Nothing. That's when I finally reported her missing."

"This was Monday, September 14th?"

"Yes, Detective."

She swallowed hard, her voice quivering. "After a week with no word, I knew something was terribly wrong. I just never imagined... it would end like this." She broke down again, shaking her head in disbelief.

Mac suddenly spoke up again, this time more courteous and polite towards the fragile secretary, much to his partner's relief.

"Pardon the interruption," he said, his curiosity piqued. "You said Judith would never miss her appointment with Heather. Why?"

"Judith was everything to Heather," Cheryl said, her voice trembling. "She completely turned her life around—a complete 180. She was mentoring her, helping her cope with... the fallouts.

I honestly don't know what Heather is going to do now that she's gone."

"Fallouts?" Charles asked, narrowing his eyes.

Cheryl hesitated. "It's best if you speak to Heather, Detectives. She can give you a better understanding of why Judith was the best at what she did."

Rising from the single-seater sofa, Cheryl stepped out into the waiting area and called Heather into the office.

As they waited, Charles' thoughts drifted back to the letter from the killer:

Through their deaths, I've liberated their victims, unshackling the innocent from their torment.

Their victims. What did he mean by that?

Heather entered the room clutching a tissue, her body trembling with grief.

"Heather, please have a seat," Charles said gently.

As she settled in, he continued, "As you know, we're investigating Ms. Barlow's murder. Cheryl tells us that Judith changed your life. Can you explain what that means?"

Heather's eyes lit up despite her sorrow. "She was a goddess, Detectives," she said with the utmost respect. "She helped me see the light in every aspect of my life. Under hypnosis, she made it clear to me what needed to change for me to experience true happiness."

Charles leaned forward slightly. "What kind of changes did you make?"

Heather exhaled, still grief stricken. "First, she made me realize I was in a toxic relationship with my ex-fiancé. We were together for five years, and when he proposed, I thought we had a future. I trusted him completely—he was a devout Christian, and I never imagined he would betray me. But, Judith helped me see the truth—he was a liar, a cheater. So I left him. Now, I live alone."

She dabbed at her eyes with the tissue before continuing.

"I also quit my job. Judith opened my eyes to how my company had exploited me for years—passing me over for promotions, undervaluing my work, and never compensating me fairly. So I walked away. Now, I'm self-employed. I make just enough to get by."

Heather swallowed hard before adding, "And lastly, I sold my house upstate. Judith warned me that the neighborhood was on the decline, that it would only get worse. Before everything fell apart, I got out. Besides, with Henry gone, I didn't need such a big space anymore. Now, I live in a small apartment in Hell's Kitchen with my cats. My life is simple. And Judith was the only person I could trust...and now she is gone!"

Tears spilled down her cheeks as she stood abruptly, seeming to be overcome with emotion. Cheryl must have overheard Heather from the waiting area, and almost barged inside and rushed to her aid, wrapping an arm around her and subsequently leading her out of the office to calm her down.

Mac let out a frustrated sigh. "What was all that about, Charles?" he asked. "Why are you asking her all these personal details? None of this has anything to do with the case."

Charles shook his head. "It might have *everything* to do with the case, Mac. In his letter, the killer referred to 'their victims'—meaning the people lying dead in the morgue may have preyed upon others before they themselves were hunted down. What if our victims weren't as innocent as they seemed?"

Mac stared at Charles as if he had lost his mind. "I don't buy it. But, we've got nothing else to go on, so if you think it's worth looking into, lead the way."

With that, the detectives gathered the details of Heather's ex-fiancé, Henry, and her former employer to verify whether Judith's claims were true—or if she had an agenda of her own.

Following his hunch that the killer was "liberating" people like Heather, Charles reached out to Henry Banks, her ex-fiancé, to learn more about their past. He arranged to meet Mr. Banks at his office at The Bank of New York on Park Avenue.

"Detectives, please, come in and have a seat," Mr. Banks said, shutting the door to his corner office behind them.

"Can I get you anything? Coffee, perhaps?"

"No, thank you. We just need a few minutes of your time," Charles replied.

"What can I do for you?"

"We're investigating the murder of Judith Barlow. We understand your ex-fiancée was a patient of hers."

Upon hearing the name, Banks scoffed. "When I saw the news, I couldn't help but feel relieved—which goes against everything I believe in. That woman was a menace. A conniving, forked-tongued witch!" He slammed his fist on the desk, his face tightening with anger.

Charles shot Mac a glance, a facial expression that suggested a possible motive.

"I know how this sounds, and I realize it could make me a suspect, Detectives. But I can assure you, whoever killed her did the world a favor."

"What made you despise her so much?" asked Charles. "We were informed that you had been unfaithful to Heather."

"That is a blatant lie!" Banks shouted, his voice cracking with emotion. His colleagues, intrigued by the commotion, raised their heads from their desks and peered through the glass of his office window. His eyes welled up with tears. "Heather was my world—my everything! I loved her more than anything, and thanks to that devil, she's now living in some dump in Hell's Kitchen."

"So, are you saying Ms. Barlow lied to Heather under hypnosis?" Charles pressed. "Why would she do that? What did she stand to gain?"

"I'll tell you exactly what she had to gain—my hard-earned money and Heather in the palm of her hand." Banks leaned forward, his hands gripping the edge of his desk. "Heather was so convinced I was cheating that Judith insisted she see her three times a week. She manipulated Heather into believing those absurd things. We had a beautiful home upstate where we planned to raise a family. It was everything we wanted. Then, out of nowhere, Judith convinced Heather the neighborhood was unsafe and we needed to sell and move!"

He scoffed bitterly before continuing, "And why? Because I told Heather we needed to cut back on spending—including her sessions with Judith. That's when things changed. Heather must have mentioned it to Judith, and that's when she turned up the manipulation, ensuring her pockets were lined nice and thick."

Banks ran a hand through his hair, frustration mounting. "Not long after Heather broke things off with me, I found out she had already listed the house and quit her job. She boasted how she adored her boss. He was kind and understanding. It didn't make sense why she would have left such a stable position—until it hit me. She had been asked to put in extra hours at work because they had just acquired a major new account. A colleague needed her support, meaning long hours at the office, which meant she would have to cut back on her sessions with Judith. And that?" He shook his head. "That wasn't going to work for Ms. Barlow."

Banks suddenly stood up, his voice filled with venom. "I'm glad she's gone. She can't hurt anyone else the way she hurt me and Heather or the countless others who fell into her web of deception!"

Charles and Mac sat in stunned silence. How could the world see this woman as a goddess, a beacon of hope—yet beneath the surface, she had been a master manipulator? At that moment, Charles knew: Judith Barlow's vice had been power and greed.

"We won't take up any more of your time, Mr. Banks," Charles finally said as the detectives stood to leave. "Thank you for speaking with us."

They exited the office and made their way back to the precinct in the Gran Fury. As soon as they arrived, Charles and Mac began piecing together a new motive, pinning their findings to the evidence board.

For the first time in his career, Charles took the initiative to set up a task force room. He then called for an urgent meeting with Captain Stevens.

The Captain strode into the room and took his seat at the head of the table. "Okay, Coffey, what have you got for me?"

"Captain, we believe we've identified the killer's motive. We now suspect he's targeting individuals who harm others—but do so behind closed doors, without public scrutiny."

Captain Stevens leaned forward, intrigued. Charles moved to the board, pointing at their first victim. "Jeremy Wilkins—a well-respected man, surrounded by friends, always in the right social circles and all-round good guy. But at home? He didn't care enough to provide for his own family."

He moved to the next photograph.

"Vincent Childs. Another beloved figure, admired by many. But behind closed doors, he was a fraud. He was forging near-priceless artworks and selling them, pretending to be a legitimate broker."

Finally, Charles pointed at the last image—the one that had just shattered their previous assumptions.

"And the coup de grâce—Judith Barlow. A world-renowned hypnotherapist, revered for her courage in facing The Night Stalker and surviving the ordeal. People worshiped her. But in reality, it seemed she was manipulating her patients, diving into their minds and planting false truths to benefit herself—making them believe whatever would make her richer and more powerful."

Charles turned back to the room. "These three victims all have one thing in common: They were bad people. That's it. They were just bad people."

Captain Stevens studied the board for a moment before asking, "Do you have the evidence to support these theories?"

"No, Sir. Not yet," Charles admitted.

"That's why we called you here. We need a task force dedicated to gathering that evidence—to deep-dive into the lives of these three victims and uncover any commonalities or anomalies that might lead us to the killer. I propose we form three teams, one for each victim."

Charles stood at the front of the room, waiting for the Captain's response. Captain Steven was reluctant but his proposal sounded solid. "You can have Bradshaw and his men. I want a weekly report, Detective. You're in charge now. Get to it." With that, the Captain stood and exited the room.

Charles turned to Mac, who looked less than thrilled—no doubt already calculating how much of his drinking time was about to be sacrificed due to the impending overtime.

As the investigation teams began delving into the lives of the 'Boroughs Three', as they were now being called, a dark cloud descended across the Harlem River.

At 313 E 187th Street, inside the Solomon Temple Baptist Church in the Bronx, something evil was stirring.

Chapter 6

Room to Breathe

Tyreese Williams was a bright and ambitious nineteen-year-old young man, brimming with potential and a future that many would envy.

The Williams family was a cornerstone of the Belmont community, a tight-knit neighborhood tucked away in the South Bronx. At the helm of the family stood Tyrel Williams, a respected local pastor and an unwavering pillar of strength within the community. His presence was deeply embedded in the fabric of Belmont, so much so that there was scarcely a place he could go without being recognized. Whether it was for a friendly conversation or a heartfelt prayer for a neighbor in need, Tyrel was the person to whom everyone could turn for guidance, support and solace.

"Tyreese! Come over here, boy," Tyrel called out to his son, who had been engaged in conversation with a few of the older women from the congregation after the Christmas Day service in 1987.

As Tyreese approached, Tyrel addressed the women with a knowing smile. "Please, won't you tell these fine young ladies what I've taught you about the struggles of our people?"

Standing tall, Tyreese responded with confidence, "Yes, Sir. You can't separate peace from freedom because no one can be at peace unless he has his freedom."

Tyrel nodded approvingly. "And who, pray tell, said that?" he inquired, his gaze fixed firmly on his son.

"Malcolm X, Sir," Tyreese answered without hesitation.

A proud grin spread across Tyrel's face as he turned back to the women. "You see, ladies? Now, I know Malcolm X was a devout Muslim, but truer words could not have been spoken by any man. And I assure you, my boy here understands the struggles we've all endured during those dark and trying times." As he spoke, he placed a firm yet reassuring hand on the shoulder of one of the elderly women, a silent gesture of solidarity and warmth.

Tyrel had always seen his son as an instrument—one he could take out and play at just the right moment. Tyreese, for his part, understood this well and respected his father for it. He knew that at every church gathering, community picnic, or town hall meeting, he would be called upon, showcased as a beacon of hope for the people. It was a role he embraced, for he understood the deeper purpose behind it.

For Tyrel, it was imperative that the community had someone to look up to—someone to stand for them, as he had done decades earlier when he stood on the steps of the Lincoln Memorial, listening to his idol and close friend deliver the now-immortal words, "I have a dream..."

Born on May 30, 1931, Tyrel Bernice Williams had been a hungry and compassionate young man from an early age. He had an innate passion for people and an unwavering commitment to serve. Whether it was assisting with collections at his local Baptist church or helping Mrs. Drifus into her car, Tyrel had always possessed a deep-seated desire to give back to his community.

His pursuit of knowledge eventually led him to the University of Pennsylvania, where he studied under esteemed professors such as William Fontaine, the university's first African-American professor, and Elizabeth F. Flower, a renowned professor of philosophy. It was there, within the halls of academia, that he first laid eyes on a young man who would become both his idol and his confidant—Dr. Martin Luther King Jr.

As time passed, Williams and King grew close, bound by their shared experiences of oppression and their relentless pursuit of justice. Tyrel felt an unshakable conviction to be a part of the movement, to stand alongside King in the fight for civil rights. He felt compelled to make a difference. However, the true spark that ignited his passion came on April 4th 1967, when King delivered his groundbreaking speech, Beyond Vietnam: A Time to Break Silence, at the Riverside Church in New York City, where Tyrel worked.

King's words struck a deep chord within him. He had witnessed firsthand the devastating impact of war on his community—the young men who left for Vietnam and never returned, the broken families left in the wake of their absence. He had been there to console grieving mothers who had lost their sons and wives who had been widowed too soon. All that remained were ashes, and it was Tyrel who held the broom.

As Dr. King continued his crusade across the nation, Tyrel took it upon himself to carry the torch in New York, preaching to anyone who would listen about the immorality and injustice of the war.

But then came the day that shattered him.

On April 5th 1968, as he stood before a crowd in Hartley Park, Mt. Vernon, delivering a powerful message about oppression and wartime struggles, he received the devastating news. Jesse Jackson had called to inform him that just the night before, on April 4th , Dr. King had been assassinated. A wound was torn into Tyrel's soul that day—a wound so deep that no words, no prayers, and no passage of time could ever fully heal it. It was in that moment that Tyrel vowed to dedicate his life to ensuring that the struggles and oppression his generation had endured would not befall the next.

From that point forward, he immersed himself even further in the movement, solidifying his place as a guiding force within the Belmont community. His presence became synonymous with leadership, resilience, and unwavering faith. The weight of it all was something he carried with the utmost pride.

One crisp December evening in 1987, as the children excitedly prepared for their upcoming Christmas play, Tyrel Williams made his way down to the church to check on Ms. Myrtle's progress with the rehearsal.

"What a fine play we're going to have this year, Ms. Myrtle," Tyrel remarked warmly as he walked down the center aisle of the church, his fingers gliding over the polished wooden pews, a ritualistic gesture that seemed almost second nature to him.

Ms. Myrtle, busy ushering the children into a straight line on the stage, turned at the sound of his voice. She let out a soft giggle. "Why, Pastor Tyrel! I wasn't expecting to see you here this evening," she said, tucking a loose strand of grey hair behind her ear.

Tyrel's gaze swept over the children, his expression beaming with approval. "You all look absolutely lovely tonight," he addressed them warmly before his eyes landed on one girl in particular. "And if I may say so, Mary-Beth Blanchard, you look magnificent, young lady," he added with a grin, stepping closer to the thirteen-year-old who had been cast as Mother Mary.

The girl blushed under the pastor's attention but remained quiet, her hands folded neatly in front of her.

"Carry on, Ms. Myrtle. Don't let me get in your way," Tyrel said as he stepped back, settling himself comfortably in the front pew, his hands folded across his lap.

As the rehearsal unfolded, Tyrel found his gaze continually drawn to Mary-Beth. There was something about her—so young, so innocent, so delicate. She captivated him.

When the rehearsal concluded, Tyrel rose to his feet, clapping enthusiastically. "As the Psalmist said, 'Children are a heritage from the Lord.' We are truly blessed to have your bright, young faces here today. And come Christmas morning, the entire community will witness the wonderful gift you've all prepared for them!"

"Thank you, Pastor Tyrel," Ms. Myrtle said, her face glowing with gratitude. "It means the world to them that you came." She then turned to the children, gently instructing them to gather the props and prepare to leave for the night.

As the children shuffled down the aisle, eager to return home to the warmth of their families, Tyrel reached out and placed a firm, yet gentle hand on Mary-Beth's shoulder. She halted at the touch, turning to look up at him as he rested his other hand on her opposite shoulder.

"Mary-Beth," he said, his voice low and soothing.

"Yes, Pastor?" she asked, her eyes wide with curiosity.

"What's the hurry? You are the star of the show, you know that don't you?" he said with a warm smile. "Come with me to my office. Let's get you a nice, warm cup of hot chocolate, okay?"

She hesitated for a moment, then nodded slowly. Taking her by the hand, he led her toward his office, away from the departing children and Ms. Myrtle.

At the same time, Tyreese, following his mother's instructions, made his way through the heavy snow toward the church. He had been sent to retrieve the donations for the 'feed-the-homeless' initiative, which had been locked away in his father's office. Frustrated, he braced against the cold, the wind biting at his skin as he made the two-block journey from home.

As he reached the front of the church, he spotted Ms. Myrtle pulling the door shut behind her.

"Tyreese?" she called, her voice filled with concern. "You're going to catch your death out here! What are you doing, child?"

"Evening, Ma'am," he replied, shaking the snow from his coat. "Mama sent me to collect the donations."

"Oh, I'm sure your father will bring them home himself," Ms. Myrtle assured him. "He's in his office now. Go on home before you freeze to death." She offered him a kind smile before making her way down the street.

Tyreese frowned. *If Papa was already here, why had Mama sent him out in the cold to fetch the donations?* The thought confused him as he pushed open the church doors and stepped inside.

The sanctuary was dimly lit, the flickering glow of candlelight casting long shadows against the walls. As he walked past the pews, he paused at the altar, his eyes drifting to the solid wooden cross made from the finest oak, standing tall behind the offering table. To its left, the American flag swayed gently in the draft; to its right, the state flag stood proudly. His gaze lingered on the inscription carved into the wood: Do this in remembrance of Me.

Would he one day stand where his father stood? Would he follow in his footsteps, delivering sermons to a congregation that respected him? Shaking the thoughts from his mind, he continued toward the back of the church, nearing the door to his father's office.

It was closed, but light crept through the gap beneath it, casting restless shadows against the floorboards. Tyreese knew that when the door was shut, his father was not to be disturbed.

Still, the thought of returning home without the donations worried him. He knew his mother would demand an explanation, and if he failed to remind his father, she'd have every right to be upset.

Sighing, he reached for the handle.

As he pressed down on it, he heard muffled voices from inside. His father's voice was deep, steady, deliberate.

"The Lord our God has found favor with you, Mary-Beth," Tyrel's voice carried through the heavy wooden door. "You are truly a child of God. The Lord has spoken through me and has instructed me to become close with you. Our Lord endured much pain and suffering, just as we do. But do not fear, for our rewards for this suffering lie in the Kingdom of Heaven. We are not to question His will. If it is His will, then it must be done. Do you understand, Mary-Beth?"

Tyreese froze.

His pulse pounded in his ears as he strained to listen.

Mary-Beth was in there with him.

To him, Tyreese assumed that his Father was counseling her; he knew the young lady from the neighborhood and the congregation. He didn't want to interrupt his Father while he was working. His grip tightened on the doorknob. He hesitated before easing the door open just an inch, allowing a fraction of warm light to spill into the hallway.

And then he saw her.

Mary-Beth's face was contorted in pain, silent tears cascading down her pale cheeks. A trembling hand was clamped over her mouth, muffling whatever sound she wanted—needed—to make. That hand belonged to his father.

Tyreese's breath caught in his throat.

For a moment, he simply stood there, unmoving, his mind processing what his eyes were seeing.

And then, ever so slowly, a smile spread across his lips.

Not a smile of horror. Not one of sorrow.

But of relief.

For years, he had concealed his own secret, one that set him apart from the righteous path his father had laid before him. His interests had never truly been with the church, nor with its teachings. Instead, he had been drawn to something far darker—the occult.

Since his early teenage years, Tyreese had immersed himself in its doctrines, its rituals, its power. And now, as he stood there, watching his father—the great, holy man of Belmont—exposed in his sin, he felt vindicated.

His father was no different.

His father was tainted, just as he was. As he listened to his father's hollow prayers spill into Mary-Beth's ears, Tyreese's heart swelled with euphoria.

She was getting what she deserved.

And this—this—was only the beginning...

"Tyreese!" The name boomed through the room, the voice echoing from a loudspeaker nestled in the top left corner.

Tyreese opened his eyes. His vision blurred and unfocused, his eyes struggled to adjust to the light. The air was thick with the scent of damp earth and fresh vegetation, the unmistakable aroma of nature and water filled the air. A cool, clammy sensation clung to his skin, beads of moisture forming along his arms. He attempted to move—but his body refused to obey. Panic surged as he realized he was completely paralyzed.

"Wake up, Tyreese. It's your birthday." The voice returned, softer now, almost soothing.

Tyreese's lips parted as he forced out a hoarse whisper. "Papa?" His vision sharpened, revealing that he was neither in his bedroom nor anywhere remotely familiar.

"Tyreese. Just remain calm. You are safe."

The voice was not his father's. That much was certain now. His gaze flickered upward. Above him stretched a vibrant canopy of green, thick foliage intertwined with wildflowers in a breathtaking array of colors. It was beautiful—yet deeply unsettling.

Terror gripped him. "What's going on? Why can't I move?! Where am I?!" His voice cracked as fear took hold.

"Relax, Tyreese. Your questions will be answered in time. For now, listen to the sounds of nature."

A flicker of static hummed through the speaker before the soft, rhythmic symphony of the rainforest filled the air. The shrill cries of macaws, the steady drone of insects, the rustling of unseen creatures moving through dense underbrush—all of it surrounded him.

With panic taking full control, he screamed for help, his voice raw and desperate, tears spilling onto his cheeks. He screamed until his throat ached, until exhaustion dragged him under like an unseen force, pulling him into a restless, unwilling sleep.

Some indeterminate amount of time passed. Tyreese oscillated between intense panic and drifted in and out of consciousness. All of a sudden, a voice—familiar now, but no less unsettling—broke through the silence.

"Wake up, Tyreese."

It seemed he had passed out. His eyes snapped open. "Who are you?!" he bellowed. Almost immediately, he began to hyperventilate.

Then, the voice returned, measured and calm. "Now, Tyreese... That is not the question you should be asking. Rather, you should ask—who are you?"

Tyreese's jaw clenched. "I know who I am, fool! It's you I don't know, man!" A low chuckle crackled through the speaker.

"The sedative I administered causes temporary paralysis. Don't worry— you'll be able to move soon."

Silence fell upon the room again, and then the voice added, "You must be starving. And after all, it's your birthday!"

"My birthday's March 4th, man!" Tyreese yelled.

"That's right. Today is March 4th, 1988. Happy 20th birthday, Tyreese."

His stomach twisted. "What?!"

"Tell me, what was the last thing you remember?"

Tyreese squeezed his eyes shut, forcing his mind to search the darkness. "I was driving home... I had just left Dymon's place in Harlem when... when..." He hesitated, the memory dissolving before he could grasp it. "I—I don't know. I can't remember anything else."

"That's right," the voice confirmed. "I know it all seems confusing, Tyreese. But in time, everything will become clear."

Then, silence returned once more and remained. The voice disappeared despite Tyreese's curses and cries.

Hours slipped by. Slowly, sensation crept back into his fingers. Tyreese flexed his hands, feeling the cold, unyielding surface beneath them—steel. His legs twitched, regaining function, until finally, he managed to shift his weight, pushing himself into a seated position on the steel platform bed.

His head throbbed. The jungle sounds still played over the loudspeaker, an eerie reminder that he was utterly alone.

His feet touched the ground—damp, rough gravel, cool against his skin. He took in his surroundings. The room was unlike anything he had ever seen; it resembled a jungle, an untamed wilderness.

Thick green vines draped from the ceiling, their leaves glossy and the flowers bloomed—reds, purples, and yellows in contrast. Along the walls, wooden crates were stacked in precise rows, each overflowing with soil and lush vegetation, the air dense with their earthy perfume.

It was breathtaking.

It was horrifying.

"Good morning, Tyreese," the voice cutting through the sounds of the rainforest.

Tyreese turned toward the speaker, fists clenched. "Who are you!?" he shouted. "Where am I, man!?"

"Calm down, Tyreese. All will be revealed in time. But first, you must be hungry. Please—eat. I have provided ample food."

Tyreese's eyes darted around. "There ain't no food here, man!" he snapped.

"You're expecting Mama's home cooking?" the voice responded sarcastically.

Frustration boiled over. Tyreese let out a bloodcurdling scream. "HELP!" His voice cracked. "SOMEBODY HELP ME!"

The voice didn't respond. Instead, the jungle sounds simply resumed.

His knees buckled. He collapsed onto the gravel, his fists pounding against the cold ground. He sobbed, chest heaving, mind racing. How? Why? He knew he had done wrong in his life, but what had he done to deserve this?

Then, the voice returned.

"I'm sure you want to know why you're here, Tyreese, but first—introductions are in order, don't you think?"

Tyreese said nothing.

"Fine, I'll start. I'm Michael. Very nice to finally meet you, Tyreese. You are my fourth visitor here. I have been looking forward to our time together."

Tyreese's stomach clenched. "I don't care who you are, man! Let me the hell out of here!"

"Now, now, Tyreese. That's not a very good start, is it? We have *plenty* of time to explore those emotions of yours. But first—eat. We wouldn't want you to starve now, would we?"

The hours dragged on. Hunger gnawed at Tyreese, twisting his insides. His muscles ached, his head pounded, and still, no food appeared. Only a grimy bucket of water rested beside his bed.

Tyreese hesitated, then lifted the bucket to his lips. The water was murky, flecks of dirt swirling beneath the surface. The first sip was foul—the water tasted like a mix of mud and rancid water. He gagged but forced himself to swallow. His mind solely focused on surviving. He drank until nearly half was gone, his stomach churning in protest.

Still, no food.

As exhaustion overtook him, he collapsed onto the bed. The room spun. His mind drifted.

Then—a scent came from the vent parallel to the loudspeaker.

Familiar. Mouthwatering.

Bacon.

His stomach writhed in agony as Michael's voice sliced through the speaker. "Good morning, Tyreese. Before we eat, I have just one question for you...

Tell me—what is her name?"

Tyreese's breath quivered. "Who!?"

"Solve the riddle, and you'll eat."

Michael's voice recited slowly:

> *"I'm a name that's timeless, from a tale so wild,*
> *Where a girl falls down a hole, quite beguiled.*
> *Through wonders and puzzles, I wander with grace,*
> *Who am I, this curious girl, in a magical place?"*

Tyreese's lips moved silently. His mind scrambled for the answer to the riddle.

Then it hit him.

"Alice!" Tyreese exclaimed loudly.

"And who is Alice to you, Tyreese?"

His blood ran cold.

"I don't know anyone named Alice."

"Are you sure?"

And then—the jungle sounds resumed.

"AHHHHHH!" Tyreese's scream tore through the air, raw and guttural, carrying the weight of sheer desperation. His voice cracked under the strain, the anguish woven into each syllable as though it might physically rip through his throat. His chest heaved violently, each breath a struggle against the suffocating grip of despair. His entire body trembled, not from cold, but from the overwhelming helplessness that had wrapped itself around him like an unshakable force.

"Listen... listen, please!" he gasped, his voice begging. His breath hitched as he fought to steady himself. "I don't know anyone named Alice... really, truly." His words spilled out in a rush, his tone laced with hopelessness. "If it's someone I should know... if it's someone from my past... just tell me. Please."

Michael moved to compliment Tyreese, albeit sarcastically "Very good Tyreese. Finally some manners."

Once again, silence filled the room for a few moments as Michael's voice disappeared and the jungle sounds resumed.

Tyreese stilled, his muscles tightening as he forced himself to shut out everything—the eerie sounds of nature, the sterile scent of damp earth, the crushing fear pressing down on his chest. He focused only on his breathing, each inhale slow and deliberate, each exhale trembling with restraint. His pulse pounded against his skull, his breaths shallow, controlled.

A pause. Then, the voice returned. Smooth and patient.

"Tyreese, I truly *want* to help you... but I need you to help me first." The voice softened, almost coaxing. "Who is Alice to you?"

Tyreese clenched his jaw, his mind pushing past the exhaustion, the fear, the hunger. He reached deep into his memories, past the pain and confusion, searching for something—*anything*—that would give him an answer.

And, as his thoughts drifted back in time, a single conclusion began to form.

It was late January when Tyreese received a call from Dymon, summoning him to their usual hangout—the abandoned factory in Harlem. The 'Factory,' as they called it, was their meeting ground.

Tyreese arrived to find Dymon standing motionless in the far corner of the dimly lit area. The cold air clung to the walls—the scent of rust and old machinery lingering in the silence. Dymon's back was to him, his eyes locked on the stained concrete wall in front of him. He stood rigid, unyielding, as though trapped in a memory too deep to escape.

The silence between them seemed heavy as Tyreese approached, his footsteps echoing softly across the empty space.

"Dymon," Tyreese whispered, placing a hand on his friend's shoulder. He could feel the tension beneath his fingers, the heaviness of the moment pressing down on them both.

Dymon did not turn. His voice, eerily calm yet charged with something Tyreese couldn't quite place, sliced through the silence.

"It's time, man."

A frown tugged at Tyreese's brow. "Time for what?" he asked, his voice laced with unease.

Dymon finally shifted, turning his head just enough to glance at Tyreese, his expression unreadable. "They sent me to be your guide." His words were slow, yet purposeful.

Confusion twisted in Tyreese's chest. "What are you talking about, man?" His frustration bubbled to the surface, his patience wearing thin.

A slow, unsettling grin spread across Dymon's face, his eyes gleaming with a strange element of intent. With a deliberate motion, he turned fully to face Tyreese, the space between them shrinking, the tension thickening.

"You have been chosen," Dymon said, his voice etched with pride. "Chosen by the master." The words hovered in the air, heavy and foreboding. Tyreese stared at him, his mind struggling to grasp the gravity of what had just been said.

"The master needs flesh," Dymon continued, his voice taking on a darker edge. "The flesh of a virgin. A young, beautiful woman." He paused, letting the words settle like a noose tightening. "You've been chosen to prove yourself. To prove your commitment."

A cold dread seeped into Tyreese's veins. His body stiffened, his heart thudding against his ribs. Never had he imagined that he would be the one called to serve.

He inhaled sharply, trying to anchor himself to the reality of the moment. Then, with a strange sense of understanding, a shift in his resolve, he placed a hand on Dymon's shoulder and pulled him into a firm embrace.

There was no turning back now.

Alice Duvall was a 16-year-old honors student at Horace Mann, the kind of girl with a future as bright as the city lights. In 1987, she had finished at the top of her class, and the celebrations were long overdue.

The Copacabana was the perfect place to kick off the night—a legendary nightclub, renowned and glamorous. Alice and her friends had been looking forward to this for weeks, their excitement bubbling over as they danced beneath the flashing lights, the music pulsing through their veins.

As the night blurred by in a haze of laughter and music, Alice decided it was time to head home. Her friends begged her to stay for just one more dance, but Alice, ever responsible, declined. With a final wave and a bright smile, she slipped out the doors and stepped into the night. She had no idea that the wheels of fate had been set in motion long before their night out had even been planned.

Dymon was the architect of it all—the mastermind. For weeks, he had followed Alice, watching her, memorizing her routines, waiting for the perfect moment to strike. The group had given Tyreese a test, and it was Dymon's job to ensure that the task was completed. Alice Duvall would be his sacrifice.

He had carefully orchestrated everything. Knowing that Alice's friends loved a good party, he had planted fake flyers in their lockers—promising one night only free entrance to the Copacabana for under-21s. When he confirmed that the girls were planning their big night out, he paid off the bouncer at the door.

Alice's parents were creatures of habit—consumed by work, lost in their jet-setting lifestyle, hopping from one tropical destination to another. Dymon knew Alice would take her usual route home, a short walk through Central Park, too close for a cab, too familiar to feel dangerous.

And so, as Alice strolled through the park off Fifth Avenue, Tyreese followed her in the shadows, Dymon's perfectly orchestrated plan was now falling into place, down to the finest detail.

The night air was crisp, the city buzzing in the distance. Alice's heels clicked against the pavement as she neared the crosswalk by the Thomas Moore Statue. It was quiet, too quiet.

Then—footsteps.

Her pulse quickened. She glanced over her shoulder. Nothing but darkness, the dim glow of lamp posts barely cutting through the gloom. Still, the feeling gnawed at her. She quickened her pace. The footsteps behind her did the same.

Fear gripped her chest. She broke into a run, her breath ragged, her heartbeat hammering in her ears. The sounds behind her grew closer, more urgent.

She sprinted toward Greyshot Arch, desperation fueling her every step. As she reached it, gasping for air, a hand shot out from the shadows.

A scream never made it past her lips.

A gloved hand clamped over her mouth, an arm snaking around her waist, lifting her off the ground. She thrashed, kicked, clawed at her attacker's arms, but the grip only tightened. She was dragged off the path, into the suffocating darkness of the bushes.

Her body hit the ground hard. Pain shot through her as she scrambled, trying to fight back, but then she saw her attacker.

A man in a dark mask. No features, just hollow cut-out holes for his eyes and mouth—gnashing teeth and lifeless eyes visible through the openings. He loomed over her trying to catch his breath from the struggle and the adrenaline; his chest rising and falling as if he were caught in some primal trance.

He muttered to himself, chanting something foreign, something unsettling, over and over.

Alice's world shattered in an instant.

Her screams were swallowed by the night.

It was done. The ritual was complete.

There was a grim sense of finality in the air as he stood over her, the weight of his actions pressed down like an unbearable force.

The master had been served...

At that moment, Tyreese was jolted back into the harsh reality of being confined to a box as the familiar, cold voice crackled through the loudspeaker above. The walls of the box-like space around him felt suffocating, closing in with each passing second.

"Who was she to you, Tyreese?"

The question reverberated in his mind, and Tyreese knew, deep down, that he would have to answer for his crimes. He didn't see what he had done as a "wrong" or immoral act, but more like a task, a mission he was compelled to complete. However, the teachings of his childhood, raised in the Church, echoed in his mind—the sharp distinction between being a saint and a sinner.

He understood what Michael needed to hear, the truth that had to be voiced.

"She was my target, Michael," Tyreese said, his voice strained, his steps erratic as he paced back and forth, wracked with sheer agony.

"YOUR TARGET!?" Michael's voice thundered through the loudspeaker, filled with disbelief and rising anger.

"Are you telling me, Tyreese, that you feel no remorse for what you've done?" Michael asked, his voice now injected with rage.

"I do, I do feel remorse, man! I hurt that girl, and I'm sorry!" Tyreese cried out, he said the words but they felt rehearsed to Michael.

"You grew up in the Church, Tyreese. You know the biblical phrase 'An eye for an eye,' right?" Michael's voice softened as he tried to guide Tyreese through his own turmoil.

"I think you need to truly understand what you have done, Tyreese. You need time to come to grips with it, and the only way we can get you there is through time. Time with me," he said, his words fading away as the ambient sounds of the jungle filled the space once again.

Tyreese collapsed onto the bed, his cries echoing in the emptiness of the room, desperate for relief. But, the darkness never brought him the peace he longed for. He simply wished for death, and yet, it never came.

The next morning, Tyreese awoke with an unfamiliar sensation, a peculiar shift in his body. The hunger that once clawed at him had vanished. Instead, it felt as if he had eaten, and eaten well. He sat up slowly, his body still weak from the days of deprivation, but something was different. As he glanced down at himself, he noticed something unsettling: his chest was covered in soil—thick, dry, rich earth clinging to his skin.

Confused and unsettled, Tyreese raised a hand to his face. He could feel the gritty texture of dirt covering him, its taste now overwhelming in his mouth. With horror, he turned to his left and heaved violently. The force of the vomiting took over as he expelled a stream of brown soil, the earth pouring out of him relentlessly. He heaved again and again, until there was nothing left in him except for the bitter remnants of the soil that had somehow found its way into his body.

In stunned disbelief, Tyreese stared at the mess around him. How did this happen? Where did the dirt come from? The questions swirled in his mind as he was joined once again by Michael's voice.

"Feeling better this morning, Tyreese? I hope you enjoyed your meal. I prepared it just for you," Michael's voice mocked, smooth and casual, as though nothing was out of the ordinary.

Tyreese's blood boiled. "What did you do to me, man!?" he shouted, still battling the nausea that churned throughout his stomach.

"But Tyreese, you said you love bacon, right?" Michael's tone was oddly playful, as if he was testing Tyreese's sanity and taunting him.

"That wasn't bacon, Michael! That was dirt!" Tyreese screamed, his voice breaking with anger.

"No, Tyreese, I think you're mistaken. It was 100% prime cut bacon," Michael replied, his words chilling.

Tyreese paced in agitation. "I don't know what kind of game you're playing, but I'm done with it!"

Michael's response was calm, almost dismissive. "Suit yourself, Tyreese. There's still so much bacon left on your bed. I'm not sure how you're going to consume it all," he said with a laugh, before the sound of his voice faded, leaving Tyreese alone again with nothing but the oppressive jungle noises.

The room felt suffocating, its very air thick with dread as Tyreese's mind began to unravel. The bed was now plastered with more soil, the overwhelming presence of the earth almost inviting him. The smell of the soil, the weight of the decision ahead, consumed him as he knelt down, his trembling hands reaching out. The damp earth, a strange temptation.

As he dug through the layers of soil, he noticed a strange wetness beneath the dry, crumbling topsoil. A faint, almost sweet aroma lingered as he uncovered a piece of bacon, glistening with maple syrup, buried within the dirt. Tyreese's breath quickened, and without hesitation, he shoved it into his mouth. The taste was an uncanny mixture of sweet and earthy, the syrup clinging to the dirt as it slid down his throat. It was familiar in a haunting way, a twisted reminder of the life he once knew.

He dug deeper, the bacon now an increasingly strange part of the dirt, swallowing mouthful after mouthful as his stomach ached, urging him to stop. But, he could not. With each bite, the hunger grew, and the bacon, the syrup, the dirt—all mixed together in a twisted, grotesque fusion that filled him. And then, as he could eat no more, the remnants of the dirt and swine seemed to settle within him, weighing him down, a permanent part of his existence. This was his life now.

As the days slipped by, and April bled into May, the air grew warmer with the first hints of Summer setting in. Tyreese found himself descending deeper into a trance-like state. His mind became increasingly detached from reality, sanity and dignity escaped him and the ritual of consuming soil became second nature. He began to savor the dirt, appreciating its texture and flavor as if it were a delicacy. He played with it, experimenting, creating combinations like a chef concocting new dishes. Michael, ever the observer, would engage him in long, probing conversations, asking about his past, his involvement with the occult, and the twisted events that had led to the violation of Alice Duvall.

One morning, Tyreese woke up startled, the remnants of a nightmare still clinging to him. But something was wrong—everything was wrong. The smell in the room had changed. No longer was it the familiar scent of earth and decay. Now, it reeked of cleanliness.

When his eyes adjusted to the light, he realized that the room had changed completely. The walls were now made of cold, brushed steel. Not an ounce of dirt lay on the floor; it was pristine and empty. All the soil, all the plants, had vanished. Panic surged through him as the familiar comfort of his previous surroundings was stripped away.

"What's going on!?" Tyreese screamed, his voice cracking with desperation. "Where is my food?" he demanded, his heart racing as he pounded the walls like an animal. For hours, he shouted, cupping his hands over his ears to block out the unbearable silence. In panic, Tyreese began to frantically pull handfuls of nothing towards his mouth; left hand, right hand, trying to devour the soil that he hoped was there.

Then finally, Michael's voice cut through the stillness, sharp and commanding. "Tyreese!"

Startled, Tyreese jumped to his feet, staggering toward the loudspeaker.

"Please, help me, Michael!" he cried, his voice raw with fear as tears and mucus spilled down his cheeks and upper lip.

"It's time to say goodbye, Tyreese," Michael said, his tone calm, yet final.

"No! No, please, Michael! Don't leave me here! Please!" Tyreese begged, his voice breaking.

"It's time to move on, Tyreese," Michael said gently, his voice distant. "Each one of you needs my time, and my time with you is up."

"No! Please, Michael! I've learned so much from you! I was wrong to hurt Alice... I understand now, please!" Tyreese cried, crumbling to the floor in despair.

"I believe you, Tyreese," Michael's voice softened, but there was no mercy in his words. "Your heart is worthy now, you cannot be the person that is remembered here.

You do not get to have a gravestone plastered in marble and granite whilst your victim deals with the trauma you left permanently tattooed in her memory! I will make sure that does not happen here Tyreese, you will get no GLORY!"

The finality of Michael's words echoed through the silence. After what felt like an eternity, his voice returned to a tormented and broken Tyreese. This would be the last time Michael would speak to him.

"Are you hungry, Tyreese?" he asked, his voice calm once again.

"Yes! Yes Michael, I'm hungry," Tyreese responded, his voice trembling with fear and resignation. Suddenly, a loud noise erupted from the vent across the room—the same vent that had once carried the intoxicating smell of food. At first, it was a low rumble, but it quickly grew louder, intensifying with every passing second. Without warning, the vent exploded, and a flood of soil poured out, cascading over Tyreese. He stood frozen, trapped in the inevitability of what was to come.

With a twisted sense of acceptance, Tyreese opened his mouth wide, letting the dirt rush in. It poured down his throat, choking him as it blocked his airway, each breath more desperate than the last. Unable to draw in any air, Tyreese fell to the floor, gasping for breath that would never come. As the world around him began to fade, he cast one final heavy glance at his surroundings before his eyes closed, and then everything went black...

"Unit 42 to Central," the officer's voice crackled through the police radio, his words sharp and urgent. His soaked uniform clung to his body, the rain pouring down relentlessly on the evening of June 1st, 1988. The streets were slick, and the usual hum of the city seemed muffled under the heavy downpour.

A brief static buzzed before a calm, yet strained voice responded, "Central, reading you 42, over."

The officer's grip tightened around the radio, his pulse quickening as his eyes scanned the darkened streets ahead, barely illuminated by the flickering streetlights.

"Central," he continued, his voice lowering as though the words themselves were too heavy to speak, "We need someone from the Manhattan task force down here, *now*. Corner of Terrace and West Drive, Central Park... We have another one."

He wiped the cold, relentless rain from his face with a trembling hand, his eyes locked on the lifeless figure of the African-American boy lying motionless on the park bench. The wet fabric of his jacket clung to his skin, but it was the sight before him that held his attention, more chilling than the storm itself. His radio, still attached to his lapel, buzzed erratically, the static sharp and jarring in the otherwise silent night. In the distance, the wail of approaching sirens grew louder, cutting through the thick air, signaling the start of yet another chapter in this grim, unrelenting and heart-wrenching investigation.

Chapter 7

You Make Me Sick

"Where do we stand, people?" Captain Stevens asked, his voice commanding as he walked into the dimly lit briefing room, the weight of the situation heavy in the air.

His boots clicked sharply against the polished floor with each step, the sound echoing through the tense silence. As he reached the head of the long and cluttered table, he paused, his eyes scanning the room. With deliberate calm, he took his seat—the chair creaking under his weight—and leaned forward slightly, his gaze locking onto Detective Coffey.

"I have a press conference in one hour Coffey; you better have something for me to feed to the wolves!"

Charles stood up and made his way over to the evidence board.

"Victim number four—Tyreese Williams—found in Central Park on June 1st and victim number five—the latest, Becky Torres—found in the Bronx on September 8th.

Like the other victims, their first and last names match the initials of the street intersections where they were found. Both victims have had organs removed as seen here and here," Charles explained, as he pointed to the crime scene photos.

"And, as always, a birthday card has been left on the body of the victim and addressed directly to me," Charles added as he moved along the board pointing towards them. "Both contain a cryptic message from the killer, however we have not managed to decipher them as yet."

Charles continued, "As for the first three victims, we have a common name that keeps coming up—"Michael"; no description or last name, it's as if he is a ghost. We are checking with CCTV cameras in and around the restaurant area where Ms. Barlow allegedly had dinner with him as she had mentioned in her date book, however this is still under investigation."

He looked over at Detective Bradshaw, who had zero interest in participating in the briefing. Instead, he stood at the window gazing out of it inspecting the traffic below, one hand in his pocket and the other glued to his lips with a cigarette.

"In closing, Sir, our investigations into the 'Boroughs Three' are still ongoing; a few more witnesses are still to be interviewed and leads coming into the task force are being followed up by Ortega and Muniz. I have split the task force into a further two groups: One will focus on Tyreese Williams—headed by Detective Bradshaw, and the other will focus on Ms. Torres—myself and Mac will be following the leads on that victim, Sir. "

Charles waited for the hammer to fall.

"Not much to work with, Detective, but I'll take whatever I can get," Captain Stevens muttered, his voice permeating with frustration yet tinged with a resigned determination. He ran a hand through his hair, his mind already racing through the sparse details they had.

With a sharp, authoritative tone, he added, "Have the summary on my desk in thirty minutes!" He didn't wait for a response. He subsequently turned on his heel and walked out of the briefing room. The heavy door swung shut behind him with a soft thud as he made his way down the long corridor. His footsteps echoed throughout the otherwise quiet hallway as he headed back to his office.

"What the hell do you think you are doing, Coffey?" Bradshaw demanded, who had by this time extinguished his cigarette in the nearest ashtray.

"Who are you to tell me what I will or will not do?"

"It's not my goddam fault that the killer is after me Bradshaw, this is just the way it is. I don't like it any more than you do!" Charles snapped, who had by this time made his way over to Bradshaw.

"Well I think you are involved somehow; what would a mastermind like this want with a 'nobody' like you?" Bradshaw responded mockingly.

"I have no idea!" Charles said, who was now in Bradshaw's face. Mac made his way over to Charles and placed a hand on his shoulder.

"It's exactly what he wants, Charlie boy; don't give it to him," Mac said calmly.

Charles kept his gaze fixated on Bradshaw; both men could not stand to be anywhere near each other. Charles was above all else a rational man, but Bradshaw knew how to stir up the buried rage within him.

"Go and interview the father of Tyreese Williams, for both our sakes!" Charles instructed, his voice firm. He turned and walked away briskly from

Bradshaw, his footsteps breaking the tense silence of the briefing room. As he pushed the door open and stepped into the hallway, it swung back, briefly creaking on its hinges. The sound of laughter—mocking and unbothered—drifted in from behind him, but Charles didn't look back. He couldn't afford to. Once outside, he climbed into the Gran Fury, his movements sharp with irritation. Without thinking, he slammed his hands down hard on the steering wheel, the impact vibrating through his fingers.

It wasn't long before Mac climbed into the passenger seat beside Charles. He had a concerned look on his face, but he didn't say anything. He didn't know what to say.

"What am I doing wrong, Mac?" Charles asked his veteran partner. His voice was strained with exhaustion and doubt, the weight of the case pressing down on him. His grip tightened on the wheel as his mind raced, trying to make sense of the mess they were caught in.

"Ignore him, Charlie boy," Mac replied, his tone casual but carrying the kind of experience that came from years of being in the trenches. "He just wants the spotlight—he's always playing the game for the glory. You know that?"

Charles let out a heavy sigh, the words offering a small measure of relief, but the frustration still clung to him. He put the car in gear and pulled away. They headed out of the city, the concrete jungle giving way to the quieter, grittier streets of Queens. As they made their way toward the North Corona neighborhood, Charles' thoughts remained clouded, but he had one focus now: getting to 102nd Street and finding answers.

As the vehicle cruised through the dark, winding corridors of the Midtown Tunnel, the tunnel lights flashed by in quick succession. One light followed the next, illuminating their surroundings only to be swallowed back into the void, creating a rhythm that seemed to gather in Charles' mind. With each flicker of light, his thoughts grew heavier, the faces of the victims flashing before his eyes like haunting specters. Their tragic deaths, their mutilated bodies—each felt like a silent marker of their suffering.

Why did he remove his heart? The chilling image of Tyreese Williams' ravaged body resurfaced, the brutality of his murder unwavering from his thoughts. The heart had been taken with such calculated cruelty and precision—Charles couldn't help but wonder what twisted motive lay behind it. There had to be some significance, some purpose, but it remained just out of his reach.

His thoughts quickly turned to the fifth victim. *And Becky's liver... The same question lingered in his mind. Why these specific body parts? Why remove them with such care? What could the killer's goal possibly be?* The connections between the victims' mutilations seemed to be right there in front of him, yet they felt elusive, like fragments of a puzzle that refused to lock into place.

Unable to keep the thoughts to himself any longer, Charles broke the silence, his words spilling out in frustration. "I can't place my finger on it, Mac..." His voice carried the weight of his confusion, the unsolved mystery pressing down on him. "It's puzzling... What does he want with the organs?"

Mac, still quiet beside him, stared out the window at the flashing lights, his face etched with thought. The seconds seemed to stretch, and then he finally spoke. His voice was calm and measured, like the steady hand of someone who had weathered many storms before.

"I can't think like he does, Charlie boy," Mac said slowly, his gaze never leaving the window. "He's got an agenda—something we can't fully understand yet. But I'm sure, whatever it is, it's only a matter of time before it includes you." His words hung in the air, rich with a quiet certainty, as if Mac knew this killer's game far better than Charles did. The unsettling feeling that the killer was closing in, not just on the victims, but on Charles himself, crept through him.

Charles and Mac turned into 102nd Street, locating the house nestled in the quiet neighborhood—number 3740. The old black gate, its paint chipped and worn, squeaked on its hinges as it reluctantly swung open, revealing the narrow path which led to the front door. The cold air of the morning brushed against their faces as they walked toward the entrance, their footsteps crunching on the gravel driveway. Charles had already met Mrs. Torres before, back when he had been the one to deliver the heartbreaking news about her daughter's tragic death.

He reached for the doorbell, the chime echoing faintly within the house; he pushed the door open slightly and stepped inside.

"Mrs. Torres," Charles greeted her softly as he entered, making his way to the sofa where she sat, her posture sagging under the weight of grief. Her tired eyes lifted slowly, her face a portrait of sorrow.

"Once again, we're so sorry for your loss," Charles continued, his voice warm and empathetic. He gave a gentle pause before asking, "Would you be open to answering a few questions?"

Mrs. Torres nodded slowly, her eyes lingering on him. She could see the sincerity in Charles' expression, the deep sadness behind his professional demeanor, as if he, too, felt the weight of her loss. "Thank you," she whispered, her voice quivering as she wiped away a tear. "What can I help you with, Detectives?"

Charles hesitated just a moment, his gaze softening as he looked at her. "Did Becky ever mention a man named Michael?" he asked.

Mrs. Torres frowned, as she sifted through her memories. "No... Not that I can remember," she replied, her voice uncertain. "My English, it's not too good," she added quietly, a note of self-consciousness creeping into her tone.

Charles smiled gently, his voice steady and reassuring. "It's okay, Mrs. Torres. You're doing just fine. Can you remind us when you last saw Becky?"

The older woman's eyes seemed to cloud with sadness as she closed them briefly, recalling the day.

"It was June 21st, a Wednesday morning," she said, her voice distant, as if trying to piece together the events. "She came home late the night before. Mrs. Antonio had asked her to look after little Maria again—had to work the night shift. Becky... she was always so willing to help." She paused for a moment, wiping her tears with the sleeve of her worn jersey, trying to steady herself.

"She ran down the stairs that morning, and she shouted, 'Goodbye, Mama, I'm off to school,' like she always did. I wish... I wish I had kissed her goodbye, like I always did," her voice cracked, breaking under the weight of regret. The tears fell freely now as she bowed her head, unable to hold back the pain any longer. "I never thought I would not see her again!"

Charles could see the anguish he had inflicted on Mrs. Torres, the weight of her grief unmistakably clear in her tear-soaked face. The raw, painful emotion radiating from her made it impossible to continue the interrogation and so he decided to let the questioning wait.

"We'll leave you in peace now, Mrs. Torres," Charles said quietly, his voice softening as he stood from his seat. He gave her one last look before turning toward the door, leaving her alone in her sorrow, her wails echoing through the silence of the living room. Mac, clearly unsettled by the decision, watched Charles for a moment, then followed him outside.

"What the hell was that about, Charles?" Mac said, catching up to his partner on Mrs. Torres front porch.

"We need more information from her!"

Charles turned to him, his expression firm but calm. "No, Mac," he replied, his voice steady. "We can get what we need from the neighbors. Like she said, Becky was the heart of this neighborhood. She cared for all the children, looked after the families who barely scraped by. There's more to learn from them."

Mac was not convinced, however the two detectives then set off down the street, their footsteps purposeful as they moved from door to door, searching for any signs of life behind the closed entrances.

At one home, Charles stopped and called out to the woman who appeared on the other side of a mesh-laced door. "Mrs. Antonio?" he asked.

"Yes?" she responded, her voice tentative.

"We're Detectives Coffey and Mackenzie," Charles introduced themselves. "May we come in?"

Mrs. Antonio hesitated for a moment before opening the door and ushering them inside. She led them to the modest living room, where they were invited to sit down, the quiet hum of the neighborhood surrounding them.

As Mrs. Antonio stepped into the living room, the sudden sound of a child crying echoed from upstairs. Without missing a beat, she paused and turned toward the stairs.

"Excuse me for a moment, please," she said, apologetically as she hurried up the stairs, the sound of her footsteps fading. It quickly became apparent that it was a crying child calling for her attention.

After a few moments, Mrs. Antonio returned downstairs, her face drawn with exhaustion, as if those brief moments upstairs had drained her entirely.

"Sorry, Detectives," she apologized, her voice quieter now, as if carrying the weight of unspoken sorrow. "It's my little girl, Maria. She was having a fit again." Her head lowered, as if the burden of her child's condition had taken a toll on her own spirit. Charles, ever methodical, gently steered the conversation back to their purpose. "We've been informed, Ma'am, that Ms. Becky Torres helped you with Maria. Is that correct?"

At the mention of Becky's name, Mrs. Antonio's face shifted with a deep sadness, her shoulders seeming to sag as if a piece of her own strength had been taken away. "Yes," she responded, her voice thick with emotion, as though the loss of Becky had shattered a fragile lifeline. "She was a wonderful young woman. She even helped me get little Maria to the clinic when I had to work. She helped me just before she went missing—Maria was having fits every hour. I asked Becky to take her to the clinic for me. She was an angel." Tears began to cascade down her cheeks as she spoke, her sorrow spilling over.

Charles, noting the depth of the woman's grief, pressed gently, "We also understand she didn't just help Maria, but other children in the neighborhood as well? She cared for several kids?"

"Yes, that's correct, Señor," Mrs. Antonio replied, her voice carrying a sense of reverence for Becky's role in their lives. "She took care of all the children for us who couldn't afford not to work." Her eyes seemed distant as she remembered Becky's constant care.

Charles paused, his thoughts momentarily clouded by the stark contrast between the image of the beloved, selfless young woman and the tragedy of her untimely end. The community had clearly lost someone irreplaceable.

"So, in your opinion, Ma'am, was there anything unusual about Becky or her behavior?" he asked, reluctant to probe deeper into the possible complexities of Becky's life.

Mrs. Antonio shook her head, her face contorting with the weight of grief. "No! She was an angel, Señor. She only ever had one problem with Mrs. Garcia," she said, her voice trembling slightly. "But that wasn't Becky's fault."

Charles leaned forward, his curiosity piqued. "What happened to Mrs. Garcia?" he asked.

Mrs. Antonio sighed, her face shadowed by the painful memory. "It was when little Luis died," she said softly. "You see, little Luis also had fits, Señor. That evening, Becky was taking care of him when it happened. He was shaking uncontrollably, and nothing would stop it, not even what Becky tried. Eventually, he stopped breathing. Mrs. Garcia rushed home when Becky called her at work, but she was too late. It was so tragic, but Becky did everything she could to help him." Mrs. Antonio dabbed at her eyes with a tissue, her voice quivering with emotion.

"That's why we trusted Becky," she continued, her tone now full of conviction. "Little Maria and Luis weren't the only children in the neighborhood with epilepsy. Becky, God rest her soul, was the one person we could always rely on to help us." Her voice softened with the gravity of the loss, and it was clear she was in need for the conversation to end.

Charles, recognizing her exhaustion and the depth of her grief, nodded respectfully. "Thank you for your time, Ma'am. And again, we're sorry for your loss."

As they stood up and made their way out of Mrs. Antonio's house and toward the Gran Fury, the weight of the conversation lingered in Charles' mind. He couldn't shake the stark contrast between the selflessness of Becky Torres—the way she had cared for the children of the neighborhood—and the tragic events that had led to her untimely death. Mrs. Antonio's recounting of little Luis's death, and the pain it had caused Mrs. Garcia, was haunting. If there was any clue to be found about Becky's life or any secret she might have kept, Mrs. Garcia's perspective was likely to be crucial. They had already visited Mrs. Garcia's home, but their knock had been met with silence.

Unphased, Charles and Mac continued canvassing the neighborhood, speaking to other mothers with children who had been in Becky's care at one point or another.

The pattern was consistent in every conversation: Becky was universally described as an angel. She had helped all of them care for their children, taking them to the clinic when they were sick, always without hesitation or questioning. Not once had she doubted the legitimacy of the children's ailments; she had simply done what was needed. The image of Becky as a selfless caretaker was now undeniable, but still, something about the circumstances of her death didn't add up.

The next day, Charles and Mac decided to visit Becky's school to speak with her guidance counselor. Maybe she had some insight into Becky that no one else could offer.

Mrs. Hernandez, the school guidance counselor at Forest Hills High School, greeted them in her small office. Her eyes became somber as she began to speak about the girl she had known.

"Becky was a top student here, Detectives," Mrs. Hernandez said, her tone etched with sadness. "She excelled in her academics, was outstanding in sports, and was always the first to lend a hand to someone in need. We've truly lost a very kind soul."

Charles nodded, absorbing the description of Becky's character. "So, you couldn't find any fault with her?" he asked, pressing gently.

Mrs. Hernandez hesitated, then replied, "No, Detectives, I can't say anything negative about her. She did go through a very traumatic experience—there was a child who lost their life—but I'm not at liberty to divulge the details of that conversation."

The counselor's reluctance to share anything further only frustrated Mac, who could feel the tension in the room. His patience snapped. "The girl is dead!" he barked at Mrs. Hernandez. "Anything that was said to you in confidence is no longer confidential."

Charles shot Mac a sharp look, a reminder to compose himself. Turning back to Mrs. Hernandez, he spoke calmly, "If you can tell us anything, Ma'am, anything at all, it may be important."

Mrs. Hernandez sighed deeply, her hands folding in front of her as if gathering the strength to reveal something that weighed heavily on her. "I had asked for Becky to come to see me after the incident," she began. "We were concerned about her well-being. During a routine locker inspection of the students, we found four bottles of Benadryl in her possession.

One might assume that they could have been intended for self-harm. When I questioned her about it, she told me that she had a severe allergic reaction to the change of season and she was simply self-medicating."

Charles and Mac exchanged a look. This new information was troubling. The discovery of the Benadryl bottles and Becky's explanation raised more questions than it answered. *What had happened to her, and how much of it had been kept hidden behind her caring demeanor?*

"Did you inform her mother about the incident?" Charles asked, his tone steady and hopeful for a truthful response. He was looking for clarity, something to help make sense of the situation.

"We didn't feel the need to contact her mother at that time," Mrs. Hernandez replied, her voice measured. "There was a valid explanation for the medication, and we didn't think it warranted further action."

Charles listened carefully, but the answer didn't sit right with him. The hesitation in her voice suggested there was more to the story. They sat and spoke informally about Becky and life at the school, however nothing else of significance seemed to emerge from the conversation. He could feel that the line of questioning was nearing its end, and with that, he knew it was time to move on. He thanked Mrs. Hernandez, for her time, nodded politely and excused himself, Mac following suit without uttering a word or even glancing in the counselor's direction.

As they exited the school grounds, Charles' mind was already racing. The thought of so much medication in the possession of a 15-year-old troubled him deeply. *How could someone so young have access to that much Benadryl, and what was the true purpose behind it?*

The next morning, Charles decided to pay a visit to the local drugstore—a place he had frequented for years. He knew Mr. Findley, the friendly neighborhood chemist, who always made sure Charles' prescription medications were ready for pickup at the end of each month.

"Mr. Findley, good morning," Charles greeted as he stepped into the familiar, neatly organized store.

"Detective," Mr. Findley replied, his smile wide and genuine. "Wasn't expecting you until the week after next. Everything alright?"

Charles shook his head, a slight smile tugging at his lips, but his focus quickly turned serious. "I'm not here for my medication today, Mr. Findley. I wanted to ask you about something regarding a case I'm working on."

The mention of a police investigation instantly caught Mr. Findley's attention. He had always been fascinated by crime novels and the idea of being involved in law enforcement, often reminiscing about childhood games of "cops and robbers." His face lit up with enthusiasm, a twinkle of excitement in his eyes.

"What can I help with, Detective?" he asked, practically beaming with the thrill of being part of something important.

Charles wasted no time. "What can you tell me about Benadryl?" he asked, his voice lowering slightly, aware of the sensitivity of the matter.

Mr. Findley tilted his head slightly, considering the question. "Well, it's commonly used to treat symptoms of allergies and allergic reactions. Why do you ask?"

Charles hesitated, knowing he couldn't reveal too much, but he needed to get to the heart of the matter. "I can't get into too much detail, as it's an active investigation, but... is it dangerous to children?"

The question hung in the air, and Charles found himself holding his breath as he awaited Mr. Findley's response.

"Well, Detective, used incorrectly, it can be quite harmful to children," Mr. Findley answered, his voice taking on a more serious tone. "The key ingredient in Benadryl is diphenhydramine. If a child takes more than 25 milligrams, it can cause hyperthermia, tachycardia, and in some cases, even seizures."

Charles' stomach dropped. It was the revelation he had been waiting for, the connection he had been searching for. The possibility that Becky had been administering Benadryl to induce seizures in the children she cared for was now a very real theory. But, it wasn't enough—he needed hard evidence to prove it.

"Mr. Findley, you've been a great help, thank you," Charles said, trying to hide the relief in his voice as he gathered his thoughts. "I appreciate you taking the time to speak with me. I'll see you soon."

With that, Charles turned and walked out of the drugstore, the door chiming softly behind him, leaving Mr. Findley with the hope that his input will somehow aid in the investigation.

Charles made his way to the precinct, where he planned to meet up with Mac. As he walked, his mind was already piecing together the next steps in the investigation.

"Mac!" Charles called out, spotting him in the briefing room once again, his mouth full of something clearly unappetizing from the hotdog vendor down the street. Charles couldn't help but shake his head, the familiar scene almost comforting despite the gravity of their work.

"I visited an old friend of mine today—a chemist," Charles continued, his tone shifting from casual to more urgent. "He told me that Benadryl, if given in the wrong dose, can actually cause seizures!"

A spark of hope flickered in Charles' eyes as he spoke, the pieces of the puzzle finally starting to merge together. They were getting somewhere, and for the first time in a while, it felt like they might have a lead. If they could just figure out how Becky had been administering it, maybe there was a connection to Michael somewhere in her story—something that could finally make sense of it all.

Mac, who had been nonchalantly wiping his hands on his shirt, looked up, a hint of interest creeping into his expression for the first time in their conversation. "So, what now?" he asked, his voice more focused, clearly ready to move forward.

Charles took a deep breath, his mind already turning to the next step. "I think it's time to visit Mrs. Garcia. We need to find out what happened with Luis's body. That might hold the answers we've been looking for."

As the investigation into the string of murders progressed, Charles and Mac grew increasingly frustrated in their attempts to speak with Mrs. Garcia. Despite multiple efforts to visit her home, they struggled to gain her cooperation. Realizing that they would have a better chance of speaking with her in a controlled environment, they made the decision to formally request that she come down to the precinct for an official interview.

"Mrs. Garcia, thank you for coming in today," Charles said gently, his voice calm as he and Mac took their seats across from the grieving mother. The atmosphere in the room was heavy, and Charles could sense the tension in her posture, her hands clenched tightly in her lap.

"Firstly, we want to express our deepest sympathies for the loss of your son," Charles continued, his words sincere. "However, we do need to ask you a few questions regarding his death."

Mrs. Garcia sat in silence, her eyes cast downward, barely moving an inch. The sterile surroundings of the police station seemed to overwhelm her, the walls closing in as she was reminded of the struggles that her immigrant parents had faced in the past to provide a better life for her and her siblings. The sight of the precinct, a place she had always associated with hardship, made her uneasy.

"Thank you, Detective," she muttered quietly under her breath, the words barely audible as she fought to maintain her composure.

Charles could see the discomfort building in her body language, her stiff posture portraying her distress. He leaned forward slightly, offering a soft but reassuring tone. "Mrs. Garcia, please remember that you're here voluntarily. You are not under arrest, and you can leave at any time if you so choose. We just need some information to help us understand what happened, okay?"

She nodded faintly, but her eyes remained fixed on the table, her hands trembling slightly.

"Mrs. Garcia," Charles continued, his voice steady, "we would appreciate it if you could walk us through the evening of June 14th—the night your son passed away. Anything you can tell us about that night will help."

Mrs. Garcia took a deep breath, her eyes welling up with tears as she began to speak, her voice wavering. "I was at work," she said softly, her words starting to break through the tense atmosphere.

"The foreman called me to the phone, and when I picked up, it was Becky. She told me that Luis was having one of his fits, and no matter what she did, he wouldn't stop shaking. She said she'd already called the ambulance and that I needed to come home immediately."

Her voice cracked as the memory flooded back. "I dropped the phone right there, ran to my cleaning supervisor and told him I had to leave. I didn't have a ride, and the bus was late, so I just started running. Ten blocks... I ran all the way home.

When I got there, the street was full of blue and red lights. I saw Becky sitting on the curb, crying. When the police let me through the yellow tape, I ran to her and asked her what happened. She just looked up at me and said, 'Luis se ha ido'."

Mrs. Garcia paused, her breath hitching in her throat as the tears spilled down her cheeks. "I collapsed right there. I don't remember anything after that."

As Mrs. Garcia retold the harrowing story of that night, Charles could feel the burden of her grief. The anguish in her voice mirrored a pain he knew all too well—a pain he had experienced himself so long ago. It was a pain that seemed impossible to ease, a loss that left a permanent scar.

"Thank you, Mrs. Garcia," Charles said softly, his voice filled with compassion. "We know this is incredibly difficult for you, and we appreciate you sharing this with us."

"Can you tell me what happened to your son's body? Was he buried or cremated?" Charles asked cautiously, aware that he didn't know the family's religious practices or cultural preferences.

"He's been buried, Detective," Mrs. Garcia replied, her voice quiet but firm.

Charles hesitated for a moment, carefully choosing his next words. He had to tread lightly; he could see how deeply her grief ran, but the case demanded the truth, no matter how painful it might be.

"Mrs. Garcia, we have a theory. We believe your son's death may not have been an accident. We'd like to request permission to perform an autopsy to confirm our suspicions. Would you consent to this, Mrs. Garcia?"

Her reaction was immediate and fierce. "Absolutely not, Detective!" she shouted, her voice trembling with both anger and sorrow. "My son died because he was sick! He's been sick for a long time... What do you mean it wasn't an accident?"

The sudden outburst took Charles by surprise, but he remained calm, trying to keep the situation under control. "We're not implying anything malicious, Ma'am," he said carefully. "We're just asking for your consent to confirm our suspicions, that's all."

Mrs. Garcia's face twisted in torment. "I do not give you consent!" she snapped. "Please, just leave me and my family alone, okay?" She stood abruptly, clearly angry and offended, and subsequently turned toward the door. Without another word, she exited the interview room, leaving Charles and Mac in the stillness of the aftermath.

The tension in the room was palpable as they both realized that, at least for now, they were at an impasse with Mrs. Garcia. They had hit a wall, and it was clear they wouldn't be getting any further with her cooperation.

Once the commotion had died down and Charles and Mac had spent time carefully compiling all of their findings, Captain Stevens called for a meeting in the briefing room to assess the progress on the ongoing murder investigations.

"Coffey, where are we with the investigation into Ms. Torres' death?" Captain Stevens asked, his tone both direct and expectant.

Charles stood up and walked to the murder board, his mind working through the details. He pointed to various notes and photos on the board, explaining the current status. "We've conducted interviews with the girl's family and people in her neighborhood. By all accounts, she was a saint—her loved ones described her as an angel. But, after a thorough investigation at her school, we found something troubling. An incident occurred where in her locker the teachers discovered four bottles of Benadryl. After consulting with a medical expert, it seems that she may have been using it on the children to induce seizures. In one tragic case, a child even died as a result. Our psychiatrist has suggested that this could be a case of Munchausen's Syndrome by Proxy."

Charles paused for a moment, then continued, knowing he had to lay out all the facts. "However, we're unable to confirm any of this as the mother of the deceased child refuses to allow an autopsy. We also haven't been able to find any direct connection to "Michael"—the suspect in the previous cases. But, the similarities between this case and the others are hard to ignore.

At this point, we don't have anything else concrete, Sir."

Captain Stevens sat in silence, his gaze cold and unwavering as he processed the information. Charles could feel the weight of the Captain's disappointment bearing down on him, but he stood his ground. "Is that all you have, Detective?" Captain Stevens broke the silence with his sharp question, his stare cutting through Charles like a knife.

Charles could feel his heart rate quicken, but he kept his composure. "Yes, Sir. For now, that's all we have."

Captain Stevens shifted his attention to Bradshaw, his seasoned detective. "Bradshaw, what have you got for me on the Williams case?" he asked, his tone slightly more hopeful.

Bradshaw, standing a little straighter, replied, "We have a promising lead, Sir. We've got a close friend of the late Tyreese in our interview room—Mr. Dymon Reese."

The mention of a lead seemed to lift some of the tension in the room. Captain Stevens' face brightened ever so slightly. "Good."

"We've run into a bit of a snag," Bradshaw continued. "He keeps repeating the same phrase over and over again—'voluntas domini facta est.' We believe it's Latin, but we're not sure what it means. We've already requested a translator to come in. But don't worry, Sir, we'll get something out of him."

"Alright. That will be all," Captain Stevens said, his tone dismissing any further discussion on the matter.

As the meeting concluded, Charles knew that he hadn't met the Captain's expectations. But this wasn't the end—not for him, and certainly not for Becky's case.

He was determined that he and Mac would keep digging, no matter what it took to uncover the truth.

When Charles and Mac returned to their desks, Charles noticed a letter placed on his desk—one that had been delivered earlier. He opened it eagerly, almost like a child tearing into a Christmas gift. Unfolding the piece of paper, he read the brief, cryptic message:

You are better than you think, Charles.

Becky and Tyreese were just pawns in our game. However, we are all kings and queens and pawns, aren't we?

At the moment, I have the upper hand.

Your move.

The words sent a chill through Charles. Another letter.

Chapter 8

The Seventeen

As the sharp chill of early Winter settled over the landscape in the later months of 1988, Michael Radford found himself completely immersed in his latest macabre undertaking.

The changing of the seasons seemed to parallel the shifts in Michael, and with meticulous precision, he had been laying the groundwork for his sixth victim. Each passing day brought him closer to executing the sinister plan he had crafted with the utmost determination. He worked tirelessly, his focus razor-sharp, while the cold, biting air outside mirrored the chilling and methodical nature of his handiwork.

Through the dim glow of the cabin's porch light, Michael ushered a frail and disoriented Belinda Wei through the wooden door. The effects of the sedative were beginning to wear off, and in her semi-conscious state, the short journey from the car to the porch—followed by the struggle of ascending a few steps—had proven to be an arduous task for the sixty-one-year-old woman.

In her current state, vulnerable and feeble, no one would have suspected that she was, in reality, one of the most powerful figures behind a sprawling underground pedophile ring operating throughout New York City.

For years, Belinda had remained hidden in plain sight, her small laundromat in central Queens serving as nothing more than a carefully constructed front—an innocuous business venture that not only sustained her cover but also funded the far more sinister enterprise in which she truly specialized.

Her laundromat had no shortage of customers—many of whom were loyal, unsuspecting patrons, particularly from the city's growing Asian immigrant population, which had surged throughout the early to mid-1980s. To the neighborhood, she was merely a kind and elderly woman, a grandmotherly figure who dedicated herself to making life easier for the families and individuals she encountered daily. No one could have imagined that behind her warm smile and helpful demeanor lurked the mastermind of a vast and horrifying criminal network.

Belinda had perfected the art of customer satisfaction. She provided an all-inclusive laundry service—washing, pressing, ironing and folding—ensuring that busy professionals, parents, and working-class families had one less burden to worry about.

Each morning, mothers and fathers would drop off piles of clothing and linen—sometimes entire suitcases full—before rushing off to work or taking their children to school. Throughout the day, the laundromat buzzed with activity, with a steady stream of customers coming and going. By late afternoon and into the evening, the cycle repeated itself as parents retrieved their fresh laundry on their way home from long, exhausting workdays.

However, Belinda's dedication to her clientele extended far beyond simple customer service. She made a point to personally deliver laundry orders to clients' homes rather than entrusting the task to an employee. This wasn't just an act of goodwill—it was an opportunity. Through these seemingly innocent home visits, she meticulously gathered personal details about her clients: their careers, their family structures, their daily routines and habits; even their likes and dislikes. This information became invaluable when it came to her true business—the underground black market of human trafficking.

Children were her primary commodity, though on occasion, an adult would be targeted based on a specific request from one of her more "exclusive" clients. With an intimate understanding of her customers' lives, she could easily identify potential targets. Every innocent interaction within the laundromat was, in reality, a step toward fulfilling her twisted and lucrative enterprise.

Now, however, the predator had become the prey. And, as she stumbled into the cabin, her mind clouded with the remnants of sedation, she had no idea that she was about to become the latest chapter in Michael Radford's own dark story.

Michael had spent the past several weeks carefully integrating himself into Belinda Wei's world, assuming the role of a wealthy yet enigmatic entrepreneur with questionable business dealings.

His approach was calculated—subtle, yet deliberate. To establish trust, he became a regular at her laundromat, routinely dropping off baskets filled with an assortment of his own clothing—shirts, jackets, chinos, bedding—always accompanied by a lighthearted remark about "helping an old lady out" with her business.

Belinda, ever the shrewd businesswoman, accepted his patronage with gratitude, seemingly unaware that her newest client was studying her just as intently as she had profiled countless others before him.

After a few weeks of friendly exchanges and routine visits, Michael decided to take the next step in his plan. One brisk Tuesday morning, just as Belinda was unlocking the gates to her laundromat, he arrived earlier than usual. He had spent ample time observing her daily habits and routines too, knowing with certainty that he had at least thirty uninterrupted minutes before the first wave of customers would begin arriving with their loads of laundry. This window of opportunity was crucial.

Belinda, taken aback by his unexpected presence at such an early hour, approached the gate with mild curiosity. However, as she noticed the familiar sight of his usual laundry basket in hand, she dismissed any suspicions and buzzed him in.

"You're early today, Mr. Radford," she remarked as she unlatched the door.

Michael responded with an easy grin. "You know me, Miss Wei—always chasing that big green buck before the others get to it, plus a man's gotta look good while doing it."

Belinda chuckled and nodded. "I understand, Mr. Radford, and please, call me Belinda."

"Only if you call me Michael," he countered smoothly, stepping inside as she held the door open for him.

Wasting no time, Michael steered the conversation toward the real purpose of his visit.

With an air of casual confidence, he mentioned that he owned a secluded cabin down in Staten Island—a property, he hinted, that provided the perfect setting for conducting certain types of business transactions without interference. The emphasis on words like "remote" and "secretive" was deliberate, spoken just subtly enough to pique Belinda's interest without revealing too much too soon.

She listened, intrigued, though she made no immediate comment. Sensing this, Michael decided to plant one final seed before taking his leave. As he gathered himself to go, he nonchalantly suggested that, at some point, he could take her to the cabin for a weekend getaway—an opportunity to escape the chaos of city life and, perhaps, explore whether the location might be useful for her own business dealings. He even hinted at the possibility of a profitable partnership, should she find the location suitable. Belinda didn't press for details, but Michael could see the curiosity flicker in her expression. He had successfully baited the hook.

Before stepping out, he casually mentioned that he would return the following evening to collect his freshly laundered clothing. Then, with the ease of a man who had just concluded an ordinary business discussion, he exited the laundromat, leaving Belinda to wonder about the mysterious invitation he had extended.

What she did not realize, however, was that within the next two weeks, she would indeed visit Michael's cabin. But, the "joint business venture" she imagined, would be nothing like what she had in mind. Instead, she would be part of a plan far more sinister—one in which she was not the architect, but the canvas.

Belinda's slow, shuffling steps would have evoked sympathy from any on-looker. She clung weakly to Michael's forearm as he guided her across the warmly lit bedroom of his secluded cabin. Despite the sunlight streaming through the elegant bay window, bathing the room in a golden hue, Belinda's sole focus was on reaching the bed—her body, still sluggish from the lingering effects of sedation, yearning for rest.

She had been unconscious for more than an hour, having slipped into darkness shortly after they left Queens. Now, barely aware of her surroundings, she struggled to orient herself. Michael, however, remained patient, steadying her as they crossed the plush carpet towards her new, albeit temporary, residence.

The bedroom had not been furnished with such care in over a year. The only lingering trace and memento of its previous occupant was a framed photograph resting on the nightstand—a quiet memorial to Judith, the woman who had last claimed this space. The queen-sized bed, typically adorned with a dozen decorative pillows, had been neatly prepared for Belinda's arrival. The luxurious Egyptian cotton sheets were turned down invitingly, and a duck-feather duvet, crisp and pristine, lay in wait. Every detail of the setup exuded warmth and comfort, as if pulled from the glossy pages of a high-end interior design magazine. A soft, light green quilt was draped elegantly at the foot of the bed, adding a final touch of refinement.

To the left of the bed, a solid oak nightstand stood with careful arrangement. A vintage dark wood frame held the image of a beautiful woman with hazel-brown hair—a face that caught Belinda's bleary eye, though she lacked the clarity to truly absorb its significance.

Next to the photo, a tall, slender white candle stood in an antique-style holder, accompanied by a small box of matches. A wooden coaster, seemingly part of a matching set, rested at the corner of the table closest to the bed.

On the Oregon pine floor beside the nightstand, a pair of neatly placed white slippers—small, delicate, size 5-6—awaited their intended wearer. Positioned carefully, they faced the very door through which Michael had just led Belinda.

With great effort, Belinda summoned the strength for one final step before collapsing onto the bed. She exhaled sharply, her breath ragged, as Michael carefully adjusted her position. He placed a supporting hand on her back, his touch surprisingly gentle as he wedged an extra duck-feather pillow behind her to prop her up.

Belinda sighed, her eyelids fluttering shut almost instinctively. Michael, saying nothing, moved toward the large bay window. With a smooth pull, he drew the majestic white curtains closed, dimming the light that had flooded the room moments earlier.

Then, without a word, he exited through an adjacent door. Belinda heard the faint creak of the door as it swung shut behind him, but she did not see him leave. Her body felt impossibly heavy, her mind drifting, sinking. All she needed was a few minutes. Just a few minutes to close her eyes.

Michael returned minutes later through the same door he had exited through, but now with a cup of tea in a saucer. Belinda slowly opened her eyes to see him place it on the table just beside her.

"A cup of chamomile tea for you, Belinda," he said.

She thanked him with a quiver in her voice and just stared up at Michael into his eyes for a few seconds as he simultaneously looked back down into hers. She hesitantly took a sip of tea and placed it back down on the saucer.

"Are you comfortable, Belinda?" Michael asked politely, still staring down at her.

"Yes, thank you Michael," she answered politely, her eyes now closed again.

"Rest your eyes, Belinda. It's been a busy night; I'm sure you must be tired?"

"I am a bit tired."

Michael wore a soft smile, but she did not notice it, for her eyes were heavy, with her body and mind in need of much rest. Her heart was pounding, but the need to sleep was even more overwhelming.

The next morning, Belinda woke up feeling slightly groggy but a lot more refreshed than when she had arrived. She cast her eyes to the table next to her and noticed the cup of chamomile tea, now cold and of which she had only had one sip the evening before.

The room was quiet, and Michael was nowhere to be seen or heard. Belinda wondered what time it was and whether she had been sleeping for the whole night or only an hour. The curtains were still drawn, but the energy was different. The room now possessed a subtle scent of lavender and sandalwood. Her eyes caught sight of the red numbers of the digital alarm clock radio on a dressing table to her right; it read 6:32 a.m.

Suddenly, the door opened beside the table and Michael popped his head inside, almost as if he had sensed her awakened state.

"Go back to sleep, Belinda," he whispered as if not to awaken her too much. "It's still early."

And so, Belinda closed her eyes and went back to sleep. She was still tired and felt unexpectedly comfortable and at ease.

She awakened a little over an hour later – noting the clock to display the time 7:44 a.m. She heard what she thought was a fish eagle call in the distance. There was a fresh hot cup of black tea on the saucer beside her, the steam still dissipating from it, with a saucer of milk placed next to it for her.

She sat up in bed and looked around the room. She now noticed a beautiful black dream catcher hanging from the back of the closed door which she first came through yesterday. It was about two feet in length and possessed white and light brown feathers and correspondingly colored beads.

The curtains now open, Belinda noticed the breathtaking view from her bed, through the bay window and out onto the lake. On either side of the beautiful bay window, Belinda noticed there were two shelves precisely the same height. Both shelves displayed several pot-plants and small garden ornaments such as fairies and gnomes, snails and tortoises, as well as some precious stones. On the one wall between the two doors – the one leading outside onto the porch and the other to the rest of the house – there were six violins mounted on the wall almost in the shape of a large clock. It truly was a sight to behold!

Beside this magnificent display, the only other thing occupying the wall, there was a magnificently framed painting of a butterfly. The entire painting was just of the butterfly itself, down to the finest details and colors. To Belinda, it appeared to have been an oil-based painting. The work of art was encapsulated within a light gold frame.

Belinda also noticed a very large oak bookshelf which stood about seven-feet high. There were a handful of books placed upon the middle of three shelves, with the lower and upper bookshelf completely empty. The impressive piece of furniture seemed somewhat excessive for the minimal number of books which occupied it.

A small rectangular table stood adjacent to it; it was much like one that would be expected to be found in a doctor's waiting room. It had magazines ranging from housekeeping and linen to simple country life, as well as a handful of books stacked on top of one another, which at first glance all appeared to be romance novels. There was also a newspaper beside the pile of books and sprawled out magazines. Belinda also noticed a deck of playing cards on the table.

"Do you read much, Belinda? Please help yourself to whichever books you feel like reading. There are a couple of novels and lengthier ones to delve into, but I've also found a few that are lighter reading material; magazines as well – as you can see. The daily newspaper will be delivered for you and the magazines will be changed out every couple of days just to make your stay more comfortable, pleasant and informative."

Belinda had a very perplexed look upon her face, and then she spoke.

"What is this Michael? All of this? You drug me or whatever you did, bring me here and it's set up like a holiday home; you are behaving like a relative looking after me. Is this the cabin you wanted me to visit?"

Michael simply responded by saying, "All in good time, Belinda. Just make yourself comfortable. Rest, relax, read, enjoy the fresh air."

"Right there – you keep saying these things but..."

"But nothing, Belinda!" Michael spoke sternly for the first time with her and she did not expect it.

His face became red and he just stared at her, without blinking and without uttering another word.

She felt an overwhelming urge to scream, desperate for some kind of response or clarification, but as soon as she parted her lips to speak, no words emerged. Instead, the expression on his face conveyed a chilling message, as if to warn her that even attempting to ask another question would lead to some harsh consequence. His posture and the intensity of his gaze made his intentions unmistakably clear, and she understood the gravity of the situation without needing any further explanation.

The next morning, Belinda stirred from her sleep to the irresistible aroma of freshly ground coffee wafting through the air. The scent was so alluring, it pulled her from her grogginess almost immediately.

Her heart raced with anticipation as she called out for Michael, her voice laced with a sense of urgency. As though he had been waiting for her to summon him, he appeared at her door, gliding in like a well-trained host, carrying a medium-sized mug of steaming coffee, just as he had done before. She couldn't help but notice that the bookshelf, once empty – save for a few items – was now adorned with a collection of new books, their spines neatly arranged.

With a warm smile, Michael greeted her and casually mentioned the new additions to the bookshelf, offering her the opportunity to choose one and dive into a new read. Though she heard his words, the kindness in his gesture failed to reach her. The events of the previous evening still loomed heavily on her mind, clouding her thoughts. In fact, she'd been haunted by a nightmare about it throughout the night. Michael, sensing her distraction, left her to her own devices, giving her the space to sip her coffee in solitude and gaze out the bay window at the peaceful lake, or perhaps to pick up one of the books he had so thoughtfully provided—though she doubted she would find solace in either.

Belinda delicately lifted the cup to her lips, taking a small sip of the steaming coffee to assess both its temperature and flavor. The warmth spread through her mouth, and she found the taste to be just right—rich, smooth, and perfectly brewed. A satisfied smile graced her lips as she took another sip before setting the cup down momentarily. With a quiet sigh, she pushed the covers aside and rose from the bed, slipping into her light pink bathrobe. As she tied the sash securely around her waist, she moved towards the bookshelf, her fingers lightly brushing against the spines of the books as she examined their titles. Tilting her head slightly to the right, she tried to make reading them a bit easier.

The bookshelf contained an eclectic mix of subjects; these ranged from the importance of rest and sleep to human anatomy and physiology, from musical instruments to interior decorating. Belinda also noticed a handful of children's books and a third year law textbook on the protection of minors in the United States.

And then – suddenly, without warning – a voice broke through the silence. Belinda was startled and then Michael spoke again.

"I know you're not in prison, Belinda, but would you like to call someone sometime? A friend, a daughter, a grandchild perhaps?"

Belinda turned her gaze away from the bookshelf and faced Michael with an expression of quiet skepticism. "And you would allow me to make a call, Michael? What if I tell them where I am?"

"So, where are you, Belinda?"

She looked around the room, realizing that she had no idea where she was, except for Michael's claim that they were in Staten Island. And, at this point in time, she did not know what to believe.

Michael continued, "I don't think you would want to do that anyway, Belinda. You might just put those closest to you in harm's way. But, of course, you're welcome to say 'Hello' and assure them that you're safe."

Belinda stood motionless, her gaze fixed on Michael as his offer echoed in her thoughts.

Choosing to err on the side of caution, she silently turned toward the bookshelf, selected a book from the neatly arranged collection, and walked over to the chair beside the bed. Without uttering a word or acknowledging his question, she sat down and began to read, leaving Michael without an answer as he quietly exited the room.

"Wakey, wakey, rise and shine Belinda, I have your coffee." Michael said, as he entered the room the following morning.

Belinda groaned softly, her voice still thick with sleep. "Michael, it's so early. Would you mind closing the curtains again so I can sleep for another hour or two?"

Michael hesitated for only a moment before responding with an apologetic nod. "Yes, of course, Belinda. My apologies—I didn't realize how early it was. It's just past 5 a.m. How silly of me."

The days drifted by in a blur, each blending seamlessly into the next. Solitude became Belinda, as she found herself surrendering to the natural rhythms of her body, allowing herself to sleep whenever she needed rest. When she was awake, she alternated between reading the books carefully selected for her, and immersing herself in the quiet rituals of sewing.

Each stitch was deliberate, a small act of focus that anchored her in the present moment. Time seemed to stretch indefinitely, the hours marked only by these quiet, repetitive tasks.

One morning, Belinda was jolted awake by the sudden clatter of metal striking the floor—a pot or pan had evidently fallen in the adjacent kitchen. A hushed curse followed, Michael's frustration evident despite his attempt to keep quiet.

Blinking against the darkness, Belinda turned her head toward the clock. The red numbers glowed in the dim room: 4:36 a.m.

Before she could process the noise further, the high-pitched whistle of the kettle pierced the silence, though it was swiftly cut off—Michael must have turned it off quickly. Moments later, she heard the distinct sound of his footsteps approaching. The bedroom door creaked open, and without hesitation, Michael seemed to march into the room almost as if he were annoyed. He moved directly to the bay window and, with a sharp tug, threw open the curtains, allowing the soft pre-dawn light to spill into the room.

"Michael, is everything okay?" Belinda asked, confused.

"Yes, Judy. I mean, Belinda."

"It's still dark outside, why are you opening the curtains now?"

I just thought we could have a cup of coffee, you and I? Out on the deck. Freshly ground, just the way you like it.

Belinda was very confused, even mildly irritated.

A wooden rocking chair sat on the porch, gently swaying in the cool morning breeze as it overlooked the serene expanse of the lake. Michael, standing near the entrance of the deck, gestured for Belinda to join him outside and offered her the seat. He then disappeared into the house momentarily, returning with a sturdy wooden chair that he had retrieved from another room. With a measured step, he carried it onto the deck, placing it a few feet away from the rocking chair.

He ensured that it too faced the undisturbed water – the lake casting a mirrored reflection of the moon.

Michael settled into his chair, his posture relaxed, yet purposeful, and waited for Belinda to join him. She stepped onto the porch hesitantly, her expression still clear with annoyance and tiredness. As she lowered herself into the rocking chair, she exhaled softly, trying to steady her thoughts.

Once she had adjusted herself comfortably, Michael spoke first.

"Belinda, isn't it beautiful out here?" he asked, his voice calm and steady.

"It is, Michael," she responded, though her tone carried a note of detachment.

Michael shifted slightly in his seat before continuing. "I need to head into town in a little while. Will you be alright here on your own?"

Belinda hesitated before answering. "Yes, of course, Michael. But I must ask you—what is all this for? Why am I here?"

Michael held her gaze for a moment before responding with a cryptic smile. "Let's have that conversation when I get back, okay?"

Belinda sighed but nodded. "Okay."

Michael rose from his chair, excusing himself. He left the wooden chair behind as he stepped back into the house to prepare for his trip, leaving Belinda alone on the deck.

She sat in silence, still puzzled, sipping the last of her coffee. He had encouraged her earlier to help herself to another cup if she wanted, mentioning that he had left the brewing pot on a tray beside her bed.

After retreating to her room, Belinda's eyes fell on the deck of cards that she had noticed previously. Deciding to pass the time, she began a game of Solitaire. As she sorted through the cards, she soon realized that one of the queens was missing. Dismissing it as a minor inconvenience, she continued playing, distracting herself for another half-hour or so.

Her quiet contemplation was interrupted by the sound of an approaching vehicle. Michael had returned. She heard the ignition shut off just outside the cabin, followed by the rustling of paper bags as he stepped inside, carrying two brown shopping bags filled with various purchases from town.

He seemed satisfied to find Belinda still in her room. They exchanged a brief greeting before she mentioned the missing card.

"Michael, I noticed there's a queen missing from the deck of cards."

He met her gaze with a knowing expression. "Yes, I removed her about two years ago. In due course, I'll be removing another one to pair it off with the first. You see, Belinda, removing the queen changes the game significantly—even more so when two are missing."

He glanced at the cards in her hands. "Oh, are you playing Solitaire? The goal is to arrange the cards in a systematic order or, in some cases, to pair them off to discard them, correct? I've never been much of a card player myself. My mother used to play all the time. Those cards belonged to her."

That night, after finishing a cup of tea, Belinda reclined in the rocking chair beside her bed, drifting into a light slumber. She was startled awake by Michael tossing her duvet onto the floor, followed by her pillowcases.

"Won't you help me with your sheet, please, Belinda?" he asked, his tone even, yet firm.

Annoyed and groggy, she rubbed her eyes. "Michael, can we change them tomorrow? I'm really tired tonight."

He exhaled sharply. "I would think that you, of all people, would appreciate freshly washed and pressed linens."

As the days turned into weeks, Michael's behavior became increasingly disruptive. He began setting the dryer for their bedding and clothes later at night and earlier in the morning, disturbing her sleep. Whenever she dozed off in the rocking chair during the day or lay in bed at night, he would barge into her room, claiming he needed to ask her something or share a thought with her. At first, he would offer half-hearted apologies for the interruptions, but as time passed, he no longer acknowledged them at all.

Belinda's sleep deprivation worsened, leaving her fatigued and disoriented. On certain days, exhaustion weighed so heavily on her that even basic concentration became a struggle. She found it difficult to read, and even sew—a task that once brought her solace had now become extremely challenging.

Michael, noticing her decline, would sometimes offer her sedatives or natural sleep aids. Yet, he would then deliberately wake her up again, either by speaking directly to her or by creating loud, jarring noises throughout the house.

Decision making became increasingly difficult for Belinda. Even when Michael asked her simple questions—such as whether she preferred tea or coffee—she found herself unable to answer without great effort.

As her mind grew foggier, he introduced a twisted form of psychological manipulation: He began using "mind teasers", presenting her with small puzzles to solve in exchange for brief periods of sleep. However, as her cognitive function declined due to exhaustion, the tasks became nearly impossible for her to complete. When she failed, Michael would either deny her the opportunity to rest or allow her only a few fleeting minutes of sleep before waking her up again.

Over time, Belinda's exhaustion manifested physically. Pain crept into her limbs, and soon, she began experiencing auditory and visual hallucinations. At times, Michael feigned sympathy, acknowledging her distress. Other times, he used her fragile state to plant the seeds of delusion, subtly reinforcing her fears and anxieties.

Belinda, once a woman of sharp intellect and quiet strength, now found herself trapped in a waking nightmare—one where sleep was a distant luxury, clarity a fleeting memory, and reality an ever-shifting illusion carefully controlled by her host.

One night, Belinda's hallucinations were particularly intense, plunging her into a state of sheer terror.

When Michael entered her room to replace some magazines, he was met with a disturbing sight—she was on the floor, wildly thrashing about, as if struggling against an unseen force. Her fingers clutched the base of the bed with a desperate grip, her knuckles white from the strain, while her legs kicked frantically into the air, alternating in erratic, panicked movements.

"Belinda," Michael said, his voice firm, but calm. "There's no one here. You're safe." But his words meant nothing to her. She was trapped in her own reality, convinced beyond reason that something—or someone—was trying to drag her away. Her wide, frantic eyes darted around the poorly lit room, searching for an escape from the invisible threat. Michael sighed, frustration flickering across his face. He had tried to soothe her, to bring her back to reason, but it was useless.

She was too far gone, lost in a delusion that no amount of reassurance could penetrate. At that moment, his patience ran dry. He no longer saw the point in humoring her fear. With a shake of his head, he turned around and left the room, closing the door behind him.

Tonight was the night. He had finally made his decision.

As the hours passed, silence gradually settled over the cabin. The thrashing and frantic cries ceased and were replaced by an eerie stillness.

When Michael cracked the door open slightly and peered inside, he saw Belinda curled into a fetal position on the floor, her arms still wrapped tightly around the bedpost. She had exhausted herself into a deep sleep.

Moving with careful precision, he stepped into the room, his footsteps almost weightless as he approached her. He crouched down and gently pried her fingers away from the post, feeling the stiffness in her hands. Then, with calculated ease, he lifted her frail, unconscious form and placed her back onto the bed.

He positioned her head on the pillow, pulled the duvet up to her shoulders, and then—after a brief hesitation—tied a blindfold around her eyes. He did this ever so gently.

Michael's hands trembled slightly as he secured the fabric, watching for any sign of resistance. But, there was none. She remained perfectly still. Too still.

He pressed two fingers against the side of her neck, feeling for the rhythmic pulse of life – even a subtle one – but there was nothing.

A slow smile curled at the corners of his lips. It was done. The struggle was finally over. He had broken her. The children could rest easy now—Belinda would never wake again.

Michael stepped away from the bed, his mind already shifting gears, brimming with ideas for the night which lay ahead. His workspace had been carefully arranged earlier in the evening, every tool and material meticulously laid out in anticipation of this moment.

At the center of his desk, there lay a smooth, colossal metal hoop – its circular shape waiting to be transformed. Nearby, bottles of adhesives stood in a neat row alongside delicate lengths of suede lace, already tightly wrapped around the hoop to provide structure.

A pair of precision scissors gleamed under the dim light, while strands of fine string lay coiled and ready for weaving. The dreamcatcher's intricate web had begun to take shape at its core, with a single black bead positioned in the center, a dark eye in the midst of the delicate threads. From the bottom of the hoop, several strings dangled freely, each adorned with carefully selected beads.

At their ends, feathers of various colors and textures were secured, waiting to sway with the slightest movement of air.

Each detail was intentional.

Every element served a purpose.

Tonight would be a night dedicated to transformation.

Trained in the meticulous craft of embalming, Michael moved with steady efficiency, preparing for what came next. He retrieved a large bucket and filled it with lukewarm water, testing the temperature with his fingertips. Satisfied, he placed a fresh bar of soap and a soft sponge beside it—everything needed to cleanse the body before the final steps.

With deliberate care, he reached for a length of maroon-colored string. He started at her ankles, wrapping each of them twice before tying a precise knot, leaving exactly six inches of loose string trailing from each. His movements were slow, methodical and ritualistic. When the last knot was secured, he straightened and stepped back, his gaze sweeping over his work. It was nearly complete.

Moving into the adjacent room where he slept, Michael pulled open a bedside drawer, sifting through an assortment of small trinkets until he found what he was looking for—cotton of the finest quality, and tucked neatly within the threads, a golden two inch needle: The tools needed to complete his work.

Then, he turned back to Belinda's still form.

She was almost ready—a masterpiece waiting for its final touches. Soon, the world would see his greatest work thus far. Soon, the city would marvel at his creation. And more importantly, the NYPD would have no choice but to take notice.

This was not just art.

This was a message.

Michael brought the vehicle to a slow, deliberate stop at the intersection of Broadway and West 125th Street. The dim glow of the dashboard clock read 2:55 a.m..—he was early, but, "Better early than late", as his mother used to say. Besides, this would require patience and she wasn't like the others.

This one was different. Belinda was special.

Stepping out of the vehicle, Michael moved with practiced ease, walking around to the back of the van. The air was still, save for the distant hum of a southbound train rattling along its tracks overhead.

Manhattan, usually alive with relentless energy, was eerily silent at this hour—no blaring horns, no hurried footsteps, no voices to break the quiet. Just the rhythmic pulse of the city sleeping.

He reached into the cargo space and carefully began unloading the centerpiece of his creation—his magnificent dreamcatcher.

The frame—large and meticulously crafted—demanded an almost divine presence under the pale glow of the streetlights. Suspended within the structure was Belinda, her lifeless body seamlessly woven into the elaborate design. Strands of ribbon cascaded around her, feathers swayed in the light breeze, and beads of various colors glistened in the faint light. She had been transformed—no longer merely flesh and bone, but a piece of macabre artistry, a symbol of something far superior than herself.

Despite the weight of the frame, Michael handled it with precision. His strength was more than sufficient, and Belinda, in death as in life, remained small and delicate, but no longer despicable.

Taking a moment, he surveyed his surroundings: The street lights flickered intermittently, casting fleeting shadows against the damp sidewalk. The towering buildings, once imposing in the daytime, now loomed like silent sentinels in the dark. The city, in these early hours, felt like his own.

With a devoted hand, he checked each knot securing Belinda's wrists, ankles, torso, and neck. He tested their hold, ensuring they remained taut and unyielding. Satisfied, he let his gaze drift downward, resting upon her face.

In death, she looked strangely harmless.

Michael exhaled slowly, pressing his middle and index fingers to his lips before gently touching them to her forehead. His gesture was neither rushed nor hesitant.

"Goodbye, Belinda."

His voice was barely above a whisper, but carried the weight of finality. For a moment, he simply stood there, his head bowed, eyes closed.

Then, in a soft breath, he uttered, *"Voluntas Domini facta est."*

With his task complete, Michael climbed back into the driver's seat, closing the door with a quiet thud. He felt neither relief nor sorrow—only a strange, subdued satisfaction, accompanied by the gentle hum of exhaustion settling over him. There was no need to rush back to Staten Island. He had time.

As the engine purred beneath him, he considered taking a detour. Perhaps a slow drive toward Central Park. Maybe he'd stop, take a walk, even feed the pigeons with the loaf of bread he had in a plastic bag behind his seat.

Then he drove away, leaving behind his meticulously prepared showpiece, perfectly positioned for its grand reveal. Now, time for rest was upon him...

A blood-curdling scream shattered the crisp morning stillness at the intersection of Broadway and West 125th Street. The chilling terror rang out, echoed off the buildings and cut through the cold air like a blade.

Bethany Jenkins had always been an early riser. She had planned to get a quick workout at Riverside Park before the weight of her daily responsibilities took hold. It was her only quiet time before the world stirred awake—before her five-year-old daughter would climb sleepily out of bed, before the noise and chaos of life resumed once more. But, this morning was different.

Nothing could have prepared her for what she was about to see. Bethany, still groggy from the early hour, gripped the steering wheel of her MK1 Ford Escort as she sipped from her flask, the lukewarm coffee doing little to sharpen her senses. Her eyes felt heavy, her mind still sluggish from sleep. As she turned onto West 125th Street, she barely noticed the massive shape in the road ahead—until it was nearly too late.

The obstruction loomed in front of her, sitting squarely in the middle of the intersection. A dark, hulking form seemed to appear out of nowhere.

Bethany's instincts kicked in—she jerked the wheel sharply to the right.

Screech!

The tires shrieked against the asphalt as the car skidded, the sudden motion sending her heart slamming into her ribs. Panic seized her chest. She fought to regain control, but the violent swerve had already sealed her fate.

At sixty miles per hour, the Ford Escort spun wildly out of control.

Then—impact.

The front of the car slammed into the sidewalk with a brutal force, metal crunching as the bonnet crumpled inward, ramming hard against a fire hydrant. A deafening hiss erupted as water gushed from the broken hydrant, creating a misty veil in the air. The sudden jolt left Bethany gasping, her body thrown forward against the seatbelt.

For a few seconds, everything was a blur.

Her breath came in short, shallow gasps. The world tilted around her. Then, as the initial shock faded, she slowly reoriented herself. The realization struck her—she had crashed. With trembling hands, she unbuckled her seatbelt and pushed the car door open, stepping onto the pavement. Frustration flared for a moment as she glanced at the damage—her car, her only means of transport, now crumpled against the hydrant.

But, all that frustration evaporated as she turned her gaze toward the object which she had swerved to avoid.

Her pulse quickened. Her feet carried her forward, hesitant, uneasy.

The surrounding streetlights offered little illumination, but as she drew closer, the shape became clearer. It was large, positioned unnaturally right in the middle of the road. Something about it made her stomach churn.

Then—realization struck.

A scream ripped from Bethany's throat, raw and primal—the sound of pure, unfiltered terror.

Her legs buckled. She tried to move, but the horror before her paralyzed her. A strangled gasp escaped her lips as her body swayed unsteadily. She stumbled backward, her knee colliding with the unforgiving asphalt. Pain shot through her, but it barely registered.

She had to get away.

Another scream tore from her as she pushed herself up, staggering toward her car. Her vision blurred, her breath shallow and ragged. Run. Move.

Do something. But, her limbs felt useless, her thoughts a fragmented mess.

Somewhere behind her, a door creaked open. A shopkeeper had emerged, drawn by the commotion—his eyes locking onto her with concern and confusion. Bethany turned toward him, desperate.

"Call the police! There's a body over there!" she cried, her voice trembling with fear.

For a moment, the man simply stood there, stunned. Then, without a word, he turned and rushed back into his store.

Bethany didn't wait to see what he would do next.

She threw herself back into the driver's seat, slamming the door behind her. Her hands shook violently as she fumbled with the keys, the engine sputtering before roaring back to life.

As she reversed and drove away from the scene, the horrific display in the road grew smaller and smaller in her rearview mirror. However,the image was already burnt into her mind. And, no matter how far or fast she drove, she would never truly forget it.

As Detective Coffey raised the yellow tape that cordoned off the area—a familiar motion that he had performed countless times before—he noticed that something was different. This time, the tape felt unusually taut in his hands, almost as if it had been wrapped with a silent disdain.

The afternoon cool air seemed to vanish from his lungs, leaving him breathless, and with it, a piece of his own spirit seemed to fade away, as though each breath carried the weight of everything he had experienced. For a moment, he paused and allowed himself to be truly present in the here and now—something he had not done in a long time.

The familiar, suffocating heaviness of anger, frustration and the relentless burden of his work washed over him. It was as though he could feel the same emotions burning through the young rookie's eyes as they observed him entering the scene, each of them hardened by the horrors they had witnessed. Their souls seemed worn down, already scarred by the darkness they had been forced to navigate, yet it was clear the worst had not yet passed. A fleeting thought crossed his mind, almost like a whisper:

Was it wrong to feel so alive?

He wondered to himself, *Why now? What have I done to deserve this? If this is the penance I must pay, then surely, I'm already in Hell.*

With deliberate caution—as if performing a sacred and somber ritual—Detective Coffey carefully pulled back the shroud that concealed the grim truth beneath it. Each movement was measured—a quiet reverence in his actions—though there was no escape from the inevitable. He approached with caution, aware of the horrors he was about to uncover, yet accepting that it was something he could not avoid.

The woman's form seemed delicate, almost fragile, her age unmistakably etched into the lines of her face. Time—it seemed had not been kind to her—her features, once vibrant, now appeared worn and weathered. But there, despite the ravages of age, was a smile, frozen on her lips as if caught in some long-forgotten moment of peace.

However, her body told a far darker story. Beneath the smile, it bore the grotesque marks of violence—mutilation and suffering that could not be hidden by the passing of time. It was difficult to reconcile the image of this frail, elderly woman with the capacity to inflict pain on another. Yet, as Coffey's eyes lingered on the scene before him, he knew the answer to that question all too well. He had seen enough to understand the darkness that had taken root, a truth that hung heavily in the air, unspoken but deeply understood. Michael knew what she was capable of.

At that moment, Coffey turned to his seasoned partner and spoke.

"The likeness is uncanny, Mac! Just as we anticipated, the cause of death seems to have been sleep deprivation. Look at her face—a striking resemblance to the Barlow case!"

He continued, visibly captivated and disturbed by the sheer enormity and twisted spectacle of the victim as he slowly circled the horrifying contraption—a nightmarish depiction of a dreamcatcher.

"I just don't get it, Mac, I can't wrap my head around why he'd choose to desecrate this frail, old woman like this! What kind of a monster would then also choose to remove both of her feet?"

Chapter 9

Closer

Six years had passed since the death of Belinda Wei, but the weight of the case still clung to Charles like a second skin. Flashbacks of the graphic images invaded his thoughts constantly and overwhelmed him to the point of debilitating anxiety. They were intrusive and disruptive to his daily life—both at work and at home.

Late one evening, he stood alone in the dimly lit briefing room, his gaze fixed on the murder board that stretched before him. The faint glow of the desk lamp illuminated the faces of the eleven victims—their photographs pinned up in grim succession. Each picture told a story, yet together, they alluded to nothing but a haunting mystery. He moved his eyes from left to right, methodically tracing the names beneath each photo.

"Jeremy Wilkins, Vincent Childs, Judith Barlow..." The list seemed endless, but despite the years of painstaking work, nothing had brought them closer to uncovering the truth.

Charles and his team had interviewed every possible witness, chased down every lead, and spoken to every family member, friend, and acquaintance connected to the victims—anyone who might hold a thread that could unravel this twisted web. And yet, the only clue they had was a single name: Michael.

No last name. No identifying features. Just the name that seemed to appear at the center of every victim's life like an uninvited shadow. The more they dug, the clearer it became—Michael wasn't just a random figure in these people's stories: He was the constant and the common denominator. This much was clear: Each victim had, in some way, wronged someone—whether through a crime committed or harm inflicted—and Michael was the one who exacted punishment. He wasn't merely an observer; he was the avenger, the deliverer of justice, and no matter how far Charles and his team went, the mystery of Michael only grew darker and more elusive.

Charles continued to scan the board, his eyes flicking from one pinned photo to another, each thread of red string a reminder of the puzzle he was still trying to solve. As he stared, his thoughts drifted once again to his strange and unsettling interactions with Michael, who had communicated through cryptic clues deliberately left for Charles to discover. He recalled the dreamcatcher that had mysteriously appeared outside his neighbor's apartment the night before Judith Barlow was found dead, and the solitary rare flower, placed with eerie precision, just outside his own door on the night Tyreese's body was discovered.

Then, there was also the incident with the leaking rooftop of his own apartment, which, in a chilling coincidence, coincided perfectly with the death of Becky Torres. These strange symbols all blurred together in his mind as he reflected on the surreal, almost theatrical nature of the events that had come to define the case.

Amidst all the darkness, one moment stood out—a rare and fragile thread of hope: The rescue of the seventeen children who had been held captive by Ms. Belinda Wei near the docks. That singular act of salvation was the only instance in which Michael's actions had led to an undeniably positive outcome.

And, while Charles could, in some sense grasp the twisted logic behind Michael's motivations, he could not bring himself to condone them. Understanding did not equate to approval, and it certainly did not justify Michael assuming the roles of judge, jury and executioner.

As Captain Stevens locked his office door, he noticed the light still flickering in the briefing room. Something about the stillness in the air made him pause, and he slowly made his way toward the room. There, he found Charles, hunched over the murder board, lost in thought, his eyes vacant and distant. The weight of the case had clearly taken its toll on him, and Captain Stevens could see it in the slump of his shoulders and the faraway look in his eyes.

"Go home, Detective," Stevens said, his voice calm but firm as he stopped beside Charles, his gaze locking onto the detective's weary face.

Charles didn't respond immediately; he merely lowered his head—the shame and exhaustion evident in his posture. "I'm not sure I'm up to the task, Sir," he admitted quietly, his voice thick with anguish. "We've spent all this time chasing a ghost. Nothing's adding up. No breakthroughs. Just dead ends."

Evidence of burnout hung on every word he spoke.

Captain Stevens studied him for a moment before speaking, his tone reassuring yet resolute. "He's not a ghost, Detective," he said, placing a hand on the back of the chair where Charles sat, his words slow and deliberate. "He just hasn't made a mistake yet. All serial killers are built the same—eventually, they'll slip up. And, when that happens, we'll be there, ready."

The Captain stood for a moment, his eyes narrowing as he reflected on their next step.

Then, in a move that showed he had thought this through, he added, "In the meantime, I've come to a decision. We could use some outside help, Charles. The media is crawling all over us, basically stating that the city is on its knees, begging us to keep them safe. I know as much as you do that the team is doing everything in their power to solve this. However, I've arranged for the FBI to send us a profiler from their Behavioral Sciences Division—one of their best, according to them. He'll be here in the morning to discuss the cases."

Charles looked up, still unsure but thankful for the support. Stevens gave him a small nod, his expression softening. "Get some rest, Detective," he urged. "We have a busy day ahead. We'll keep pushing."

With that, Stevens rested a firm hand on Charles' shoulder—a silent, yet meaningful gesture of encouragement and solidarity. Then, without another word, he turned and began making his way toward the narrow doorway leading out of the briefing room.

Just as he reached the threshold, a sudden thought struck him. Pausing, he looked back over his shoulder. "Have you seen Bradshaw, Coffey? I haven't seen him in a few days."

Charles, still grappling with the weight of the moment and the realization that the case was now being turned over to the FBI, shifted his gaze toward the Captain. "He mentioned having a promising lead that he believed would 'break the case wide open.' That's when I last heard from him, Sir."

Stevens gave a brief nod, his expression tightening with concern.

"Let me know as soon as you hear from him," he said, before slipping quietly out the back door—leaving Charles alone with his thoughts once again.

He stood staring at the murder board for a few minutes—his mind neither focused nor absent—before making his way back home as the Captain had suggested.

As the moon ascended into the night sky and gradually descended with the passage of time, Charles lay wide awake in his bed, staring up at the ceiling in the quiet darkness. The stillness of the early hours did nothing to ease the turmoil swirling through his mind. He tossed and turned, restless and consumed by guilt, unable to escape the overwhelming weight of his thoughts and fatigue.

Also, the feeling that he had failed his team, the victims, and even himself gnawed at him relentlessly. He could no longer deny it—he had come to a point where outside help was no longer a choice, but a necessity. The realization that they couldn't solve the case on their own and had to rely on another agency to find answers, only deepened his sense of defeat. He had always prided himself on being capable, but now that hope seemed distant and fragile, lost in the echoes of his self-doubt.

As the warm steam from Charles' freshly brewed cup of coffee rose into the air the next morning, Captain Stevens approached the detective's desk with a purposeful stride. Without hesitation, he spoke in a commanding tone, his words cutting through the quiet hum of the office.

"Coffey, Mac," he called, his gaze steady. "He's waiting for us in the briefing room."

Charles and Mac, sensing the gravity of his words, followed closely behind Captain Stevens as he made his way towards the heavy doors of the briefing room. With a swift motion, he pushed them open, revealing a figure standing directly in front of the murder board, examining the collection of victims' photos with a focused intensity. The man, impeccably dressed in a light grey suit with a subtle sheen like sharkskin, stood still, almost as if he was absorbing the tragedy laid out before him. The only glimpse of his shirt was the edge of a white collar, just barely visible between his jacket and neck.

Charles, still holding his coffee, instinctively took the first sip as they entered the room. His eyes didn't immediately drift toward the man, but his presence seemed to shift the energy in the room.

"Detectives, I'd like you to meet Special Agent Landon Rayne from the FBI headquarters in Washington D.C.," Captain Stevens announced, his tone businesslike, but edged with the weight of the introduction.

The moment the name Landon Rayne reached his ears, Charles froze. It was as if the world came to an abrupt halt, the rush of everything else around him fading into a heavy, deafening silence. He hadn't heard that name in over seventeen years, and now, standing before him, was a face that carried the burden of time, a boy who had once been a fixture in his life, a distant memory now thrust into his present.

Charles blinked, his grip tightening on the coffee cup, but he barely registered it as his eyes met Landon's gaze across the room. The shock was immediate, almost overwhelming, but the familiarity in Landon's eyes was strangely reassuring.

"Charles... is that really you?" Landon's voice broke the silence, and with a sense of urgency, he moved towards Charles, extending his hand.

The moment Charles heard that voice, everything snapped into place. Without thinking, his instincts took over, and before either man could say another word, Charles reached out and pulled Landon into a tight embrace. He squeezed him, his eyes shutting against the rush of emotions that flooded over him.

"It's good to see you, Charlie," Landon uttered warmly, his voice thick with unspoken understanding as he pulled back, gently holding Charles by the shoulders. He saw the tears in Charles' eyes and knew exactly why they had surfaced.

Captain Stevens watched the scene unfold, his expression unreadable, but Mac's voice broke through the stillness.

"I take it you two know each other?" he asked, his tone curious yet filled with the undercurrent of something more.

"Charlie and I go way back," Landon replied, his smile fading. It was as if his pride in seeing his old friend again was tempered by the circumstances of their reunion.

Landon's gaze then shifted to the murder board, and he took a few steps toward it. "So, Charlie," he said, his voice lighter, yet carrying the weight of the moment, "Captain Stevens informed me that you're heading up the investigation, correct?"

Charles, still coming to terms with the surreal turn of events, cleared his throat, a formal tone slowly returning, despite the lingering disbelief that all of this was actually happening. "That's correct," he replied, his voice steady, but his mind still grappling with the fact that Landon Rayne—the very person who had been a part of his past—was standing here, now a crucial part of his present.

Landon nodded, his expression becoming more serious. "Well, gentlemen," he said, his eyes narrowing as he studied the board, "It appears that we have gathered an abundance of information about our suspect, yet there is absolutely no tangible evidence to confirm his identity.

On the surface, your suspect seems to anticipate your every move with remarkable precision, displaying an uncanny ability to plan in advance, and he appears to be a master of manipulation. However, Charlie, I don't want to jump to conclusions before I've had the chance to thoroughly analyze the cases at hand. Still, it's clear that this individual has positioned you as the central figure in a complex web. There is an undeniable connection between you two, and together, we will uncover exactly what it is."

In that moment, a profound and unsettling realization washed over Charles, gripping him with an undeniable force. He suddenly understood that the time had come to face the darkest, most painful chapters of his past—those very emotions he had spent years trying to suppress and forget. No longer could he hide from the memories that had haunted him for so long. The weight of the truth was heavy and unrelenting. The success of solving this case, the ability to prevent another victim from becoming just another name on an ever-growing list, hinged on him confronting the demons he had long avoided. The future, and the lives of those still at risk, depended on him. He knew that the painful reckoning he had spent so much time evading was now inevitable.

Charles, Mac, and Captain Stevens stood quietly, their expressions serious and focused, their gaze never leaving Landon as he continued to speak. His voice seemed to hang in the air, deliberate and measured, as he carefully began to unravel the investigation, methodically linking each piece of evidence like threads being woven together.

As Landon moved from one end of the murder board to the other, his pace steady, a faint grin played at the corners of his lips, though he made an effort to keep it hidden from the others. The sight of his meticulous work laid out before him on the board filled him with a quiet satisfaction—a deep sense of pride and accomplishment in the complex web that he had created.

to be continued

FROM THE MINDS OF

SEAN J. TOWSEN & CRAIG S. PALMER

HEXADECAGON

A CITY ON ITS KNEES

HEXADECAGON

A CITY ON ITS KNEES

SEAN J. TOWSEN & CRAIG S. PALMER

TP

HEXADECAGON: A City on its Knees is the gripping first installment of a psychological thriller set against the gritty, volatile backdrop of the late 1980's and early 1990's in New York City—a city on the edge of chaos. Ronald Reagan sits in the White House and Rudy Giuliani leads an aggressive federal crusade against the Mafia, tightening the noose around the city's underworld. But, beneath the surface of political victories and high-profile prosecutions, something far darker stirs.

Detective Charles William Coffey, an average investigator, finds himself thrust into the center of a chilling manhunt. Alongside him is Peter "Mac" Mackenzie—a washed-up, seasoned detective whose best days are long behind him. Together, they are tasked with tracking a methodical and enigmatic killer known only by one name: Michael.

As the string of murders unfold throughout the five boroughs, the pursuit of Michael becomes more than just a case. It evolves into a psychological descent that forces Charles to confront buried truths about himself.

Haunted by visions, manipulated by riddles, and pushed to the brink, Charles begins to understand that Michael's game is not merely one of murder—but of transformation. With every step, the hunter becomes more like the hunted, and Charles begins to question whether he is chasing a killer with reason and purpose, or whether he is being led somewhere far more personal.

Twisting through alleys of suspense, soaked in noir atmosphere, and punctuated by sharp moments of dry wit and surprising levity, HEXADECAGON: A City on its Knees is as much a character study as it is a psychological crime thriller. It is a story where loyalty is fragile, the mind is a battlefield, and the most dangerous truths are the ones we hide from ourselves.

In the end, it's not just a serial killer that Charles must find—it's the man he is becoming.

HEXADECAGON

A CITY ON ITS KNEES

Sean Towsen is an emerging voice in the psychological thriller genre, known for his intricate plotting and a keen insight into the human mind. Drawing on years of experience in storytelling, Towsen is finding a profound passion in crafting fictional narratives that delve deep into the complexities of the human psyche, masterfully intertwining suspense with emotional resonance.

Born in 1987 in Johannesburg, South Africa. At an early age, Towsen enjoyed creative writing and the performing arts. As the years matured, Towsen found himself studying and working in the field of Marketing. Obtaining a Marketing certification from the University of Stellenbosch in Cape Town (UCT) in 2018 and in 2019 then pursuing a Master of Business and Administration (MBA) certification and graduating with a distinction from the London School of Economics (LSE).

Working alongside his co-author and life long friend, Mr. Craig S. Palmer. The duo have been a creative force since 2006 when their passion for music collided and a band was formed. Towsen's and Palmer's passions lead to creating vibrant lyrics which in turn secured them a record deal with a U.S based record label. In 2013, Towsen made the decision to step down from the band, yet the two remained close and worked on numerous other projects over the coming years. Currently, working together to create and publish their first novel.

Eager to establish himself as an up and coming author. Towsen's dedication to the craft is evident in his meticulous approach to character development and plot construction. He draws from years of trying to understand true crime investigations and motives of the criminal mind.

His ability to evoke tension and provoke thought has earned him a growing audience eager to explore the darker facets of human nature.

With a rich background rooted in the world of creative expression, cultivated through years of experience in his career. Towsen brings a unique narrative sensibility to his writing. His undeniable enthusiasm for storytelling fuels his ability to craft immersive, atmospheric worlds that draw readers in and hold their attention. Drawing inspiration from the nuances of everyday life, he has a talent for turning ordinary moments into powerful, emotionally resonant stories. His work often explores deeper themes and ideas, leaving a lasting impression that stays with readers long after they've turned the final page.

Now residing in a town east of Johannesburg, South Africa. Sean Towsen invites readers from across the globe to join him on a journey through the shadows of the psyche, promising tales that are as unsettling as they are unforgettable.

Craig Palmer is a registered psychologist in independent practice, having obtained his Master of Arts (MA) in Counselling Psychology (with distinction) in 2013.

Born in 1983 in Durban, South Africa, and growing up in the quiet city of Pinetown, Craig's early years were shaped by an enjoyment for English Comprehension as a subject, and a passion for the written word. This led him to excel at writing essays from a young age.

After his Primary school years in Kwazulu Natal, his family relocated to the Gauteng province in 1996, to a town just outside of Johannesburg.

After High school, Craig's thirst for knowledge and drive to establish a meaningful career path and help others, led him to further his studies at the University of the Witwatersrand (WITS), whereby he majored in Law and Psychology. Even as an undergraduate student, Craig had a fascination with peoples' minds, with very specific interest in Criminal Law and Psychopathology.

After obtaining his undergraduate university degree, Craig made the decision to complete his postgraduate studies in Psychology, moving forward with his Honors and Masters degrees at the University of Pretoria (TUKS).

Aside from his career in the field of psychology, and interest in crime, Craig is also the co-founder of a long-standing metal band, which is currently signed to a USA-based record label. After graduating from university in 2013, Craig was able to devote more time and energy into his passion, oftentimes obsession for music. Aside from his main band, Craig also has a music side project, which he launched in more recent years. He is also an avid music collector.

Craig started out as – and continues to be – the sole drummer and primary lyricist for both of his bands, the longer standing and primary one of which he formed over fifteen years ago with the co-author and lead author of their upcoming debut novel – Sean Towsen.

Though a first-time author, Craig injects into their first novel, his first-hand knowledge of psychology and over twelve years' experience as a practising psychologist, contributing to him becoming an emerging voice in the psychological crime thriller genre.

Hexadecagon: A City on its Knees will be their first piece of work as novelists and new authors, however, it is certainly not the first time this duo are working and writing together on a creative level, nor is it Craig's first time writing and completing a professional product of the written word:

As a postgraduate student at university, Craig naturally gravitated towards narrative theory and narrative therapy; concepts such as 'identity', 'characters' and 'scripts' only furthered his interest and passion in the written word and for the mental health sector. In fact, submitted in partial fulfilment of the requirements for his Masters degree (Cum Laude), Craig's mini-dissertation was entitled 'Caught between Christianity and the hard rock: A narrative study.'

Today, Craig stands and remains an extremely driven individual – in his career, as a family man and as a musician. And now, in his early 40's, with writing ingrained in his blood, one can be sure that the hunger which Craig experiences in all other facets of his life will undoubtedly be at the helm for him once again as he begins to forge a new passion and possible second career path, a pen in one hand and a blank piece of paper in front of him.

Synopsis

HEXADECAGON – A City on its Knees is the gripping first installment of a psychological thriller set against the gritty, volatile backdrop of the late 1980's and early 1990's in New York City—a city on the edge of chaos. Ronald Reagan sits in the White House and Rudy Giuliani leads an aggressive federal crusade against the Mafia, tightening the noose around the city's underworld. But, beneath the surface of political victories and high-profile prosecutions, something far darker stirs.

Detective Charles William Coffey, an average investigator, finds himself thrust into the center of a chilling manhunt. Alongside him is Peter "Mac" Mackenzie—a washed-up, seasoned detective whose best days are long behind him. Together, they are tasked with tracking a methodical and enigmatic killer known only by one name: Michael.

As the string murders unfold throughout the five boroughs, the pursuit of Michael becomes more than just a case. It evolves into a psychological descent that forces Charles to confront buried truths about himself. Haunted by visions, manipulated by riddles, and pushed to the brink, Charles begins to understand that Michael's game is not merely one of murder—but of transformation. With every step, the hunter becomes more like the hunted, and Charles begins to question whether he is chasing a killer with reason and purpose, or whether he is being led somewhere far more personal.

Twisting through alleys of suspense, soaked in noir atmosphere, and punctuated by sharp moments of dry wit and surprising levity, HEXADECAGON – A City on its Knees is as much a character study as it is a psychological crime thriller. It is a story where loyalty is fragile, the mind is a battlefield, and the most dangerous truths are the ones we hide from ourselves.

In the end, it's not just a serial killer that Charles must find—it's the man he is becoming.

FROM THE MINDS OF
SEAN J. TOWSEN & CRAIG S. PALMER
HEXADECAGON
A CITY ON ITS KNEES

www.ingramcontent.com/pod-product-compliance
Lightning Source LLC
Chambersburg PA
CBHW070537100726
47907CB00004B/1152